GRIFFIN'S DESTINY

BOOK THREE OF
THE GRIFFIN'S DAUGHTER TRILOGY

BY
LESLIE ANN MOORE

RIDAN

A Ridan Publication
www.ridanpublishing.com
www.leslieannmoore.com

Copyright © 2010 by Leslie Ann Moore
Cover Art by Michael J. Sullivan
Interior Layout Design by Michael J. Sullivan
Map and Photo by Ted Meyer

ISBN: 978-0-9825145-0-4
PRINTED IN THE UNITED STATES
First Printing: March 2010

*To my friends at Ridan Publishing. You saved my series and for that,
I am eternally grateful.*

PRAISE FOR GRIFFIN'S DAUGHTER SERIES

"Griffin's Daughter is ranking right up there with any fantasy I've read recently from the major presses."
—Tia Nevitt, Fantasy Debut

"This [Griffin's Daughter] is the opening tale of what looks to be a great epic fantasy."
"Griffin's Shadow is [a] superb tale that will have the audience wanting more from Ms. Moore."
—Harriet Klausner, #1 Ranked Amazon Reviewer

"[A] likeable set of characters who showed heart, and an engaging story. [R]eaders new to fantasy who liked Feist, and the Mallorean, etc, would like this too - I would recommend it accordingly."
—Janny Wurts, author of The Wars of Light and Shadow

"In her sequel to Griffin's Daughter and the second title in her trilogy, Moore introduces a deeper conflict on a grand scale. Her strong male and female characters and their abiding feelings of love and honor bring a sense of true heroism to their struggles against their obstacles."
—Library Journal

"[N]onstop action and sympathetic characterizations. Moore's narrative drive and suspenseful plot twists will leave readers eager for the conclusion to this intricate and appealing tale."
—Publishers Weekly

"Leslie Ann Moore's debut fantasy book, Griffin's Daughter (the first book of the Griffin's Daughter Trilogy), is quite an interesting book. I think it's the best romantic fantasy debut I've read this year."
—Sami Airola, Risingstar.net

CONTENTS

PART I

PART II

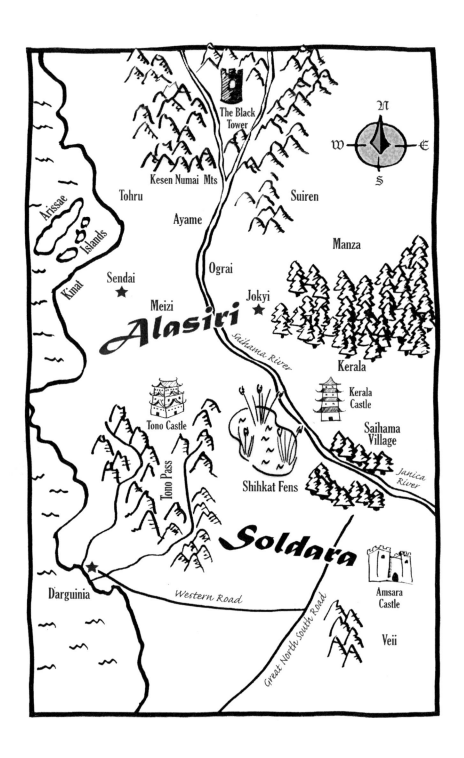

GRIFFIN'S DESTINY

PROLOGUE-MEMORIES

"Help me, Brother!"

Across a fire-blackened landscape, the cry echoes. He scans the charred surroundings, trying to locate the source, but the sound comes from everywhere at once.

"Help me, Brother! They are killing me!"

"Where are you?" he cries. "I can't see! It's too dark!"

Flames crackle to life before him, drenching the scene in lurid, crimson light. A ring of shadows twists around the figure of a man whose blood-spattered face he knows as well as his own.

"Little Brother..."

He stands frozen, hands by his sides. The shadows howl in triumph. They engulf their victim, pulling him down.

"Why do you not help me?" his brother screams as he falls. "Why are you letting them kill me?"

The shadows twist and heave, devouring their prey.

He steps backward and tumbles over the edge of a cliff...

Sadaiyo Sakehera jerked awake then sat upright, drenched in sweat.

"Goddess' tits," he whispered. Curled beside him in their bed, his wife Misune stirred but did not wake.

I remember!

Shaking with reaction from the flood of images in his head, he slipped out of bed and crouched on the floor beside the hearth. The fire had burnt down to a pile of glowing coals. Pushing a stray lock of hair from his face, he took a deep breath to slow his galloping heart.

He stared into the red light, but his eyes focused inward.

I remember all of it, just as the old man said I would! Goddess…What have I done?

What will I do now?

Sadaiyo crawled back into bed and pressed himself against his sleeping wife. He thought of his parents and how they would recoil in horror if they learned the truth.

They must never know. No one can ever know!

Will you haunt my dreams from now on, Little Brother?

Damn you!

PART I

Chapter 1

ESCAPE AND PURSUIT

Magnes awoke with a start and nearly toppled from his seat on the wagon bench to the hard earth below. Knuckling the sleep from his eyes, he yawned and looked down on the stocky brown rump of the cart horse, still in harness and dozing. With the rapidly fading shreds of an unsettling dream drifting across his mind's eye, he swung his legs over the side then dropped to the roadbed.

Damn it...I didn't mean to fall asleep!

He spent a few moments stretching and kneading the kinks from his neck, then tramped off the road to relieve himself in the weeds.

When he returned, he found Gran standing beside the wagon, facing back toward Darguinia. Something about the way she held her body warned Magnes not to disturb her.

After several heartbeats, she shook herself then turned around.

"Oh, Magnes. Didn't realize you were there."

"Sorry, Gran if I startled you," he replied.

The old elven woman shook her head. "No, no, you didn't. I was just performing a farscan. I don't sense any fast moving groups heading this way from the city, praise the One."

Like a slave-catching posse, Magnes thought.

"It seems that Aruk-cho has come through for us," he said, stroking the drowsy gelding's nose. The beast shook its head and whickered.

Poor wretch, Magnes thought. *You hauled us and this wagon most of the night with no complaint, and there's still no real rest for you yet.*

Gran nodded. "So far, it seems that way, yes. But it's still early. The slave-catchers may yet come after us. Mistress de Guera won't want to let go of Ashi so easily, I fear. Let's pray she listens to Aruk-cho and allows him to persuade her."

Magnes thought about the events leading up to last night's harrowing escape from the de Guera yard.

I'm sorry Corvin and his men got caught up in all this. Despite everything, I hope it doesn't go too badly for them. They were only doing their jobs. Armina de Guera is a fair woman, and Aruk-cho will speak up for them, surely!

He shivered, remembering Fadili's terrified cries as Corvin's men threatened the young apprentice healer with their swords. Despair had nearly overwhelmed him, but then Gran materialized from the darkness. With arms raised and blue flames crackling from her fingertips she came, and their attackers fell senseless at her feet. He knew Gran possessed Talent, like all elves, and he also knew she had been a member of a powerful mage's guild. But until last night, he had no real idea of the magnitude of her strength.

He shaded his eyes against the glare of the rising sun and peered ahead past the horse's limp ears. "What of the group ahead of us?" he asked.

"They're still there, but they should be moving out shortly and then we can go."

Gran climbed into the wagon and Magnes could hear her rousing the others. A few moments later, Ashinji emerged followed by Fadili and a yawning, sleepy-eyed Seijon. Ashinji looked pale but steady as he dropped from the wagon.

"How are you feeling?" Magnes asked, searching his friend's face.

"Tired, but otherwise, not too bad," Ashinji replied. He nodded toward the verge of the road and Magnes' mouth quirked in understanding.

After they took care of their bodily needs, they shared a quick meal of bread and cheese. Fadili then saw to the horse and they piled into the wagon to resume their flight. Gran sat up front beside Magnes in order to scan the road ahead and behind with her magical senses.

The morning sky was clear and bright, the air fresh and full of the scents of damp, growing things. The road stretched ahead into the distance, rising and dipping with the land, passing through fields verdant with spring wheat, and orchards in full, glorious bloom. The wagon rolled past cottages and small manor houses, muddy farmyards guarded by belligerent geese, and pastures tenanted by complacent cows.

For a good part of the morning, they had the road to themselves, but eventually, faster carts and wagons began to overtake them, as well as individuals mounted on horses and mules. Other than a few curious looks from passersby, they attracted no particular attention. Magnes set a deliberately slow pace, so as to stay well behind the large group of people traveling ahead of them. It chafed him to have to do so, especially with the risk of pursuit from the city still so great, but the possibility the group up ahead might be an armed company also concerned him.

As the morning wore on, the sun climbed higher along with the temperature, leaving them all damp with sweat. Squadrons of dragonflies glided by on iridescent wings while legions of unseen insects shrilled in unison from the bushes and trees, their harsh chorus waxing and waning in the hot, still air.

At midday, they stopped beneath the sprawling shade of an old oak to rest the horse and eat a meager lunch of dried beef, cheese, and bread, washed down with tepid, leather-flavored water. Until now, Magnes had kept his shirt on, out of respect for Gran, but when Ashinji stripped down to his breeches and sandals, Magnes quickly followed suit. Soon, both Fadili and Seijon had also rid themselves of all unnecessary clothing. Gran finally shed her overdress, relaxing on a patch of grass clad only in an unbleached cotton shift.

Directly opposite their resting place, three pairs of horses stood nose-to-rump, flicking flies off each other's faces with swishing tails. Ashinji went to investigate. He climbed over the fence then approached the animals slowly so as not to spook them, all the while speaking in soft, singsong Siri-dar. Magnes and the others watched as he examined each horse, gently running his hands over their hides and lifting their feet. After he had finished, Ashinji returned, wiping his hands on his breeches, a look of satisfaction on his face.

"They're not prizewinners, but they're well-built and sturdy. If we can find their owners, I think we should offer to buy the bay mare and those two geldings there," he said, pointing to each animal in turn. "Gran can ride the mare, Seijon and I can ride double on the big chestnut, and you can take the piebald, Magnes."

"Sounds good to me," Magnes replied and Gran nodded in agreement. "There's a farmhouse just up the road. Fadili and I will go see if someone is around."

"Here, take this." Gran held out a pouch. "There're fifteen imperials inside. You should not pay more than ten for the three. If you do some shrewd bargaining, though, you might get the farmer to accept seven."

"I'm a very good bargainer," Magnes replied then added, "Although maybe you shouldn't stay here alone. What if…"

"Don't worry," Gran said. "No one will bother us."

"It's like you read my thoughts!" Magnes looked hard at the old woman, but she just smiled.

After packing a bag with a small supply of remedies, Magnes and Fadili hiked to the farmhouse. They found a plump, florid woman washing clothes in the front yard. After relating their cover story—they were traveling healers on their way to join up with the Imperial Army and they needed saddle horses—Magnes persuaded the farmwife to accept seven imperials, along with some of the medicines he brought, for the three horses. She didn't ask why two men required three horses. She seemed not to care.

"Could ye throw in some ol' halters, missus?' Magnes asked in his best north-country accent. The woman snorted and rolled her eyes.

"'Round back in the shed," she said, pointing over her ample shoulder.

Magnes and Fadili left her standing by her tub, counting coins.

When they returned, Magnes knew something was amiss even before he saw the grim looks on both Ashinji's and Gran's faces.

"The slave catchers are coming, aren't they?"

Ashinji nodded, his green eyes dark and dangerous. "I'm not going back," he murmured.

Magnes laid a hand on his friend's shoulder. "I won't let them take you, Ashi, I promise. Whatever I, *we*, have to do, you'll not be made a slave again." He looked beyond Ashinji to Seijon, who stood wide-eyed and shaking within the protective circle of Gran's arms. "That goes for you too, little monkey," he added. The boy managed a fleeting smile.

"We'd better catch the horses," Fadili suggested. "How far behind us are they, Gran?"

"A half-day, I'd say. They're moving a lot faster than we are and will catch up soon if we don't pick up our pace."

"Then perhaps now is the time for me to say farewell." Fadili drew himself up taller, his young face determined. "We knew I would eventually take the infirmary and go my own way. After all, that is what I'm out here for, to serve the needs of the poor. You can travel much faster now that you have horses. When the slave catchers finally reach me, you'll be long gone."

"They won't believe you when you say you don't know which direction we took," Ashinji said. "I'm certain Corvin provided descriptions of both you and the wagon." He paused then added, "They might hurt you, Fadili."

The young Eskleipan flashed teeth like white tiles set in dark earth. "I'm a Soldaran citizen. I have rights." His voice shook a little.

"They won't care about that," Gran said.

"She's right. We have to make it look like I forced you." Magnes grasped Fadili's shoulder and squeezed. Fear for his young friend's safety and fresh guilt over the necessity of involving him sat like hot coals in his gut.

"I'm not afraid." Fadili drew himself up and lifted his chin. "Do what you must."

"I can block most of the pain then plant some false memories." Gran moved to stand at the apprentice healer's back. "Don't strike until I say so."

Ashinji slipped behind her and grasped her shoulders. Magnes took a step back and raised his fist. Gran laid her palms on Fadili's temples. A few heartbeats later, his eyelids fluttered then closed. Gran's body stiffened.

"Now," she whispered.

Magnes drove his fist hard into Fadili's slack face. Blood and saliva splashed his knuckles as the force of the blow sent both apprentice and mage reeling. Only Ashinji's strength kept all three from tumbling to the ground.

Magnes rushed forward to ease the weight of the unconscious apprentice off Gran and Ashinji. As tenderly as he would his own child, Magnes lowered his friend to the rough roadbed then crouched beside him. He resisted the urge to wipe away the blood leaking from Fadili's nose and mouth.

"Are you sure he felt nothing?" Tears stung Magnes' eyes.

"I promise you he didn't." Gran knelt and touched fingertips to Fadili's forehead. "I will alter his memories now. When he wakes, he'll tell the slave posse how you threatened to kill him if he didn't cooperate. Hopefully, they'll go easy on him."

"Gods." Magnes rubbed his bruised and bloody knuckles. "The Eskleipans will be horrified when Fadili tells them what he thinks happened." The realization of how much confusion and hurt they would feel tore at his soul.

"If it's any consolation, false memories eventually fade," Ashinji said. "It might take several months, but by then Fadili should be out of danger."

Seijon sidled up to Ashinji then leaned against him like a puppy seeking comfort. Ashinji draped an arm across the boy's slim shoulders. Magnes stayed at Fadili's side, watching while Gran performed the magic they all hoped would spare their friend.

"It's done." Gran drew a deep breath. "Help me up, please." Ashinji held out his hand for her to grasp.

"I'm going to miss you, my brother," Magnes whispered. He wanted so much to arrange Fadili's limbs to more comfortable positions, but knew the deception depended on the illusion of violence.

"We must go now," Gran urged. "We don't have much time."

Magnes sighed then rose to his feet. Separation and loss were a part of life, he knew, but why did it always have to be so hard?

Working as quickly as they could, Magnes and Ashinji caught and haltered the three horses. After leading them out of their pasture onto the road, Ashinji tied the lead ropes to the halters to serve as reins.

Gran gathered some supplies into a satchel then swung aboard the little bay mare with ease. Magnes mounted the piebald, grunting as the horse's prominent spine dug into his crotch. Ashinji must have noticed his discomfort, for he said, "I'm guessing the farmer had no saddle blankets?"

"Don't know. Forgot to ask," Magnes replied through gritted teeth.

Ashinji chuckled. "I sympathize, my friend."

With spare rope from the wagon, Ashinji secured a bag, also filled with supplies, to the back of the chestnut gelding he and Seijon were to ride then quickly mounted. He reached down and grasped Seijon's wrist then helped the boy to scramble up behind him.

For a few moments, no one spoke. High in the canopy of the stately old oak, birdsong filled the branches with sweet, piping notes. A tiny butterfly, the color of the summer sky, alighted on the back of Magnes' hand and clung there, its wings opening and closing in languid sweeps.

ESCAPE AND PURSUIT

Perhaps this is an omen that everything will turn out for the best, he thought.

The butterfly fluttered away. Magnes turned to look back at Fadili and the sight of his young friend lying senseless on the road tore a groan from Magnes' lips. "Gods…We can't leave him like this!"

"We have no choice. We've done all we can to protect him. We must go now." Gran's implacable tone left no room for dissent.

"May Eskleipas always hold you in His hands, Brother. I'm sorry." Magnes wiped his streaming eyes with trembling fingers.

"May the One keep him safe," Ashinji added. "Which way, my friend?"

"Northeast, cross-country. We should reach Amsara in about two weeks, that is, if we don't run into any trouble. There's a smaller road that parallels this one, but I'm not quite sure how far we'll have to ride overland until we find it. Since the army isn't going that way, we shouldn't encounter any patrols."

"Our only hope now is speed," Ashinji commented, tugging on his ear and glancing over his shoulder. "We haven't time to conceal our trail, so we'll have to outrun our pursuers."

"Let us pray these horses are up to the task," Gran responded.

"They'll have to be," Ashinji replied, his voice grim. "Lead the way, Magnes."

Together, the little band of fugitives turned their horses' noses eastward.

∂

At sunset, they reached the secondary road and turned north once again. They rode hard until moonrise, then stopped and sheltered in an abandoned barn for the remainder of the night. At first light, they pushed on.

They rode now through rolling grasslands dotted with small stands of oak and solitary chestnut trees, populated by sheep and brown-spotted cattle. Isolated farmsteads appeared in little valleys or on windswept hilltops then fell away behind as they pressed onward. It soon became obvious their meager supplies would not last much more than a few days. Finding food in this sparsely settled land would be extremely difficult with no weapons for hunting, and they dared not stop openly at any of the farms along the way. The only alternative was the use of Gran's magic.

"At the next farmstead we come to, I'll cast glamours on us," the old mage said.

Shortly after midday, they spotted a small, thatch-roofed farmhouse standing in a little hollow about a hundred paces off the road. A stand of laurel trees across the road provided a convenient place of concealment where Ashinji and Seijon could wait with the horses.

Even after she had explained and had cast the glamour, Magnes still couldn't believe his eyes. In Gran's place, an old human woman with iron gray hair and dark brown eyes stood before him.

"By the way you're gaping at me, I can guess my glamour is convincing," Gran sniffed as she tied a scrap of cloth over her head for a scarf. "Now, hold still while I disguise you." Magnes held his breath as he waited, his eyes riveted on Gran's every move. A slight wave of vertigo, a burst of tingling along his limbs, and then...

"Ha! You'd fool your own mother, young man," the old mage commented wryly.

"What do I look like? Tell me!" Magnes demanded.

Ashinji stifled a guffaw behind his hand. Seijon gaped like a startled bird.

"You've got a shiny bald head and a big black beard," the boy squeaked. "You look like a pirate!"

"You do look a bit, uh, frightening," Ashinji agreed, his wiry body shaking with mirth. "You could pass for a pirate. I think."

"Oh, don't listen to them," Gran grumbled. "You don't look like yourself and that's all that matters."

Magnes found himself laughing as well and it felt good, in spite, or maybe because of, the danger they faced.

As Ashinji and Seijon led the horses deeper into the sheltering trees, Magnes and Gran approached the house along a gravel-strewn footpath. They moved cautiously, expecting at any moment to be challenged by dogs, but the yard remained quiet.

"Halloo!" Magnes called out. "Anyone at home?" He and Gran waited in silence for a few heartbeats before he tried again, louder this time.

"Halloooo!"

After several more moments of silence, Magnes looked at Gran and said, "There doesn't seem to be anyone around."

"No, there is someone here," Gran replied. "I can sense...*her*. I'm not sure why she doesn't come out, unless...no, no. I sense no fear. I think she must not be able to hear us for some reason."

"Let's go look inside." Magnes crossed the yard in several quick strides to the door then pushed it open. He stuck his head in and looked around. A rough-hewn oak table and two chairs stood at the center of the room. The only other furniture consisted of a cupboard against the far wall and two more finely crafted chairs beside the unlit hearth. Natural light entering from two small windows and the open door provided the only illumination.

"No one in here," he called out. He entered and stood, hands on hips, puzzled; then, it occurred to him why Gran could feel the presence of a person here, but yet, the farmhouse appeared deserted. "There must be a root cellar and that's where the owner is," he speculated.

Gran entered the room and looked around. "The woman must be hard of hearing, then," she said. "Let's get what we need and go."

In the area that served as the cottage's kitchen, they found eggs, cheese, butter, bread, turnips, a seed cake, and a large clay urn buried in the floor, filled with beer. A brace of freshly killed chickens hung from the ceiling. They took all of the eggs, a single loaf, one small round of cheese and one chicken. Magnes fished around in his pouch for a few silver coins to leave as payment.

"What's this, then!"

Slowly, Magnes and Gran turned to face their unwilling host.

The farmwife stood blocking the open doorway, a small club in one upraised fist, a plump matron ready for battle. Magnes, though flushed with consternation, could also not help but feel amused. He took a single step forward, hands folded in supplication.

"Please, missus," he said. "Me old mam an' me was just travellin' by on our way back home, an' we was runnin' outta food. We saw yer farm and I did call out but no one answered."

"So, you thought you'd just come on in and help yourselves, is that it?" the woman replied, voice sharp with sarcasm. Magnes ducked his head as if ashamed, and in truth, he was, a bit.

"I'm real sorry, missus," he murmured. "But we was goin' to pay. Me mam and me ain't thieves." The woman sniffed and slowly, the club sank to her side.

"Huh, well. Can't let it get about that I refused aid to them what's in need," she huffed.

Especially when there's money in it for you, Magnes thought. He produced two silver sols and held them out on the palm of his hand. The woman scooped the coins up and promptly secreted them away within the folds of her skirt. She flashed a gap-toothed grin.

"P'raps yer old mam would like a mug of beer before you move on," she offered, her suspicion transformed into solicitousness by the power of money. Magnes opened his mouth to politely refuse, but before he could speak, Gran stepped forward and tapped the woman on the forehead with her forefinger.

Magnes gaped in surprise as the woman's eyes grew as round as saucers. Her fat lips stretched wide to scream, but instead, she gurgled, then went rigid.

It's like she's turned to stone, Magnes thought. *No, more like wax.*

"What did you do to her?" he demanded, rounding on Gran.

"We've run out of time!" The old mage grabbed his arm and pulled. "Ashi just mindspoke to me. The slave catchers are on our heels. We've got to run!"

Magnes' heart leapt into his throat. "But...but how did they manage to catch up to us so fast?" he gasped.

"I don't know. It doesn't matter. Come on!" She led the way out of the cottage and back up the slippery path to the road. Magnes paused for a heartbeat to look back at the house.

"Don't worry about her," Gran snapped. "The spell is temporary."

Magnes turned and followed Gran's fleeing figure toward the laurel grove where Ashinji and Seijon waited. They found the two mounted and ready to ride.

"I scouted back to that little rise in the road," Ashinji said, pointing over his shoulder. "I spotted the posse. I think they may have seen me." Seijon clung with arms locked around Ashinji's waist, his face drained of all color. The big chestnut pirouetted beneath them, sensing his riders' agitation. Magnes waited until Gran had scrambled aboard her mare before climbing onto the piebald's sharp back. Even before he drummed his heels into the horse's sides, the animal sprang forward, chasing after its fellows.

ESCAPE AND PURSUIT

We'll never outrun them! Magnes thought, mind reeling in desperation. He began searching the terrain for a place where they might make a stand, but even as he did, he knew in his heart it would be futile, unless…

Unless Gran uses her magic. It's our only hope!

He urged his horse alongside hers. "We can't run anymore!" he shouted. "Gran, you've got to stop them!" She glanced at him for just an instant, but Magnes saw consensus in her pale eyes. He also saw something else— resignation.

Ashinji, who rode in the lead, pointed ahead to a hill topped by a crown of oaks. They made for it, their tired mounts laboring up the slope. At the top, the horses stumbled to a halt, sides heaving. Magnes slid to the ground and ran to the edge of the grove to look back the way they had come. He spotted the posse, riding hard, heading straight for their position.

"So, this is what it's come to," Ashinji said. He had moved to stand beside Magnes and now gazed pensively at the approaching horsemen.

Magnes glanced at his friend. Ashinji's hair had come undone, and now hung in a rumpled gold cascade across his shoulders and back. Rivulets of sweat cut tracks through the grime on his skin, and the fresh scars from the wounds that had nearly killed him traced angry red trails down his bare flank.

Even in such a disheveled state, Ashinji's beauty remained undimmed.

Magnes well understood Armina de Guera's determination to get back her most prized possession. He shivered, beset by a rush of powerful emotion, his body reacting of its own accord to feelings he dared not confront. To do so would only court disaster.

Magnes could never betray Jelena or jeopardize his friendship with Ashinji in order to make sense of his tangled desires. Some lines could never be crossed.

He shook himself and refocused on the present danger.

"Do you know what Gran is going to do?" he asked, looking over his shoulder at the old mage who now stood immobile in the center of the grove, eyes closed, arms hanging loosely by her sides.

Ashinji shrugged. "I'm not sure, but whatever it is, it will drain her. She'll be incapacitated, perhaps for several days. If we manage to escape, we'll have to find somewhere to go to ground because she won't be able to travel."

"I'm going to look for something to use as a weapon," Magnes said. It felt like a useless gesture, but he had to do something.

Ashinji put out a hand to stop him. "Magnes, promise you won't do something foolish to save me. Concentrate on protecting Seijon and getting him away. Armina de Guera won't pay those men for a corpse, so they're going to do everything in their power to capture me alive. Seijon is worthless to them, and Gran is condemned for aiding my escape, as are you. If I have to, I'll surrender to give you three a chance to escape." Ashinji spoke without a trace of fear or indecision.

"Ashi, I promised I wouldn't let you be taken and I intend to honor that," Magnes insisted. "Please don't make me say otherwise."

Ashinji sighed, and looked at his feet, then lifted his eyes to meet Magnes'. "You and my wife are a lot alike," he said softly. "You can both be downright pig-headed when you've a mind to."

Magnes chuckled. "When you see my cousin again, you can tell her that."

The two young men watched in silence as the posse fanned out to surround the hill, though they made no move to close in; instead, the riders drew rein and waited. After a few moments, a man on a white mule urged his mount forward, cupped his hands to his mouth and shouted, "Come on down, tink! You can't run anymore. You come quietly and we'll let the others go."

Ashinji bared his teeth. "They must think we're stupid," he muttered.

Magnes flicked the man a rude gesture with his finger.

Without warning, the ground at the base of the hill exploded.

Chapter 2

CONSEQUENCES

The hill lurched violently, throwing Ashinji and Magnes to their knees. Acorns rained on their heads as dust billowed in a choking cloud. Screams of terror rent the air. Coughing, eyes tearing, Ashinji crawled to the edge of the grove and stared in disbelief at the scene below.

Tree roots, flailing like the tentacles of a maddened sea creature, had burst from the earth to attack the slave-catchers.

Ashinji watched in horrified fascination as a root the thickness of a man's arm whipped around the posse leader's neck and ripped him from his plunging mule. The man struggled and tore at the unrelenting wood, his bulging eyes wild with terror. His face flushed purple before turning gray as his kicks and twists became weaker. Finally, he dangled like a broken puppet, his tongue protruding grotesquely from his mouth.

A second, then a third man each met the same fate.

The others did not wait to witness the final death throes of their comrades. Even as the three victims swung above their heads, they wheeled their panicked horses and fled. None of them looked back.

Dizzy with shock, Ashinji backed away from the slope and rose on shaky legs.

"Goddess," he whispered through dry lips.

"Ashi! There's more coming up the back!" Magnes shouted.

Too late, Ashinji remembered the posse had split up to surround them.

He whirled in time to see three men charge into the grove from the far side of the hill, swords raised. They ran straight for Gran, who remained locked in a trance, unable to move.

Gran! Ashinji cried out in mindspeech, but she did not respond. Magnes pelted forward to intercept them, Seijon hard on his heels.

"Seijon, no!" Ashinji screamed. He flung himself after the boy, straining to catch him but even as he did so, he knew he would fail.

Magnes reached the men first, barreling into them like a charging bull, knocking one man flat and sending the second one stumbling to his knees. He pinned the fallen man and started pummeling his face with his fists. The third man twisted aside and lunged for Gran.

Seijon, brandishing a tree branch, leapt in his path just as the slaver's sword swept around in a glittering arc. The blade sliced through the wood and cut across the boy's body, sending a spray of blood into the air.

Seijon fell without a sound.

Without warning, a terrible pressure grew within Ashinji's head, just behind his eyes. With a shout of rage, he loosed it like a taut bowstring. The recoil knocked him flat on his back.

Seijon's killer burst into flames.

The man dropped his sword and staggered in an erratic circle, shrieking, until he finally collapsed. Acrid smoke filled the grove with the stench of burnt flesh. The two men whom Magnes had knocked to the ground had regained their feet. The one Magnes had beaten leaned like a drunk against his comrade, his face slick with gore. Both men raised their hands above their heads.

"Please, don't kill us!" the injured man croaked.

Ashinji rose to his feet and without thinking, loosed another bolt of energy. The slave catcher flew through the air then smashed into a tree trunk with a meaty thud. His body slid to the ground, broken and lifeless. Howling with terror, the remaining slaver whirled and bolted away from Ashinji , running hard for the edge of the grove. Magnes lunged but his fingers closed on empty air.

"Let him go!" Ashinji cried. Sick with horror, he stumbled toward where Seijon's body lay and sank to his knees.

No, no, not you, Little Brother!

CONSEQUENCES

The sword had sheared open the boy's belly, making a ruin of his innards. Death had come swiftly. Ashinji drew in a shuddering breath and gently lifted Seijon's head to cradle it in his lap.

The boy's half-open eyes and parted lips made him look as if he had one last thing he needed to say. Ashinji stared into the small face—so pale and still—trying to dredge up from the darkest place in his soul a spark to re-ignite the rage that had called down fire to destroy a man, but he couldn't. The fire had burnt out, leaving only sorrow and bitter regret in its stead.

"This is my fault," he whispered. "I should never have allowed you to come with us. If I'd made you stay behind, you'd still be alive." Hot tears sliced through the dirt on his face. The air in the grove had grown thick and oppressive, as if it had become saturated with Ashinji's grief and could hold no more.

"No, Ashi. You can't blame yourself for this. Seijon knew the risks when he begged you to take him with us." Magnes came up and knelt beside the body.

"He was only a child!" Ashinji brushed a strand of hair off Seijon's forehead. "How could he possibly have known? It was my job to protect him, and I failed."

"It was all of our jobs, Ashi," Gran rasped. She had emerged from her trance and now stood behind him, and when Ashinji turned to look up into her face, he gasped with dismay. The light and strength that had always been a part of her had burnt out, and at any moment, she might crumble into ashes.

"Gran, please, you must sit down!"

The old woman shook her head. "No. If I sit now, I'll not be able to get up again. I must keep moving, at least until we've cared for the boy and left this place."

"I promised Seijon I'd get him to Alasiri. How am I going to keep that promise now?" Ashinji shook his head and a tear fell to splash on Seijon's bloodless cheek.

"Back in ancient times, oak groves were sacred to our people," Gran replied. "It will be a fitting resting place for the boy. Take a lock of his hair, Ashi, and bury it when we reach home. That way, you can keep your promise, at least in a small way."

His gaze never straying from Seijon's face, Ashinji tried to rise, but could not make his legs obey. Sudden, crushing weariness had pinned him to the earth.

"Gran, something's wrong with me." He had to struggle to lift his head to look at the mage. "I feel so tired."

"You expended a lot of energy doing what you did, Ashi." Gran squeezed his shoulder. "You are young. It won't take you nearly as long to recover. Rest awhile before you and Magnes take care of the boy."

"I'll get started." Magnes bent to retrieve a sword dropped by one of the slavers. "This will make digging easier."

He walked to the nearest tree and began scraping at the hard soil between two of the twisted roots fanning out from its base. Ashinji watched for a few moments then struggled to his feet.

"I'm all right," he said in response to the consternation in Gran's eyes, but in truth, he wondered how much longer he could keep moving. Focusing his mind on the task at hand, he managed to dredge up a reserve of strength left untouched by the flow of magic. Scooping up another discarded sword, he joined Magnes and together they chopped into the stubborn earth. The labor kept Ashinji's mind off the part he had played in the destruction of the slave catching posse.

When they judged the depression deep enough, Ashinji and Magnes threw down their swords. Ashinji bent to gather up Seijon's torn body in his arms. Carrying the boy as gently as if he were sleeping, Ashinji then laid Seijon into the grave. With Gran's small belt knife, he severed a lock of the boy's russet hair then he and Magnes covered the body, first with a webbing of branches and then a fill of soil and small rocks. To finish things off, they veiled the top in a thick covering of dead leaves. Magnes piled a small cairn of stones to serve as a marker.

When they were done, the three of them lingered beneath the spreading limbs of the ancient tree, loathe to depart, yet knowing they must. To Ashinji's heart, it felt like abandonment, even though his head knew the folly of that notion. Seijon was dead and beyond any feelings of abandonment. Even though the boy had been born on the streets of Darguinia and knew very little of the elven religion, it comforted Ashinji to believe the Goddess would recognize one of Her own and gather the boy's soul into Her eternal, loving embrace.

CONSEQUENCES

"Goodbye, Little Brother," Ashinji whispered. "I'm so very sorry."

Wordlessly, Magnes helped Gran up on her mare, then mounted his piebald gelding and waited. Ashinji twisted the lock of Seijon's hair into a knot and held it out to Gran who tucked it into her waist pouch. He then swung on his horse and the three of them left the grove behind, riding down the side of the hill through the grisly aftermath of Gran's magical defense. It would be several days before the terrorized remnant of the slave posse got back to Darguinia to report their defeat, and by that time, their quarry would be beyond reach.

Ashinji looked back over his shoulder and, for an instant, thought he saw a small figure standing at the edge of the grove, a shadow really, backlit by the glow of the dying sun. He blinked and the figure disappeared.

He fixed his eyes on the northern horizon. The exhaustion he had kept at bay until now pulled at his limbs once more. He covered his face, weeping, and thought about how badly he needed to feel Jelena in his arms again.

&

They took shelter that night inside an ancient mound whose sides had partially collapsed, allowing access to the burial chamber below. Many such mounds dotted this part of the country, along with crumbling walls and weed-choked towers, the remains of an extinct civilization that had once ruled here. Magnes explained that no one knew much about the mound builders. Their world had fallen long before the coming of the Soldarans, and folk hereabouts viewed them with a mix of awe and superstitious dread.

"No one will bother us in here," he stated. "I'm certain the locals give this place a wide berth. They won't dare approach, no matter what they see."

The rubble from the cave-in made a convenient ramp on which to lead the horses down into the burial chamber. Looking around, they could see robbers had looted the grave long ago, leaving behind only a few pottery shards and fragments of animal bone.

After Ashinji and Magnes had cleared an area of debris and had unpacked their meager supplies, Gran spread a blanket on the floor and lay down, closing her eyes. While Magnes built a small fire, Ashinji scrounged some sticks with which to hang their chicken over the flames.

As the bird began to sizzle, dripping fat into the fire, greasy smoke rose through the ragged hole in the roof and swirled away into the star-spattered sky. Ashinji assumed spit duty, turning the bird at regular intervals so it would roast as evenly as possible. After a while, Magnes moved to wake Gran but Ashinji shook his head.

"You won't be able to rouse her. She's in a profound state of trance, something practitioners call 'mage sleep'. I doubt she'll stir for at least another day," he explained.

"You look done in, yourself," Magnes said. "Maybe you should try some of that 'mage sleep'"

"I don't know the technique. I'm not trained." Ashinji rubbed eyes stinging with fatigue. "I'll be all right in the morning, I think."

They ate their meal in companionable silence, washing it down with swigs of tepid water. When they had finished, Ashinji set aside a portion of the chicken for Gran, then banked the fire while Magnes saw to the horses. The animals whickered and stomped restlessly as Magnes did what little he could to groom them. "They're hungry," he commented. "We'll have to let them graze a bit tomorrow."

"I hope you're right about folk not wanting to approach the barrow," Ashinji replied. "I'd hate to have to fight off horse thieves."

Magnes grunted and shook his head. "I'm sure the locals are convinced this place is haunted. They won't risk getting themselves snatched and drained of their life force by some hungry ghost." He chuckled, then added, "Or by a soul-stealing elf!"

Ashinji tossed a blanket onto the packed earth and lay down with a grimace. "Ai, Goddess, but this ground's hard," he sighed. Magnes, finished with tending the horses, threw his own blanket down beside Ashinji and settled on his back. The two young men lay for a while in silence, staring at the shadow-cloaked ceiling of the barrow.

"I saw what you did to those men, Ashi," Magnes said, breaking the quiet. "I had no idea your magic was so strong." In the dark, his voice sounded a little awed.

"I didn't know, either. I mean, Gran has told me my Talent is very powerful, but it's been blocked since childhood, for reasons that don't seem very compelling right now."

CONSEQUENCES

A wave of guilt washed over him, so powerful and bitter it tore a sob from his throat.

"What kind of a monster am I, Magnes?" He looked at his friend and sensing the other's confusion, added, "I murdered two men. "

"What are you talking about, Ashi? You didn't murder…"

"Yes, I did!" Ashinji cut him off, nearly choking on the pain. "The…the one man, he, he…Ai, Goddess! He begged me for his life! I could have let him live, but…but I, I…"

"Ashi, please don't do this to yourself," Magnes pulled him into an embrace.

Ashinji covered his face with his hands and gave in to his tears, so lost in self-loathing he could not accept or acknowledge the comfort his friend offered.

How can I ever face Jelena again? How can I even think of touching her, making love to her, with the blood of a murdered man on my hands? When she finds out what I've done, she'll hate me. Goddess, I couldn't live with that!

"Ashi, Ashi…please…" Magnes murmured, stroking his hair. "You did nothing wrong. Those men attacked us. We were defending ourselves. You are not a murderer. Gods, I can't stand this!"

Magnes pried Ashinji's hands from his face and kissed him.

Ashinji gasped and recoiled in shock.

Magnes jerked back, nearly falling into the fire. "I…I'm so sorry, Ashi!" he stammered. "I only wanted to, to make you feel better…I didn't mean…" He fell silent and looked away.

Ashinji let out a ragged sigh. The storm had passed, leaving behind a quieter, but no less intense guilt in its wake.

"Magnes."

Magnes flinched, as if stung by the sound of his name.

"Look at me…please."

The two young men stared at each other for several heartbeats. In the semi-darkness, Magnes' eyes gleamed with such raw need, Ashinji thought he might weep anew.

"Ashi…" Magnes whispered, breathing hard now as if locked in a fierce struggle with something he dare not allow to win.

Trembling, Ashinji hugged his knees to his chest, afraid of this perilous new landscape he must now traverse. He chose his next words with care.

"Magnes, you are, and will always be, my friend," he murmured, "But…"

"No, Ashi. You don't have to say anything. I know, believe me. I know all too well." Magnes squeezed his eyes shut, and a single tear leaked out, sparking in the fire's glow. "You are Jelena's husband, and I know how much you love her. I'm human, you're an elf. We're both men. I know all this!" He groaned and covered his face with shaking hands. "But, it still hurts to be so near you and not be able to…to…" His voice stuttered into silence.

Ashinji swallowed hard and raked his hands through his hair, unsure of what to say to ease his friend's pain.

"This makes no sense to me at all." Magnes dropped his hands and continued in a hoarse whisper. "I've never been attracted to other men before, never, until the day I met *you*. I felt something for you from the very first moment. I locked those feelings away, buried them deep, especially when I saw how you looked at Jelena. I don't know why they've chosen to resurface now."

"We've been through a lot together," Ashinji replied in a gentle voice. "I owe my life to you, Magnes. If not for your healing skills, I would have died a slave. That kind of thing forges an unbreakable bond between people. It creates a kind of love."

"Love is a very strange thing," Magnes replied. "I loved a girl once, back home in Amsara. I still love her, but she's married to another man, and even if she weren't, it would be impossible for us to be together. Yet, I still hold on to the fantasy that I could actually have a life with her." He stared at the barrow ceiling as he spoke, as if doing so made it easier to confess all of the secret agony in his heart.

"I don't want to feel this way about you, Ashi. It's too confusing and painful! I've got to push this out of my heart somehow, yet find a way to hold on to that other kind of love we can share."

He looked into Ashinji's eyes.

"I love you, Ashi," he declared. "There, I've said it once and I promise I'll never say it to you again. Now you must promise me you'll say nothing to Jelena about any of this. I couldn't bear the thought of her knowing how close I came to betraying her trust."

"What you've said to me will always be just between us, I swear," Ashinji replied. His heart ached at the profound sadness in Magnes' eyes, but he knew he could never give his friend what he so desperately wanted.

For a while longer, the two young men regarded each other in silence, then Magnes said, "You have to find a way to forgive yourself for what you had to do, Ashi."

"I don't know if that's possible." Ashinji picked up a stick and stirred the dying fire.

"Yes, it is." Magnes extended his hand as if to touch Ashinji's arm, then let it fall to his lap.

"Then you must take your own advice, my friend," Ashinji said.

"What do you mean?"

"Your father's death was an accident. You need self-forgiveness as much as I do, Magnes."

After a few heartbeats, Magnes nodded. "I have to go home, put things right with Thessalina and face what I did," he said. "I just pray it's not too late."

"Trust your sister to see the truth," Ashinji replied.

"Jelena once told me she thought you were the most beautiful thing on this earth, Ashi," Magnes murmured. "She was right."

"No, my friend," Ashinji replied, his voice catching as more tears threatened. "I am so far from that. My wife is the most beautiful thing on this earth, not me."

Magnes sighed and shook his head. He lay down and turned away from Ashinji, as if he could no longer bear to look upon what he so fervently desired but could never have.

For a very long time, Ashinji remained awake staring into the fire, too exhausted and emotionally raw to sleep. When he finally did lie down, he could only toss and turn.

When the sky beyond the broken edges of the barrow turned pearl gray with the coming dawn, Ashinji rose and climbed the rubble slope out onto the side of the ancient grave. He sat cross-legged in the dewy grass and watched the sun lift itself over the horizon to begin its daily journey across the heavens.

When he heard the scuffle of footsteps on the slope behind him, he didn't need to look to know who approached. Magnes came up beside him and held out a hunk of cheese and a piece of bread. Wordlessly, Ashinji took the food and began to eat. Together, they stared into the distance, two friends sharing a meal in the quiet of the morning, each one knowing nothing would be the same between them ever again.

Chapter 3

A CHANGE OF HEART

You have a body for me?"

"Yes, Highness," the old man said. "A man of middle years, dead less than a day."

"Excellent. Take me to it."

Prince Raidan Onjara did not fear death, having witnessed it many times during his long career as a physician, but as he followed the elderly healer along the dirt path leading to the man's cold room, he felt a twinge of apprehension.

What if the plague could not be stopped?

The prince had arrived in Tono three days ago. Since then, he had examined the bodies of five victims, though none had been fresh enough to yield acceptable samples.

All five were okui and had recently come into contact with hikui folk. According to the local Chief Constable, many people in the district had fallen sick, and the purebloods now seemed to die as easily as the mixed-race folk. This had led to some ugly confrontations, and increasing demands by some okui that all hikui be forced to leave the district.

With Lady Odata away in Sendai for the war council, the thankless task of keeping the peace in the valley now fell to her eldest son, an untested youth just barely of age. Raidan had felt no surprise when the beleaguered chief greeted his arrival with such overt relief.

Having no time to spare for anything other than the mission that brought him to Tono in the first place, Raidan had been forced to declare himself unavailable for peacekeeping duty, much to the consternation of the chief and his staff.

From first light to well after sunset, Raidan and his small escort rode from one farmstead to the next, interviewing the healthy and examining the sick. From modest cottages to prosperous manor houses, the prince encountered the same thing; people feared the plague and the imminent invasion by the Soldarans—purebloods and mixed bloods alike.

That evening, as the prince and his men dined at a local inn, word came to them of the old healer and the newly deceased man lying in a cold room behind the healer's cottage. Not wishing to waste a single moment, Raidan abandoned his dinner and took to the saddle, leaving his escort behind.

Trudging along behind the old man, his worn leather satchel bumping his back, Raidan made a mental list of the samples he needed: blood, saliva, hair, skin, and discharge from any swellings or sores.

Let my brother scoff and cling to the belief that magic is the only way! The future lies with science, not magic, and if the elven people are to advance, they will have to give up their reliance on Talent and embrace the new learning.

That is, if we manage to survive both the plague and the Soldaran invasion.

A three-quarter moon hung like a clipped silver coin amid a thick field of stars. The old healer led the way through a stand of trees to the side of a hill, holding a bull's-eye lantern above his graying head to light their way. Its golden beam fell upon a stout wooden door set into the side of the grass-covered hill.

"He's right inside, milord Prince, lying on the lowermost shelf at the back," the old man said. He gripped the heavy iron ring handle and heaved the door open, then led the way along a sloping passage deep into the interior of the hill.

The passage ended in a circular chamber constructed of tightly fitted, whitewashed stone. Raidan looked around, impressed with the old man's workroom. Wood shelves, filled with a variety of pots, jars, and caskets, ran along the curve of the walls on either side of the door. A complete kit of dissection tools hung on pegs attached to a table at the center of the room. At the very back, three shelves had been recessed into the wall. Only one held an occupant—the lowest, as stated.

A CHANGE OF HEART

"I'll need your assistance, healer," Raidan said as he stepped over to the body and pulled back a fold of the heavy shroud, revealing the dead man's face.

"Of course, milord," the old man answered. "I have specimen jars, salt, vinegar. Just tell me what you need." He hung the lantern from a hook embedded in the ceiling, then turned to wait upon the prince, who stood gazing with pensive eyes at the waxen features of the corpse.

"This is a man who's been struck down in the prime of his life," Raidan said.

"Just so, milord. 'Tis a tragedy."

"Help me carry him to the table."

While Raidan managed the head and shoulders, the old healer took the legs and feet. Together, the two men wrestled the corpse onto the table, where Raidan pulled the sheet away to reveal the entire body.

"I like the design of this dissection table," he commented as he dropped the shroud to the floor and pushed it aside with his foot.

The old man squared his bony shoulders and grinned. "I designed it myself, your Highness. The top is glazed ceramic, and you see here, these channels along the sides? Perfect for the drainage of body fluids. I also put drains in the floor..."

"Yes, yes, very impressive," Raidan cut in. The healer gulped and fell silent. "I need to get started now," the prince added. "There's a lot of work to do."

"I can hang your cloak on the peg by the door, Highness. I also have an extra apron if you would like," the old man offered meekly.

"Thank you, yes, and light another lantern if you have one." Raidan eased his satchel off his shoulder and let it slip to the floor. As the healer scurried to comply, the prince continued his preliminary examination of the corpse. All the telltale signs of the plague were present—purplish swellings under the jaw, a blackened, protruding tongue, hemorrhage from eyes, ears, nose, and mouth.

No doubt I'll find blood at the anus as well, the prince thought.

"Jashen," the healer said.

"What?" Raidan threw a sideways glance at the old man.

The healer pointed to the corpse. "His name was Jashen. Jashen Hosha.

He was a farmer. Owned a decent-sized spread just south of here." The old man sighed and shook his head. "I don't know what his poor wife's going to do. Two little ones and a third on the way."

Raidan rummaged in his bag and withdrew a small leather case. He eased it open and removed a pearl-handled scalpel. "Has the woman no other family to assist her?" he asked, brow furrowed in concentration as he carefully cut into one of the swellings, releasing a gush of black fluid.

"Suka is a northerner," the healer replied. "She's got no family anywhere near Tono, sad to say, your Highness."

Raidan laid down the scalpel then reached into his bag for a collection spoon and vial. Careful not to allow any to come in contact with his skin, he scooped a small amount of the black fluid into the vial and sealed it.

Over the next hour, he and the old man worked in silence. It seemed only fitting they do so, out of respect for the deceased. To Raidan, the dissection of a body must always be done with reverence, for only through careful examination, using the logic of science, would its inner workings be revealed, and by extension, the mind of The One.

After collecting the samples he needed, Raidan washed his hands in a basin provided by his host, then helped the old man replace the corpse in its niche. He stowed his specimens with care in his satchel, then fished out a small leather pouch. He upended it and three coins—two gold and a silver—clinked onto his open palm.

"The gold is for the widow. See that she gets it. The silver is for your trouble, healer."

The old man nodded and folded the coins into his gnarled fist. "Thank you, milord," he murmured, bowing deeply. "It has been an honor to assist you."

"Let's hope tonight's work yields some answers. The fate of our people could depend on it."

Raidan lifted his bag to his shoulder and collected his cloak from the peg by the door. He then followed the old man back up the tunnel to the outer entrance, leaving the dead farmer to rest in the chilly darkness.

A Change of Heart

❧

The following morning dawned gray and cool. Fat clouds, heavy with rain, scudded by overhead, carried north on stiff winds from their birthplace over the western ocean. Raidan sat on a bench in the shelter of the inn's large covered porch, wrapped in his cloak, impatient to be away.

Out in the inn's front yard, the prince's entourage bustled back and forth, readying their horses for departure. Raidan sighed irritably and rose to his feet.

What is taking so long? Where is my horse?

He paced along the length of the porch, attempting to rein in his temper, self-aware enough to know that lack of sleep contributed to his ill humor. An outburst now would be undignified and unfair.

"My lord prince!" Raidan's aide Kasai trotted across the yard to the porch. He sketched a quick bow. "Your horse has a loose shoe," he explained between quick breaths. "The inn has no on-site blacksmith, so someone's been sent to the next village to fetch one." The man bowed again. "I'm sorry for the delay, your Highness."

Raidan cursed. Kasai kept his gaze fixed on his boots. Raidan took a deep breath. "I know this isn't your fault. These things happen. It's been a hard week for all of us. How long do you think it'll be?"

Cautiously, Kasai looked up. "I can't say for sure, my lord, but the village is not far and the stable boy left right away. It shouldn't be too long. Perhaps you'd rather wait inside where it's warmer?"

Raidan nodded, temporarily mollified. He followed Kasai back into the inn's common room and commandeered the most comfortable chair while his aide called for service.

A few moments later, the innkeeper herself appeared and scurried over, wiping her hands on her apron as she approached. A cloud of worry surrounded her like a fog. Raidan's eyes narrowed. The woman bowed and asked, "What can I bring you, your Highness?"

"A mug of your best beer," the prince responded, then asked a question of his own. "Mistress, even a person with no Talent at all would be able to see quite clearly how troubled you are. I hope neither I nor any of my people have been the cause of your discomfiture."

The innkeeper, a solidly built woman with silver-streaked black hair, briskly shook her head. "Oh, no, my lord, no!" she exclaimed, eyebrows raised. "You've been most gracious, my lord, no trouble at all..." Her voice trailed off, and Raidan sensed she was barely holding herself together.

"Tell me what has got you in such a state, then," he prodded in a gentle tone. The woman's hands flew to her mouth and fat tears leaked from her clear, brown eyes. She stifled a sob, gulped, then whispered, "It's my oldest boy, sir. I think he...he's come down with the plague!"

Raidan rose to his feet. "Take me to him," he commanded. "Kasai, go fetch my bag."

"Straight away, my lord!" Kasai replied and rushed to obey. Without another word, the innkeeper led the way through the kitchen into the family's living quarters, Raidan hard on her heels.

The boy lay in a small darkened bedchamber, buried beneath a mound of blankets.

"Mistress, please uncover a window. I need light to work," Raidan ordered. The innkeeper opened a shutter to allow storm-gray light into the room. Raidan approached the bed, but he needed no visual confirmation to tell him what his nose had already made clear. With gentle hands, he peeled back the layers of blankets to reveal the sick child.

"What is your son's name, Mistress?" Raidan asked.

"Tanshi, your Highness," the innkeeper whispered.

"Tanshi, can you hear me?"

The boy moaned and his eyes rolled beneath closed lids.

Kasai entered the room, carrying Raidan's satchel. He handed over the bag without a word, and backed off to stand at the foot of the bed beside Tanshi's mother.

Raidan's eyes traveled over the boy's body. Tanshi had been a robust lad on the cusp of manhood. The prince noted the telltale signs of the plague, but as of yet, there appeared to be no hemorrhage. Raidan took this as a hopeful sign. Of the many plague victims he had seen over the last week, those that did not bleed went on to recover. Still, the boy was desperately ill and could fail at any moment.

His exam complete, Raidan replaced the blankets, then turned to face the mother. "Tanshi does have the plague, Mistress, but there is cause for hope."

A CHANGE OF HEART

The innkeeper listened attentively while Raidan instructed her on her son's care and the proper dosage of the medicines he planned to leave. "Above, all, you must wash your hands after you have finished with your son. It is very important."

The innkeeper looked dubious, but nodded her head. "I will, my lord," she replied.

Raidan handed her several vials, then repacked his bag.

"You can wash in the kitchen, sir," the innkeeper said, anticipating Raidan's next request. As she led the way back into the kitchen, the woman turned and said over her shoulder, "It's those dirty hikui, my lord. They're the ones spreading this plague!"

Raidan frowned. "We don't know enough about this disease to blame its spread on any one thing, Mistress," he replied.

"Begging your pardon, Highness, but you'll not convince me!" the woman huffed. "A hikui tinker came calling two weeks ago. My Tanshi spent a fair amount of time with the man's daughter, against my wishes I might add! Now, he's sick! No one else has fallen ill. Only my son." She hovered while Raidan scrubbed his hands in the scullery basin. "I say all hikui should be made to leave Tono, my lord, and I'm not the only one!" Her eyes flashed defiance, as if daring Raidan to chastise her. The prince said nothing; he understood her attitude.

Okui folk are scared and the hikui make convenient scapegoats, he thought.

Kasai waited for him in the common room. "The blacksmith is here, Highness," he said. "Your horse should be ready within the hour."

"Very good." Raidan nodded to the innkeeper. "I'll have that beer now, Mistress, if you please."

The prince sat sipping his beer, mulling over in his mind the report he would make to his brother, the king. His thoughts—dark, grim things—swirled about inside his head dressed in shreds of horror and blood.

What bitter irony it would be if we manage to repel the Soldaran invasion, only to succumb to this human disease. Surely the Goddess would not allow such a fate for Her children!

Kasai interrupted his master's bleak reverie. "Your horse is ready, my lord prince. We await your orders."

"Pay our hostess," Raidan directed as he exited the common room into the yard. The stable lad holding his mount's reins bowed his head as the prince took charge of the horse.

When the entire party had mounted, Raidan led the group out of the inn yard onto the road leading north. He frowned at the dark clouds bulking on the horizon, then looked back over his shoulder to see the innkeeper standing in the doorway, her face a mask of worry. Raidan couldn't help but sympathize with her.

I have children too, he thought.

He turned to look at Kasai, riding beside him. "We must hurry. This has taken far longer than I'd anticipated. I want to get back to Sendai by tomorrow night."

"Yes, your Highness," Kasai replied.

Raidan dug in his heels and his horse surged into a canter. Together, the group of riders raced northward, into the storm.

&

The prince peered through the eyepiece of his scope at a smear of fluid staining a small glass plate and sighed in frustration.

Nothing!

The samples he had collected in Tono had yet to yield any clues to the nature of the mysterious essence he *knew* must be the cause of the disease. He pushed aside the scope and rubbed his tired eyes.

Could it be my collection methods? I followed, to the letter, the recommendations of Nazarius. No, that can't be the problem. What about the means of preservation of the specimens?

He picked up a specimen jar and examined the blob of tissue floating within.

Perhaps. Vinegar, wine, salt. All well and good for foodstuffs, but for fragile tissue samples? Unfortunately, there isn't anything else available, unless I incur the considerable expense of buying preservation spells from a mage, which is impractical.

Could the problem lie with my instruments? Perhaps they are not sensitive enough.

Raidan gazed at the microscope, a delicate construction of brass and carefully ground lenses. The finest maker of scientific and navigational tools in all of the Arrisae Islands had custom crafted it to Raidan's specifications.

A Change of Heart

The scope had worked beautifully on other things: the minute structure of a butterfly's wing, the round disks that floated in the blood of both people and animals.

No, there has to be some other reason, something I've not thought of yet.

Raidan stood and stretched, then poured himself a glass of wine from the carafe on his work table. He took a sip, then walked to the window of his study and looked out at the small, walled garden below. The carefully tended plants had been the pride and joy of his mother. Taya, his wife, looked after it now. The little garden had always been a sanctuary of sorts, filled with happy childhood memories.

If only those carefree days could be recaptured, Raidan thought.

Five days ago, he had stood before the full council and had given his report on the situation in Tono. Afterward, Lady Odata immediately begged permission to return home and the king had granted it. She and her people had departed Sendai that same day.

Yesterday, a rider had arrived from Tono with a message from Odata—the Soldaran Army advanced northward at a leisurely pace, as if deliberately mocking the elves. Keizo had remarked that since the humans brimmed with such confidence over their superior numbers, they apparently felt no need to hurry.

Tonight, he, Keizo, and Sen Sakehera planned to meet privately in order to finalize the war plans. All was essentially in readiness. The army was assembled and the Home Guard in place. Only the role of the mages remained to be finalized.

Keizo had insisted on using mages, and after some serious thought, Raidan had agreed. It made sense. Very few humans were capable of wielding magic, and those that could did not command the same force and power as even a modestly trained elven mage. From what Raidan knew about human magic, most of it seemed based on little more than superstition, illusion, and outright trickery.

Magic would give them a badly needed advantage, serving to counterbalance the elves' lesser numbers.

A sharp knock on his study door interrupted the prince's train of thought. "Come!" he called out.

The door swung open and a page, dressed in the livery of the king, stepped through and bowed. "Your Highness! Princess Jelena begs you to come right away. The king has fallen ill!"

Raidan's heart froze.

The half-full glass slipped from his fingers and fell to the floor, spilling wine across the mats in a blood-red spray.

The prince bolted past the startled page, through the deserted rooms of his apartments and out into the corridor. He didn't stop running until he reached the king's bedside.

Breath heavy with fear more than exertion, Raidan stood gazing down at his brother, who lay pale and sweating in the bed he shared with his Companion Sonoe, the telltale swellings already beginning to appear under his jaw.

"It's the plague, isn't it?"

Raidan looked into the eyes of Keizo's daughter, her stricken face so like his brother's, Raidan wondered how he could ever have doubted her paternity. His niece sounded more like a scared child than a grown woman. He nodded and Jelena dropped her head into her hands.

Guilt, like a landslide, rolled down upon the prince, threatening to overwhelm him.

This is my fault! I must have brought the plague back from Tono somehow!

Keizo had expressed serious misgivings about allowing him to pursue his inquiries, but Raidan had insisted, charging Keizo with backwardness in wanting to cling to magic rather than accepting the rational tenets of science.

Now, all of Alasiri will pay the price for my arrogance.

Neither Jelena nor he spoke for a time. The enormity of this disaster was too overwhelming to absorb all at once. Raidan, even with his limited Talent, felt his niece's despair beating at him like a living thing, raw and wild.

At last, Jelena whispered, "What are we going to do?" Her voice quivered with unshed tears. She moved from the foot of the bed closer to Raidan.

"We have no choice but to carry on," he replied, fighting for control. "The lives of all our people are at stake. Fortunately, everything is in place. All that's left now is to execute the war plan."

Jelena nodded. "Yes, Uncle, I agree. I wish to ride out with the army, by your side, as I would have with my father." For the first time since she had arrived in Sendai and had changed all of their lives forever, Raidan felt genuine tenderness toward his brother's daughter, and pride as well.

A CHANGE OF HEART

She has proven herself to be a true Onjara, strong and brave, human blood notwithstanding. Was it only a few months ago that I contemplated murdering this girl to safeguard my own ambitions?

Shame, like a bitter-tongued old hag, harangued him, adding to the heavy burden of guilt already weighing down his soul. Unaccustomed to this particular emotion, it did not sit well with him.

He rested a hand on Jelena's shoulder. "Are you sure you wouldn't rather stay here in Sendai with your father and Hatora?" he asked in a gentle voice. "No one would think any less of you."

"There's nothing I can do for him," she replied, glancing at Keizo then back at her uncle. "Sonoe will stay with him."

Raidan shook his head, and when Jelena opened her mouth to protest, he pressed a finger to her lips. "No, Niece. I cannot allow you to leave Sendai, and I ask you to please just listen before you bite my head off. You are not a trained soldier! Your child needs her mother. Think about what would happen to Hatora if you should fall in battle. She's already lost her father. Do you really think it's fair to put her at risk of losing you as well?"

Jelena's hazel eyes blazed in defiance; then, as Raidan's words penetrated the wall of desperate fury she had erected, he watched reason begin to cool his niece's inflamed emotions. Her face crumpled and, without warning, she leaned against him and laid her head on his shoulder.

Caught completely off-guard, Raidan slipped his arms around Jelena almost without thinking. He held her until the spate of tears had passed and she broke the embrace. Wiping her eyes on the hem of her sleeve, she lifted her chin and stared back at Raidan with calm resignation.

"You're right, of course, Uncle. My place is here with my daughter and I'm ashamed I had to be reminded of it." She paused, took a deep breath, then asked, "Is there any treatment you know of that might help my father?"

"Nothing specific, other than supportive care," Raidan replied, moving closer to the bed so he could examine Keizo more thoroughly. "My brother has a very strong constitution. I have every reason to hope he will survive." He leaned in close and spoke into Keizo's ear. "Can you hear me, Brother?"

The king moaned and his lips worked but no words slipped out.

"Don't worry, Keizo. Sen and I know what must be done." Raidan spoke in a rapid whisper. "Alasiri will not fall, not as long as there is a single elf left alive to defend her. I swear to you on the graves of our father, brother, and mother, that I will not let the humans take our land from us!"

"I'm here too, Father." Jelena came up beside Raidan and closed her hand around Keizo's. Lifting it to her lips, she kissed her father's palm, then pressed it to her cheek and closed her eyes.

"Where is Sonoe?" Raidan asked, surprised and puzzled at the absence of Keizo's Companion.

The girl shrugged. "I don't know. When I arrived to see my father, she wasn't here. He must have taken ill after she had gone out for the day. I doubt she would have left him, otherwise."

"I'll send a page to find her. She should be here with him," Raidan said. "Jelena, things are going to get difficult very soon," he continued. "As much as any of us hate to admit it, there's a good chance the elves will lose this war. We are badly outnumbered by a determined enemy." He paused to gaze deep into his niece's eyes. What he saw there reassured him. "It may very well fall to you to assume leadership of our people should the worst happen and your father, myself, and my two sons don't survive."

"But, Uncle, the elven people won't accept me as their queen…" Jelena began, but Raidan interrupted.

"The elven people may have no choice," he countered firmly. He paused to take a breath, then continued. "This is very difficult for me to admit, but I was wrong about you. When you first came to Sendai…more specifically, when we all learned the truth about you, I was angry, no, furious is a better word. Despite your protestations to the contrary, I did view you as a threat and—please don't be afraid when I say this—I was fully prepared to eliminate you." Jelena's eyes widened in shock. Her lower lip trembled, but she remained silent, her face gone pale.

"I'm a proud man, sometimes arrogant, this I know, but I like to think I'm ruled by reason and not passion," Raidan continued. "I wish I could say to you that I saw reason, but the truth is much less tidy. My wife stayed my hand, Jelena. She asked, no…" He smiled wryly. "She *ordered* me not to harm you. Taya is the only person, other than my brother, who can order me to do anything! It seems you have a destiny not even I can interfere with."

He took Jelena by the hand and led her to a cushioned bench against the wall opposite Keizo's bed, and together, they sat. Raidan kept her hand folded in his as he spoke. "I can't point to any single moment when my heart changed, Niece, but it was definitely you who changed it. You are Keizo's daughter, a true Onjara, and you are old enough to rule. Alasiri will need an adult of royal blood at the helm should the worst happen, someone able to make hard decisions. I have come to accept that this person is you."

Jelena bit her lip and lowered her head. Reaching beneath the collar of her tunic, she withdrew her Griffin Ring upon its sturdy chain. She stared at the heavy circle of white gold, then closed it in her fist. She lifted her face to meet Raidan's eyes, and in that instant, he witnessed the completion of her transformation from bastard outsider to royal princess.

"If the One decrees it, I'll be ready," she replied.

Chapter 4

Journey's End

Gran awoke from the mage sleep two days later. Her thin face still bore traces of the tremendous strain she had endured, but she seemed to have regained most of the strength she had spent to save their lives. After breaking her fast on bread and cheese, she climbed out of the barrow chamber, Ashinji and Magnes at her side.

"How are you feeling Ashi?" Gran cupped Ashinji's face between her hands, her pale eyes boring into his. The gesture reminded him of his mother.

"Better. You were right. It didn't take me long to recover."

Gran dropped her hands, nodding. "How much longer 'til we reach Amsara?" she asked.

"About ten days, if we don't encounter any trouble," Magnes replied. "The road is pretty good all the way."

"We're so exposed out here. It makes me very nervous," Ashinji said. "How likely are we to run into trouble?"

"Not very," Magnes assured. "The Imperial Army lies well to the west and the land hereabouts is thinly settled. Shepherds, mostly. Even if we do encounter any people, as long as you and Gran are disguised, they'll probably leave us alone."

"We'd better get going, then," Gran said. "We're running out of time."

"Have you sensed something new, Gran?" Ashinji asked, a thrill of fear spurring his heart into a gallop.

36

JOURNEY'S END

Gran shook her head. "No, no, Ashi. Nothing has changed." She reached out and patted his forearm. "I just meant that we can't afford to dawdle."

Ashinji took a deep, calming breath, then did some quick calculations in his head.

Ten days to reach Amsara, then another couple of days to the Alasiri border. After that, we'll need at least two days to skirt the Fens and two more to reach Kerala Castle. We can get supplies and fresh horses there for the ride to Sendai. Gran can't ride as fast as I can, so that'll add a day or two. We should reach the capital in six days, seven at the most.

And when we finally do reach Sendai...

His mind shied away from the dark thoughts now trying to push their way to the fore of his consciousness, thoughts of suffering and loss yet to be endured. He did not feel ready to face them though he knew, in the end, he must.

They packed their meager supplies then set out across the rolling countryside. The sun had nearly reached its zenith by the time they found the road. As the horses clopped along its uneven surface, their unshod hooves kicked up puffs of red-brown dust that floated away in lazy wisps on a light breeze.

They encountered no other people that day. To Ashinji, it felt like they alone inhabited the world, save for the sheep dozing in clusters by the roadside, or standing in bleating groups beneath the precious shade of solitary trees.

That night, they took shelter in the ruin of a stone tower. The tiny fire Magnes built served mainly to chase away the shadows, for the night was warm and they had no fresh food that needed cooking. Ashinji fell asleep to the sound of the horses cropping the thick, sun-scorched grass beyond the tumbled stones of the tower's fallen upper stories.

The days passed in a somnolent blur, falling away behind them like barely remembered dreams. They continued to have the road to themselves. Only the occasional herder or crofter seen in the distance reminded them that people did make this desolate area their home.

After the fifth day, the land began to change, the rolling hills giving way to flat, cultivated fields.

"We've crossed into Veii," Magnes informed them. "Amsara's southern neighbor. My father sold Jelena to Veii's duke. If she hadn't had the courage to defy my father and run away..."

"She would have escaped somehow and found her way north to me, even so," Ashinji said. "We were destined for each other."

A flash of pain twitched across Magnes' face. "You and Jelena will soon be together again, Ashi." He would not look at Ashinji as he spoke.

At sunset on the eighth day, Veii Castle hove into view like a big black ship on the horizon. The three travelers stayed well to the west of the fortress, skirting several hamlets and taking a wider detour around a large village. Gran remained ready with a glamour to disguise herself and Ashinji should they chance upon any people, but it never became necessary. They always managed to avoid any close encounters.

Twelve days after fleeing Darguinia in the mobile infirmary of the Eskleipans, the three fugitives crossed into Amsara. A stone tablet marked the border, nothing more. To Ashinji, the landscape appeared much as it had through most of Veii, but he could see by the subtle lift of Magnes' shoulders and the renewed spark in his eyes, his friend knew the look and feel of home.

They traveled for one more day and part of another before the road at last split into two branches—one heading north, the second angling to the northwest.

Magnes, who had been riding in the lead, raised his hand to signal a halt. He slid off his mount and Ashinji followed suit. "This is where we must part company, my friend," he said. He pointed to the northward path, then fixed his gaze upon Ashinji's face. "Amsara lies that way…" His voice faltered and he looked away.

"Come, my friend," Ashinji said quietly. "Let's walk a little." He looked back at Gran.

Go, she mindspoke. *I know you two need a few moments alone.*

Magnes ambled a few paces up the northward path, Ashinji a step behind, then stopped and turned to face his elven friend. He made no attempt to hide his feelings. Ashinji met Magnes' naked yearning with compassion as his only offering, but then an idea sprang into his mind.

Maybe there is something I can do for my friend. A gift to ease his pain.

"Magnes, you know we elves can communicate with each other, mind to mind," he said. Magnes nodded. "I'm not sure if it will work between an elf and a human, but I want to try it with you. If I'm successful, our minds will be joined for a time. It's an extremely intimate experience, usually shared only between two people who are very close."

Magnes swallowed hard. "Are…are you sure you want to do this now, Ashi?"

"Yes, I'm sure." He laid a hand on Magnes' shoulder. "We may never have another chance. We are friends…no, we are much more than friends. We are brothers."

"If you're sure, then I would be honored," Magnes replied. "What do I have to do?"

"Sit down first, then relax. I'll do the rest."

Ashinji wasn't at all certain it could be done, but he had to try.

Gran really should be the one doing this. After all, she's the trained mage, not I.

He had no experience or schooling to guide him, only gut instinct, determination, and the intense desire to help his friend. Perhaps he shouldn't, but nevertheless, he still felt partly responsible for Magnes' emotional torment.

No, I must be the one to fix this, not Gran.

The two young men sat down in the grass beside the path. Ashinji held out his hands to Magnes and smiled.

"Rest your palms on mine, and close your eyes," he directed.

Ashinji let his consciousness flow outward, seeking the barrier separating his own mind from Magnes'. When he found it, it dissolved before him like a veil of smoke and left Magnes' mind exposed and vulnerable. Ashinji searched for and discovered what he needed to change but before he gave his friend the gift of forgetfulness, he would give him the joy of a true bonding.

Ashinji let drop the barriers shielding his own mind and allowed his consciousness to flow like water into the pool of Magnes' being. He immediately sought to dampen his friend's shock at first contact, instinctively sending the energy of his Talent coursing along Magnes' nerves—soothing, reassuring, wrapping the other man's mind in a calm, loving embrace. He held Magnes thus, and rejoiced as the other's fear turn to wonder. He recalled the first time he and Jelena had shared the mind link. Her reaction had been much the same.

Ashinji held steady within the link and allowed Magnes to roam where he willed. He concealed only that part of his mind which held all the private experiences he had shared with Jelena. When Magnes had seen all he could, Ashinji, in turn, traveled through the myriad rooms and corridors of his friend's mind, leaving unexplored only those darkest corners he sensed the other man guarding, albeit unconsciously. Ashinji had no wish to be privy to Magnes' most sensitive secrets.

When he was done, Ashinji sent forth a ghost of himself onto the landscape of Magnes' mind, to serve as a distraction while he performed the task that would set his friend free. He felt no hesitation or doubt; somehow, he just seemed to know what to do.

Quickly, he returned to the source of pain and cauterized the wound, sealing the raw edges and spreading a soothing balm of forgetfulness over the entire area. He then withdrew and broke the link.

Magnes' head jerked up and his eyes snapped open. He stared at Ashinji for many heartbeats. Finally, he spoke. "Gods!"

Ashinji smiled.

"All elves do this, this mind thing?" Magnes stuttered.

"Yes, we all can do it, but as I've said, we almost always reserve the mind link for those we feel closest to. As you saw, it leaves one completely exposed."

"Ashi, I...I don't know what to say," Magnes whispered.

"You don't have to say anything. You are my friend and I'd gladly share the link with you again, now that I know it's possible." Ashinji rose to his feet.

After a moment's hesitation, Magnes followed suit. He glanced over his shoulder toward the north then up at the sky. "If I hurry, I should make it home by sundown," he said. He turned to look at Ashinji; the pain and longing had vanished from his eyes.

Ashinji breathed a sigh of relief. Up until that moment, he had not been sure if his attempt at psychic surgery had worked. "This is not goodbye, Magnes," he insisted. "I know in my heart we will meet again. This war may be between our two nations but it's not between us. We're linked by ties too strong to break."

"My future is uncertain, Ashi. I might find forgiveness at home or I might find myself an outcast...or worse. But if it's within my power, I'll seek you and Jelena out and we'll be reunited." Magnes drew Ashinji into a tight embrace, one Ashinji felt no qualms about returning.

Journey's End

Magnes stepped away first. He turned and approached Gran, who had been waiting patiently the entire time, sitting astride her horse and keeping watch from a discreet distance.

"So, young human," Gran said. "This is where we part company, is it?"

"Yes, my lady, it is," Magnes replied. He reached up and covered Gran's hand with his. "Chiana, it has been a privilege knowing you. I'll never forget you."

"Nor I you, Magnes." Gran stretched out her hand to caress his cheek. "You are a fine young man. May the One always guide you and keep you safe."

"Stick to this road and you should be all right. I doubt any of the castle guard will patrol this far west." Magnes turned and looked at Ashinji. "You won't know you've crossed the border until you see the swamp."

"We'll smell it long before we see it," Ashinji commented with a wry smile. He grasped his gelding's coarse mane and swung onto the animal's back. The horse sighed and shifted from foot to foot.

Magnes climbed onto his own mount and maneuvered it next to Ashinji's.

"When you see Jelena, tell her I love her and I'm looking forward to seeing her again," he said.

"I will," Ashinji replied. He and Gran watched as Magnes turned his horse onto the northbound road and, just before he urged the animal into a trot, Ashinji called out, "Magnes, wait!"

Magnes pulled the horse to a stop and waited for Ashinji to catch up, a questioning look upon his face. "Tell your sister I said 'thank you,'" Ashinji said.

Magnes cocked his head in puzzlement. "For what?" he asked.

"Thessalina could've given in to her commanders and had me killed, but she didn't. Instead, she let me live. I'm grateful to her for that."

"I'll tell her, my friend," Magnes replied. He tapped his horse with his heels and the animal lurched into a lazy trot. Ashinji watched for a moment, then guided his mount over to where Gran waited. Together, the two elves started up the northwest road.

They rode for a while in silence before Gran spoke. "What you did back there, for Magnes…"

Ashinji looked sharply at her, frowning. "You were watching us?" he asked, shocked that she would intrude into such a private thing.

"I didn't scan either of you, if that's what you think, but yes, I *kept* watch, just in case you got into trouble," she huffed. "Oh don't look so offended, young man! You are completely untrained—which is a situation that should be rectified if at all possible, I might add—and you could have easily wiped out a part of your friend's mind he needed in order to function. Psychic surgery is a procedure that should only be done by a fully trained mage." Her scowl was so dire, Ashinji flinched before it and looked down at his hands, feeling like a child caught misbehaving.

"I had to do something for him, Gran. I couldn't let him go on suffering," he said.

"You were not responsible for Magnes' pain, Ashi," Gran snapped.

"That's where you're wrong!" Ashinji retorted, looking up. "I was the source of his unhappiness! I thought of a way I might help him, so I did what I had to, and it worked."

He and Gran glared at each other for a few moments, but then the old mage sighed and shook her head. A ghost of a smile played about her mouth. "Yes, it worked," she admitted. "And now that I've finished scolding you, I'll praise you for a job well done." She paused, then said, "Tell me what happened on the hill with the slave catchers."

Ashinji hesitated, unwilling to give voice to his deed. After a few tense moments of silence, he finally said, "I don't really know. I was furious at Seijon's death. I knew I had to stop his killer before he attacked you. The energy just…came out of me. I didn't consciously call upon my Talent at all because I thought it was blocked."

"Yes, it *was*." Gran pinned him with ice-blue eyes, her brow furrowed. After a few heartbeats, she let out a sharp exhalation. "It seems, Ashi, that somehow, you have been able to overcome the block your mother put on your Talent, all on your own, which is just extraordinary." She paused to look thoughtfully into the distance. "It really is unfortunate your mother could not find the courage to go against tradition and send you to the Kan Onji. You'd have made a formidable mage."

"My mother did what she thought best," Ashinji responded, tight-lipped with anger. "You, of all people, have no right to criticize her!" As soon as the words left his mouth, he felt a rush of regret. "I'm sorry, Gran," he murmured. "I should not have said that. It was cruel of me."

"No, Ashi, you are right to defend your mother. It is true that I'm the least fit person to be Amara's judge. What I should have said was, it is a great pity your mother felt she could not send you to the Kan Onji." She looked at him and smiled. "It's not too late, Ashi. You can still become a mage, if you wish."

"I don't know, Gran," Ashinji replied. "I've never been anything else but a soldier. My warrior's skills are what will be needed in this fight. Becoming a mage is, well, it just seems like an impractical goal right now. And besides, neither of us knows if we'll even survive what's to come."

"We'll see," Gran muttered.

❧

"There they are. The Shihkat Fens. We've made it home, Gran."

The elderly mage nodded. "We may be back in Alasiri, but we've got a long way to travel yet."

Ashinji raised his hand against the glare of the midday sun off the shimmering expanse. From this distance, the Fens looked like a vast lake, but as the two travelers drew closer, the landscape resolved into a patchwork of stagnant pools slimed with brilliant green algae, weed choked sinkholes, and hillocks covered in tough, brown grasses. The warm, wet air reeked with the smell of decay.

"I know there are trails leading through, but without a guide, we'd have little chance of finding our way," Ashinji said.

"We'll have to go around, then," Gran replied, her voice low and resigned. The necessity of bypassing the swamp would add at least two extra days to their journey.

Despite the inhospitability of the land, Ashinji knew people did inhabit the Fens, making their living by hunting, trapping, and fishing. The fresher pools and running streams harbored abundant life—fish, frogs, turtles, and crayfish—while the thickets abounded with rodents and other small mammals, as well as snakes, lizards, and songbirds. Migratory waterfowl used the larger ponds as stopovers along their ancient flyways. The hardy folk who chose to live within this world were an unconventional lot, content to exist outside the normal structures of elven society.

A large chunk of the eastern end of the Fens fell within the borders of Kerala, but by tradition, Kerala's lords claimed no jurisdiction over it or anyone living there. The Shihkat Fens existed as a world unto itself, one in which, at this point in time, Ashinji had no wish to enter.

At sundown, they stopped to make camp beneath a stand of willows. They had been living off the land for several days, relying on Gran's animal charming spells to bring small game within reach and supplementing their diet with wild greens and berries

After a meager supper of cold, stringy rabbit, Ashinji hobbled the horses to prevent them from wandering too far and Gran cast a simple warding spell around the campsite. Almost as soon as he lay down on his thin blanket, Ashinji fell asleep, too exhausted to wonder or even care if Gran's wards would be enough to wake him in the event danger threatened.

The next morning, he woke to find the skin of his arms and legs dotted with itchy red welts, the result of a nocturnal insect attack. As he scratched the lesions, he wondered why Gran's wards could keep out some predators but not others. Gran herself appeared untouched.

Perhaps the miserable little bloodsuckers don't like the taste of mage's blood! Ashinji thought.

After two more days of travel, the Fens yielded to drier land and the travelers steered northeast in a direct line that would bring them to Kerala Castle. Everything around him looked familiar; Ashinji felt his spirits lifting.

At sunset, a little over a year after his brother's betrayal had cast him down into a life of slavery, Ashinji rode across the bridge connecting Kerala Castle to the mainland and halted at the outer gate.

I made it back! Against all odds, I'm home!

The gate stood shut against the coming night. Ashinji slid off his horse, walked to the postern door and pounded on it with his fist.

After a few heartbeats, the peephole slid open.

"Who goes there?" The voice sounded more irritated than challenging.

Ashinji stepped closer so the guard could see his face in the rapidly failing light. "Tell Captain Miri and Seneschal Iruka that Ashinji Sakehera has returned," he said softly. The guard let out a startled yelp and the peephole slammed shut. A heartbeat later, the postern door flew open and a pair of excited guardsmen tumbled out. Both men began talking at once.

"My lord! This is unbelievable…"

"You're alive! We were told you'd been killed…"

"At the Battle of the Saihama Fords! It's been…"

"At least a year. Lord Ashinji, where have you been all this time?"

Ashinji held up both hands and the two guards fell silent. "Please," he said in a broken voice. "Lady Chiana and I just need to rest for a while. Then we'll tell our story." He indicated Gran, still mounted, with a lift of his chin. "One of you go help the lady, and will the other please go fetch Captain Miri and the seneschal now."

"Yes, Lord Ashinji!"

"Yes, my lord!"

Ashinji squeezed his eyes shut for a moment, battling a wave of vertigo that threatened to pitch him to the ground. He had never before in his life felt so drained, not even after the times he had survived lethal matches on the sands of the Grand Arena. That kind of fatigue had always left his mind strangely energized; the sheer thrill of escaping death for him acted as a potent mental stimulant. What he felt now seemed something else entirely, as if he had expended all his energy in the effort to get back home, and now had nothing left. He didn't know how much longer he could remain on his feet and conscious.

Gran came up beside him, leaning on the young guardsman for support. She brushed his forearm with her fingertips and a warm jolt of energy flowed up Ashinji's arm and dispersed throughout his body. He instantly felt better, but guilt made him turn to Gran and chide her. "You shouldn't have done that, Gran. You need all of your strength."

"Don't tell me what to do with what's mine, young man," Gran responded. "If I choose to give away my energy, then I will and you've got no say in the matter." Ashinji saw the tenderness in her eyes that belied the tartness of her words. He sighed and kissed her cheek.

"My lord, please come inside." the guardsman begged, gesturing toward the postern door.

"Take Lady Chiana and send someone out to get the horses," Ashinji ordered. "I'll wait here."

"Straight away, my lord," the guard responded. Gran allowed herself to be led through the door, offering no resistance, head bowed, her once firm, determined step reduced to a shuffle. Seeing her in such a state, Ashinji felt equal parts guilt and gratitude pierce his heart like twin thorns.

Without her skills and strength, I might never have made it back. I owe her a tremendous debt.

Ashinji did not have long to wait before another guard, a woman this time, emerged from the postern. "L...Lord Ashinji," she stammered. "Ai, Goddess, it's true. You are alive!" She fell to one knee, grabbed Ashinji's hand and pressed it to her lips. "It was like all our hearts had been torn out, my lord, when word came you'd fallen in battle." She looked up and smiled. "But now, here you are, alive. The One is truly merciful!"

Sadaiyo, you have much to answer for! Ashinji thought. Fighting to keep the bitterness out of his voice, he replied, "It's good to be home."

He placed the horses' lead ropes into the guardswoman's hand. "Please, take the horses and see to it they get a thorough rubdown and an extra ration of grain." He gave each horse a parting slap on the neck as the guard led them away.

I owe those ugly beasts, he thought. *They've earned their extra grain and much more.*

Ashinji waited until the horses had passed through the postern before he crossed over the threshold into the lower yard of Kerala Castle. Another guard waited inside to close and bar the door for the night. "Welcome home, Lord Ashinji," the man said.

Before Ashinji could respond, a familiar voice shouted his name. He turned to see Gendan rushing toward him, sobbing, arms outstretched. Ashinji braced himself as the other man swept him into a crushing hug. For a few precious moments, all considerations of social hierarchy fell aside. They were just two friends, caught up in the sweetness of unexpected reunion.

"Gendan, I can't breathe!" Ashinji gasped, laughing. Gendan released his grip and stepped back, wiping his streaming eyes and nose on his sleeve. He opened his mouth to speak but only a wordless gasp emerged.

It took a few more moments before the captain mastered himself enough to speak. "Welcome home, my lord," he said, his voice still rough with tears. He bowed, and with that act, he and Ashinji became once again lord and liegeman. "The lady that rode in with you is in my office. One of my guards is giving her a cup of tea as we speak." Ashinji began walking and Gendan fell in beside him.

"Thank you, Gendan," Ashinji replied. "As soon as she's had her tea, have someone escort her to the keep. She's just about reached the limits of her strength."

"Begging your pardon, my lord, but you look pretty done in yourself," Gendan commented.

"That's a very polite way of saying I look like shit, my friend," Ashinji said, grinning. "It's been a long journey, Gendan. I know everyone wants to know what happened to me and where I've been, but right now, all I want is a bath and some sleep." Gran's gift of energy had all but dissipated; Ashinji felt a black wall of exhaustion looming over him, threatening to crush him at any moment.

Walking had become an exercise in sheer willpower; his feet felt like iron weights were attached to his ankles. He had to consciously order his legs to swing forward and his knees to lock so he wouldn't fall. Gendan's voice faded to a soft buzz, like a distant swarm of bees heard on a hot, summer day. He had to keep focused on walking—*swing the leg, lock the knee, shift forward, don't fall, do it again...*

He became aware he now walked amidst a crowd of excited castle folk. Gendan tried his best to keep them from overwhelming their young lord, but they kept breaking past to touch Ashinji with eager hands. He tried to acknowledge their heartfelt joy at his return, but every nod of his head, every lift of a hand, was a monumental struggle.

Gendan escorted him to the Sakehera family's private bath house and sent in a servant to assist him. After helping to scrub away weeks of road grime, the manservant stationed himself in a corner on a stool, keeping watch while his young lord soaked and drowsed in the heated water.

Ashinji did not realize he had fallen asleep until the servant woke him, then helped him get from the bath house to his own bed. His last thoughts before falling away into slumber were of Jelena and the first night they had spent together in this very bed. He imagined he could still smell her scent lingering on the pillows.

When next Ashinji opened his eyes, the golden glow of the late afternoon sun had set the shutters of his windows ablaze. He rose only long enough to use the chamber pot, then returned to bed where he promptly fell back to sleep and straight into a dream.

Chapter 5

THE PRINCE RIDES TO WAR

Jelena stood atop the broad staircase before the main entrance of Sendai Castle, her infant daughter cradled in her arms, eyes narrowed against the bright glare of the morning sun. Below, spread in neat ranks across the parade ground, the Prince's Guard waited—at ease, yet attentive. The sounds of muted conversation, jangling harness and blowing horses filled the air.

Jelena waited as well, for her uncle and for Mai. Last evening, over an intimate supper in her private apartments, Jelena had accepted Mai's offer of marriage; much to her surprise, he had insisted they wait until he returned from the war.

"You've suffered the loss of one husband already. I won't make you a widow twice," he offered in explanation. Reluctantly, she had agreed with his reasoning. Though neither one wished to dwell on it, they held no illusions. That night, they clung to each other, unable to sleep, afraid this would be their final time together as lovers.

The clatter of arms and armor drew Jelena back to the present. She turned to see her uncle, accompanied by his two sons and his aides, sweep out of the shadowy interior of the main atrium onto the steps beside her. Prince Raidan looked resplendent in his exquisite blue-lacquered armor, his dark, shining hair adorned with a simple gold coronet.

"Good morning, Niece." His handsome face was set in hard lines and sharp angles. Beads of perspiration dotted his brow.

"Greetings, Uncle," Jelena replied, then nodded to her cousins. Contrary to his usual sullen demeanor, Raidu wore a look of feral anticipation.

Perhaps the prospect of bloodshed excites my cousin, Jelena thought.

His brother Kaisik, however, looked like a rabbit caught in a snare—terrified but resigned. Jelena's heart ached for her sensitive younger cousin.

"Is Mai with you, Uncle?" Jelena strained to see over the heads of the soldiers clustered around the prince. Hatora stirred and began to whimper.

She's hungry. Jelena bounced the baby to distract her.

"I'm here, Jelena," Mai answered, emerging from behind the knot of the prince's aides. He moved to stand beside her, reached down to tickle the baby, and received a drooling smile for his efforts.

Raidan's eyes flicked from Jelena's face to Mai's and back. "I've promoted Mai Nohe to my personal staff," the prince announced. "He'll take his orders directly from me now. I hope this pleases you, Niece."

Jelena's face lit up with surprise and delight. "Yes! Oh, yes, Uncle, it does, very much!" She and Mai exchanged ecstatic glances. Jelena realized her uncle had done this thing as a favor to her; still, Mai's promotion meant much more than just an increase in pay and responsibilities. It meant the prince considered Swordmaster Kurume Nohe's son a worthy consort for his niece.

Raidan took Jelena's elbow and steered her away from Mai and the others. "Jelena, I've just come from the king's quarters. Your father is no better, but he's no worse, either, which is cause for cautious optimism. I've left detailed instructions with my chief medical assistant as to how the king is to be cared for. I've given Sonoe instructions as well."

"Sonoe has been wonderful, Uncle. She's barely left Father's side. I've practically had to force her to come away long enough to bathe and eat," Jelena said, then added, "Sonoe really loves Father, Uncle. I can see it in her eyes whenever she looks at him. It's…well, it's unfair that she's denied marriage to Father simply because she's a commoner."

"It may be unfair, but it's the way things are," Raidan replied. "Listen to me carefully now, Jelena." Jelena took a deep breath and fixed her eyes on her uncle's face. As if sensing her mother needed to concentrate, Hatora stopped fidgeting and tucked one tiny fist into her mouth.

"I am entrusting you with the defense of Sendai," Raidan continued. "I can see I don't need to tell you how vital your task will be. You must stand in for both myself and, more importantly, for the king."

Jelena nodded. "I'll not fail you, or my father," she said.

"The survival of the elves as a people, as a nation, has never before been so precarious." Raidan paused, then laid a hand on her shoulder. "Jelena, I know something of what the Kirians have planned for you, and until recently, I didn't much care. You know now that I do. While I can't tell you exactly what will happen, I do know it will be extraordinarily dangerous."

Jelena swallowed hard and clenched her hands a little tighter within the folds of Hatora's blanket. "I know the Sundering will be dangerous, Uncle, but it's necessary. The Key must be removed from me and placed within an inanimate object the Kirians can safeguard. Otherwise…"

"Otherwise, the Nameless One will use his growing power to tear the Key from Jelena's body—destroying her in the process—and use it to complete what he began a thousand years ago," Taya said.

At the sound of her voice, Raidan looked up and a tiny smile creased the corners of his mouth. "Ah, my wife has arrived, at last," he murmured. The princess approached with measured stride, dressed in lightweight silk the color of the sea at dusk. A red sash, symbol of her rank as a First Mage of the Kan Onji, bound her slender waist.

Raidan held out his hand and Taya clasped it firmly. She fastened her cool gaze upon Jelena. "Your niece knows her duty, Husband," the princess said. "You needn't worry. The Kirians will see to it that the Sundering goes as planned."

"I'm not afraid, Uncle," Jelena lied. "Both Sonoe and Aunt Taya have helped me prepare. I'm ready." She knew Raidan could see right through her brave façade by the way his eyes narrowed.

"What about my mages, Wife?" the prince asked, veering away from the subject of the Sundering.

"There are five Firsts and nine Seconds of the Kan Onji waiting at the outer city gates," Taya reported, "as well as an additional twenty or so mages from the other orders. Every order sent at least one representative. You should have more than enough magical strength."

"If only I had another troop division," the prince muttered, then added quickly, "but the mages will improve our chances, no doubt." He squinted at the sky. "It's time we were on our way. Even though the Soldarans don't seem in much of a hurry, they can still beat us to Tono if we don't move fast." He looked to his aides and called out, "Get to your mounts and bring mine!"

The knot of people gathered on the steps dissolved as the prince's aides hurried off. Raidu and Kaisik remained behind, as did Mai. The way in which Raidu stood between his father and brother reminded Jelena of Sadaiyo. Ashinji's brother, too, had often used his body thus, as not only a physical barrier, but a psychological one as well, cutting his sibling off from their father's attention.

"Kaisik," Jelena called out. At the sound of his name, Kaisik jumped as if stung, and turned to look at her. "When you come home, I'll teach you how to play Hounds and Hares," she said. She had promised to instruct her young cousin in the popular Soldaran board game months ago, but had never been able to find the time. *Now*, she thought with a twinge of guilt, *I may never get the chance.*

Kaisik smiled. "I'll look forward to it, Cousin," he replied. Raidu snorted, but said nothing. Jelena frowned and a sharp comment formed on the tip of her tongue, but reluctantly, she swallowed it.

This is no time for harsh words.

A groom arrived with Raidan's horse. The prince gestured to his sons. "You two, go mount up."

Jelena laid a hand on Kaisik's arm as he turned to go. "I'll see you soon, Cousin," she said.

Kaisik's haunted eyes belied his brave reply. "No doubt I'll have all sorts of exciting tales to tell you," he said. "Take care of yourself, and Hatora, too, Jelena."

Blinking back tears, Jelena turned to Mai and whispered, "I'm really afraid for him. He's not a soldier, Mai. He's just a scared young boy! My uncle should let him stay here in Sendai."

"He's a prince of Alasiri, Jelena," Mai replied, stroking her hair. "He is where he's supposed to be, doing what he's meant to do, which is riding to the defense of his people." He slipped his arms around her and the baby and pulled them close. "I'll keep as close a watch on him as I can," he promised, "but I'm certain Prince Raidan already has at least one minder assigned to the boy. He'll not let anything happen to his son."

THE PRINCE RIDES TO WAR

Jelena twisted in Mai's arms to look at her uncle, who stood close to his wife, speaking to her in a voice too low to overhear.

It's as if no one else exists in the world besides themselves, and nothing else matters except what they need to say to each other at this moment...I had that kind of love, once.

Jelena's brief surge of envy dissolved into guilt and she drew in a sharp breath.

"What is it, love?" Mai asked. Jelena shook her head, then reached up to clasp Mai's chin in her hand, drawing his face to hers. She kissed him hard, savoring his unique taste and smell. She wanted to implant his essence deep within her memory, so she would not forget him if the unthinkable happened.

When at last their lips parted, Mai whispered, "I love you, Jelena." He kissed Hatora's forehead and added, "Both of you."

"I know," she replied. "Come home to us."

Jelena watched as Mai collected his horse from a waiting groom and swung aboard the silver gelding with easy grace. It took every bit of strength she had not to fall apart, for was it not on these very steps that she had stood and watched Ashinji ride away, never to return?

"You're thinking of him, aren't you?"

Jelena turned to find Sonoe standing at her elbow. "Sonoe, is something wrong, has my father..."

"Keizo sleeps. There's been no change. I'm sorry. I didn't mean to frighten you, pet." Jelena breathed a sigh of relief, then refocused her attention on Mai as he prepared to ride out.

Sonoe reached out and squeezed Jelena's shoulder. "You needn't feel guilty for thinking of Ashinji, especially now."

"But I do, Sonoe. My thoughts should be only for Mai. He's the living man, the one I've pledged to marry!" Jelena's voice broke in a sob. "I couldn't even tell him I loved him, not even now, when he's riding to war and I might never see him again." She held up her bare wrist. "I finally took my wedding bracelet off last night, and it felt like I'd betrayed Ashi. Mai loves me so much, and I know it would have meant the world to him to hear me say those words, but I just couldn't, Sonoe. I couldn't." Jelena wept openly now and the baby began to wail in response.

"Hush, sweetheart, *shhhh,*" Sonoe murmured, slipping her arms around

Jelena. "Mai knows how you feel, and he accepts it. Don't torture yourself over this. Everything will be as it should, I promise." Something in the other woman's tone made Jelena turn to scrutinize her friend. Sonoe's face looked paler than usual and dark shadows smudged the skin beneath her jade-green eyes.

"You're exhausted, Sonoe," Jelena whispered, wiping her face on a corner of Hatora's blanket, then sobbed, "Oh, Hattie baby…please don't cry!" She rocked the squalling infant in an effort to soothe her.

"Here, let me take her," Sonoe offered, holding out her arms. Jelena relinquished the baby to the red-haired mage, who gathered her close, then placed the tip of a forefinger to the infant's wrinkled brow and spoke a single word. Almost at once, Hatora's tiny face relaxed and her squalls subsided.

"You're going to have to teach me that one," Jelena said, shaking her head in disbelief.

"Of course, pet," Sonoe replied, smiling.

Raidan and his entourage were at last ready to ride out. Taya stood at her husband's left stirrup, holding his dragon-crested war helm in her hands. The Prince's Guard, waiting at ease while Raidan and his staff made their preparations, now snapped to attention. As soon as Raidan gave the order, they would all leave the castle and ride through the city to join the main bulk of the army, which lay encamped outside the city gates under the command of Lord Sen.

Leaving the baby with Sonoe, Jelena hurried down the steps toward the prince. "Uncle!" she called out. Raidan paused with arms outstretched as Taya placed his helm in his hands. Jelena brushed his horse's shoulder with her fingers and said, "Please tell my father-in-law my prayers are with him."

Raidan nodded sharply. "I will," he replied. "Remember all that I've said to you, Niece."

Jelena backed away from the restless white stallion then ducked through the cluster of horses to where Mai waited. He had not donned his helmet yet; instead, he had hung it from the pommel of his saddle. He smiled as soon as he caught sight of her. Jelena reached up to lay a hand on his knee.

Before she could speak, Mai shook his head. "No, Jelena. You don't need to say anything more. I know how you feel." He covered her hand with his gloved fingers. "I'll keep you and Hatora in my heart, I promise."

THE PRINCE RIDES TO WAR

"And I'll keep you in mine, Mai. I promise," Jelena whispered.

The prince gave the order to ride, and Jelena retreated to the castle steps as the entire mounted contingent wheeled about and took off at a trot toward the castle's main gates. She moved to stand between Sonoe, still cradling Hatora in her arms, and Taya, who stood rigidly erect, hands clenched into fists at her side.

Can it be? My aunt is…yes, she's afraid! Jelena glanced at Taya from the corner of her eye. Never had she felt any tenderness for her formidable aunt until now. *It's so easy to forget she's a wife and mother as well as a powerful mage. She wants her loved ones to return home safe, just as I do.*

Jelena raised her hand as if to touch her aunt's arm. "Aunt, I know how…"

"Jelena, Sonoe," Taya snapped, cutting her off. "Come with me. We have much to do." The princess turned on her heel and marched off toward the yawning doors of the castle entrance, not bothering to look back.

و

Late that evening, Jelena kept watch at her father's bedside, as she had done every night since he had fallen ill. After a quick meal, Sonoe had gone with Taya and Amara to work on the preparations for the Sundering. Only Society business could tear Sonoe away from the king's side, but Jelena had noticed her friend seemed especially distracted of late.

Conflicted seems more accurate, she thought.

Keizo's Companion kept her mind carefully shielded at all times but Jelena needed no special ability to recognize that Sonoe appeared locked in a fierce, inner struggle of some kind.

Jelena sensed it had something to do with Keizo, but mostly with *her.* She would catch Sonoe watching her, an expression of what seemed like regret on her face and yet, her friend exuded an aura of anticipation.

Maybe Sonoe feels conflicted over her role in the ritual of the Sundering. After all, she's always believed that she, not Aunt Taya, should be head of the Kirian Society.

As Mistress of the Society, Taya would gain control of the Key once they separated it from Jelena and installed it in its new, inanimate vessel. Taya would have the final say over what the Society would ultimately do with the Key. Perhaps Sonoe worried her counsel would be belittled or ignored altogether by the princess.

Would Taya be so petty, Jelena wondered. *Surely, she'd put aside any rivalries between her and Sonoe for the greater good! I must choose to believe my aunt will act wisely, for what else can I do? My life rests in her hands, in the hands of all the Kirians. They have promised to see me through the Sundering, and I trust in that promise.*

Keizo stirred against his pillows and moaned softly. Jelena leaned forward to peer into his face, searching for any signs of consciousness, but saw none. With loving hands she stroked his hair, once as lustrous as newly minted silver, but dulled now with sickness. His body had wasted with shocking swiftness, leaving behind a shrunken remnant of a once strong and vital man.

Jelena had never before scanned her father's mind without his permission, nor could she have done so with him fully conscious. She did so now only out of her desperate need to connect with him, even if only on a subconscious level. She wanted him to feel her presence and know she loved him.

She entered her father's mind with ease—none of the usual shields stood in place to guard it—and drifted like a feather on a soft breeze down into Keizo's once meticulously ordered mental landscape, now made chaotic by sickness. Pieces of thought and memory flashed by like small lightning strikes. She found them difficult to read because of the quickness of their comings and goings, but one thing remained stable—a glowing thought form hanging stationary amidst the confusion. Jelena steered toward it, knowing this was what she had come looking for. She had found her father's core sense of himself, his unwavering knowledge of who he was, unaffected by the ravages of the plague that had so devastated his physical body.

Without hesitation, she merged with her father's consciousness as easily as she slipped into the warmth of his corporeal embrace. The rush of recognition and love which greeted her acted as a balm to her soul, easing the terrible fear burdening it since Keizo had fallen ill.

I'm here, Father.

Jelena...I've left you alone, but I don't know why. What has happened to me? Why am I so confused?

You're very sick, Father. Uncle Raidan has been caring for you, but he had to go south with the army. Sonoe and I are looking after you now.

Sonoe?

THE PRINCE RIDES TO WAR

Yes, Father. Sonoe has hardly left your side. She's been wonderful.

Sonoe…my beautiful one. I love her so very much.

I know, Father. She loves you, too.

Jelena, I loved your mother, truly I did.

I know that Father, and I understand why you two couldn't be together.

Whenever I look at you, I see her. I've carried the pain of our separation with me all these years…my child! If I'd known about you, I never…

No, Father, don't. Please don't blame yourself.

But I do, and I always will. You are my first and only born child. By right, you should be queen of Alasiri after me.

You and I both know that's not possible, Father. Your duty as king is to always do what's best for the elven people. My uncle and his sons are the rightful heirs to your crown, not me. All I've ever wanted is to live a quiet life with my family, and that's what I intend to do.

You'd have made a great queen, my daughter.

You rest now, Father.

Gently, Jelena severed the connection and withdrew from Keizo's mind. She could feel him slipping away into sleep as she emerged from the trance, and upon opening her eyes, she checked the pulse at his throat, as she had been taught by Raidan, to reassure herself her father remained stable. In the soft light of the little oil lamps hanging above the bed, Keizo's face appeared peaceful.

Jelena got up from her chair and raised her arms above her head in a long stretch, wincing at the tightness in her shoulders and back. She glanced out the open window at the night sky. A full moon hung round and brilliant in the gap between two peaks of the castle's roofs.

Sonoe should be returning soon with a report on the preparations for the Sundering, she thought.

Jelena had deliberately shielded all thoughts about the ritual from Keizo, wishing to spare him unnecessary stress. Her father needed to focus all his energy on recovery.

As the days passed and the time for the Sundering approached, Jelena's apprehension had melted into calm. The Kirians had prepped her as best they could. She felt strong and determined to survive. The Nameless One—that malevolent ghost of her centuries-dead ancestor—would be defeated and the Key safeguarded forever. They had no other options, after all.

A sudden craving for a sweet snack sent Jelena over to the pull-cord that would summon a servant to her father's bedchamber, but before she could lay fingers on the rope, the doors flew open and Sonoe rushed in. Jelena turned to face her friend, a question about the ritual on her lips, but it died before she could utter it. Sonoe's face gleamed white with shock.

"Sonoe, what..." Jelena whispered, but Sonoe cut her off with four astounding words.

"Jelena, Ashinji is alive!"

Chapter 6

HOUSE OF SHADOWS

G ods...*Magnes!*"

Magnes stopped staring into the ashes of the dead fireplace anchoring the north wall of the keep to turn and face his sister.

"Hello, Thess," he murmured.

Thessalina rushed toward him, then stopped within touching distance and simply stared, dark eyes shimmering with tears. Her mouth trembled and her nostrils flared. He couldn't tell whether she wanted to sob or scream.

She did neither. She asked him a question. "Where have you been?"

Magnes raked his hands through his thick curls.

"Can we go somewhere and sit, Thess? This is going to take awhile."

Thessalina turned and led the way in silence, up the stairs to the second floor study that had been their father's. Magnes hesitated at the threshold. All the memories of that terrible night when last he had passed through this door—sick with fear and horror over what he had done—came flooding back, threatening to breach the walls he had thrown up to confine them and sweep him away.

Perhaps returning home was a mistake after all.

He closed his eyes and sucked in a deep, shaky breath, then entered the room. Thessalina already sat at the desk, hands folded before her. Magnes approached with hesitant steps then took the chair opposite.

Thessalina remained silent, in complete charge of her emotions now, her eyes neutral. Magnes studied his sister's face and in that moment, he understood just who she had become. The little sister and childhood playmate had gone, replaced by a woman with the authority to order him imprisoned or executed. She was the duchess in all but name only, his living body her only obstacle to attaining all their father's titles and wealth.

He opened his mouth to speak but found his voice had deserted him.

"You must be thirsty. I'll call for some cider," Thessalina said. Magnes nodded, grateful for the momentary reprieve. She arose and pulled the service cord by the fireplace. While they waited for a servant to arrive, Magnes allowed his eyes to wander about the study. Thessalina had made few changes; their father's presence remained very much a part of the room, infusing the atmosphere with the residue of his personality. Magnes felt a flush creep over him; sweat prickled his brow. Against his will, he found his gaze drawn to the fireplace and it seemed as if no time had passed. The vision of his father's face, slack-jawed in death, the smell of blood and urine, the metallic taste of fear in his own mouth...

Gods, this is all too much!

Abruptly, he leapt to his feet, stumbled to the open window behind the desk, and vomited.

Thessalina appeared at his shoulder, murmuring soothing words. Magnes hung in whey-faced misery over the casement until his stomach ceased its spasms, then raised up to face his sister, stubble-roughened cheeks red with shame. Thessalina took his hand in hers, and for a few moments, became his little sister again. She pressed a cloth into his fist—a handkerchief of fine white linen embroidered with tiny yellow flowers—which he used to wipe his mouth. Grimacing with renewed embarrassment, he started to return the handkerchief, then instead wadded it up and tucked it into his waistband.

A soft knock at the door signaled the arrival of the servant. The man entered the study and bowed. "Yes, my lady?" he inquired.

"Bring a jug of cider and two mugs please," Thessalina ordered. The servant bowed again then exited the room. Brother and sister waited in silence until the servant returned, bearing a heavy pitcher and two ceramic mugs. He deposited his burden on a side table, then departed. Thessalina poured for both of them and handed Magnes a mug. He took a sip, swished the tart liquid around inside his mouth, then spat over the casement. Thessalina raised her mug to her lips, and together, they drank.

Feeling refreshed and a little more in control, Magnes returned to his chair and sat, cradling the mug between both hands. Thessalina remained by the window, waiting for him to speak.

"I don't remember attacking him, Thess," Magnes began. "That part is a blank. We were arguing. He said some things about Livie. Gods, it was ugly!" He paused to take another swig of cider. "Something came over me. I don't know what. Like nothing I've ever felt before. It was…horrible, like a red fog. I understand now what some men mean when they speak of the berserker madness."

He looked up at Thessalina and found, to his surprise, a measure of understanding. "I remember a struggle, then the next thing I knew, Father lay at my feet with…with…" He could not make his mouth form the words. He shook his head to loosen his tongue.

"A maid came in and she must have seen him. She screamed and I panicked. In hindsight I know now pure cowardice made me run. I wish I'd had the courage to stay, but at the time, all I could think of was that I'd be blamed for his murder. So I ran and I didn't stop until I'd made it all the way to Darguinia. Where better to go, if one wants to disappear? It would be as if Magnes Preseren had never existed."

His mouth twisted in a bitter smile at the flood of memories. "I changed my name and joined a holy brotherhood of humble healers, of a foreign god, no less! I thought by serving the poor and living as a simple healer, I could somehow make up for what I'd done."

He went on to recount his life as an Eskleipan and how it had eventually brought him some peace. "The daily routine helped me to deal with the pain and, finally, to get it under control."

"Why did you come back?" Thessalina asked quietly. She had remained silent throughout her brother's narrative, until now.

"I ran into someone in Darguinia, a friend. Someone you've met, actually. He had suffered incredible ill fortune and had wound up in terrible circumstances. He convinced me I needed to come home and face up to what had happened, but now that I'm here, I'm beginning to think I should have stayed away."

He looked around the room with haunted eyes. "Entering this room again took just about everything I had. I can feel Father's presence so strongly. It's as if he's still here! I feel his anger, Thess. He blames me for his death, and rightly so." He paused and drained his cup. "If I spend the rest of my life in atonement, it still won't wash me clean of my crime," he added.

Thessalina pushed away from the window and returned to her desk. She held still for several heartbeats, her eyes focused on her sun-browned hands. Finally, she spoke. "Magnes, the maid saw everything. She testified at a formal inquiry that Father attacked you, and how, during the struggle, he slipped and fell against the mantle. The magistrate officially ruled our father's death an accident."

Thessalina fell silent for a moment, then continued. "You know I love you," she stated. "You're my big brother, the one who took me riding on his pony before I was old enough to have one of my own. You taught me how to swim, and how to steal sweets from the kitchen without getting caught." She looked up at him, her face stark with hurt. "How could you run away from me, Magnes? How could you not trust me to see the truth of things? Gods, Brother! I know you could have never, *ever* killed our father on purpose."

"Thess, I'm so sorry," Magnes whispered. "I don't deserve your forgiveness."

Tears wet Thessalina's cheeks. "I would forgive you anything, Brother. Now, you have to forgive yourself," she replied.

"Someone else said the very same thing to me recently," Magnes murmured. He looked into his sister's dark eyes. "I'm not sure I know how."

A dog howled in mournful counterpoint to Magnes' words from the yard below.

Thessalina sniffed and blotted her wet face on her sleeve. "Now that you're back," she said slowly, "there's the question of your inheritance." She paused and Magnes could sense a subtle shift in her attitude, from empathy to ambivalence.

"What about it, Thess?" he prompted.

"When you disappeared and we'd heard no word from you, Father's vassals grew restless. There was even a plot, hatched by Sebastianus of Veii, to ride into Amsara and declare himself Duke! Thank the gods I had enough allies to prevent that." She picked up a gilt-handled letter opener and began twirling it in her hands. "Magnes, none of us knew if you were ever coming back. I even sent a professional Tracker to find you, but he failed, obviously. Word started going around that you were dead."

Magnes bit his lower lip. "Death may have been easier on me than what I went through," he muttered.

"I had to make a decision," Thessalina continued. "The duchy needed leadership and a clear succession. I thought long and hard and decided I couldn't wait, so I sent a petition to the capital, asking the empress to officially bestow upon me the title of Duchess and grant me all of Father's lands. I'd already led the diversionary campaign against the elves last fall, and I had the respect and support of most of Father's allies."

Magnes nodded. "None of this comes as much of a surprise," he commented.

"The empress granted my petition, Brother. I am legally still your regent, but when a year and a day have passed from the date of my petition, I will officially become Duchess of Amsara; that is, unless you decide to contest it. You are still alive, after all, and your claim supercedes mine. The empress will have no choice but to rescind my grant if you declare your intention to take back what is yours." Thessalina's next words fell from her lips reluctantly, as though they had to be pushed. "I won't fight you, Magnes, if you want Amsara back."

Ever since they had been children, Thessalina led and he, Magnes, had followed, even though he had been the firstborn. Thessalina had inherited all of Duke Teodorus' drive and ability for leadership. Though Magnes favored their father in appearance, their mother's gentle temperament formed the core of his personality.

No. Thessalina stands in her rightful place and we both know it.

"I won't contest, Sister. You should have been Father's Heir all along. I just wish he could have seen the truth of that. It would have saved all of us a lot of pain." A tangle of emotions wrapped up and stilled his voice. He closed his eyes and concentrated on breathing until the spell passed. "All I ask is that you allow me to stay on and manage the estates, like I always did for Father," he murmured.

Thessalina stood and stepped around to the front of the desk. Magnes rose to meet her and they fell into each other's arms.

"I missed you so much, Big Brother!" Thessalina mumbled into his shoulder.

"I missed you, too," he replied, stroking her dark, braided hair.

They held each other awhile longer, then Thessalina gently pushed away. A wan smile curved her lips. "You said you'd found a friend in Darguinia in bad circumstances, someone I'd met."

"Yes, and he wanted me to give you a message."

"Tell me who it was," Thessalina demanded.

"Let me give you his message first. He said to thank you for his life."

Thessalina's brow furrowed with puzzlement. "I don't recall saving anybody's life, Brother," she said. "Are you certain this friend…" She paused in mid-sentence and her eyes grew soft and unfocused. "The elf," she breathed. "Ash…Ashee…"

"Ashinji Sakehera," Magnes corrected. "You remember him now, I see."

Thessalina nodded. "One of my patrols captured him at the beginning of the fall campaign. He had been badly wounded. Shot through the shoulder. My commanders demanded he be killed and returned to the elves in pieces, but I refused. Since I couldn't send him back alive and I couldn't stomach having him killed, I sold him to a slaver instead." She paused, hand pressed to her mouth. "So, he survived. Or did he?" Magnes heard a strange catch in her voice.

"He did, though for a time, I didn't think he would. I worked as a healer at the Grand Arena. I found Ashinji enslaved at the de Guera yard, one of Darguinia's most prestigious. He was one of Armina de Guera's best fighters, but it wasn't in the arena where he nearly met his death. A fellow slave stabbed him in the back."

Magnes went on to recount the difficult feat of surgery he had performed on Ashinji. He also described the escape and flight out of Darguinia.

"You helped a slave escape his rightful owner, Brother? Do you know what would have happened to you if you'd been caught?" Thessalina frowned for a moment, then sighed. "I'm glad to hear the elf's alive and on his way back home."

Her expression grew pensive. "My men dragged him into our camp, badly hurt and in a lot of pain. He must have been so afraid." Thessalina's voice grew soft as she remembered. "But he never gave in to fear and he never lost his dignity, even in the face of the most terrible humiliation. I only spoke to him briefly, but it was enough to make me think."

"About what?" Magnes asked.

"About why we hate the elves. I'd never seen one before, other than Jelena, and she's only half-elf. I looked at him..." Thessalina paused and a stain of red crept into her tanned cheeks. She cleared her throat and continued. "I spent a lot of time just staring at him while he slept. He never knew I did that. I finally realized he was just a scared young man, hurt and alone among his enemies. I came to admire him for his courage. I knew I couldn't change the attitudes of my commanders, or of the ranks, but I could change my own."

"Ashinji sensed your change of heart, Sister. That's why he wanted me to thank you," Magnes said.

"Someday, I hope I get the chance to apologize to him and to Jelena," Thessalina murmured.

A loud knock on the study door interrupted their exchange. "Come!" Thessalina called out.

A man dressed in dusty brown leathers strode into the room, a packet clutched in his gloved hand. The silver badge of the Imperial Couriers winked on his shoulder. He touched his fist to his cap in salute and said, "My lady, I bear an official dispatch from the Soldaran High Command."

Thessalina held out her hand and the messenger placed the packet in it. She laid it on the desk, then rummaged among the clutter to retrieve a silver half-sol coin, which she dropped onto the man's palm. He saluted again and departed.

Thessalina eagerly picked up the packet. Several official wax seals affixed to cords secured the wrapper. Magnes recognized the largest—the Great Seal of Empress Constantia herself.

"What is that?" he asked, but he had already guessed the answer.

Thessalina broke the seals and unfolded the thick sheaf of papers. Her eyes scanned the contents. "These are my mobilization orders," she said, confirming Magnes' suspicion. "I've been expecting these, but I thought they would've come long before now. I'm to bring my levies with all speed to the Portanus Pass to join with the main body of the Imperial Army." She glanced at Magnes, then looked back to the papers. "I'm to leave a third of my forces behind, to act as a rear guard against any attempt by the elves to cross the border at the Janica River fords."

"That's unlikely," Magnes stated. "I'm certain there's nothing but a small defensive garrison left at Kerala Castle. Lord Sakehera, Ashinji's father, is one of the elf king's generals. He'll be at Tono, I mean Portanus, for sure."

Thessalina dropped the papers atop the desk. Her demeanor had changed again. The acting Duchess of Amsara stood before Magnes once again. "There's much to be done, Brother. I must go now. I'll see you at supper in the hall tonight?"

"Yes," Magnes replied.

ॐ

"So, how fares our cousin?" Thessalina inquired.

She and Magnes sat at one end of the massive rectangular oak table that dominated the center of Amsara Castle's great hall. A simple supper of rabbit pie, boiled turnips, salad, and apples had been sent over from the kitchen, along with a crock of last fall's hard cider.

"Very well, when last I saw her," Magnes replied. He took a bite of pie. "She and Ashinji had not yet wed, but from what I could see, they were very much in love. By the time your men captured Ashinji, he and Jelena were married and she was several months pregnant. Ashi has a son or daughter he's never seen."

"I hope, truly, that our cousin and her child will be safe," Thessalina sighed. "This war is going to be very hard on the elves. I wish..." Thessalina paused to wipe at eyes gone red. "I wish now that I had treated Jelena better."

Magnes' eyebrows shot up. "I never expected to hear you say that."

"Well, that makes two of us," Thessalina replied, taking a deep pull from her cider mug.

"There's something else about Jelena I haven't told you yet," Magnes said, setting his fork down. Thessalina looked at him, waiting.

"I know you think Jelena left Amsara to avoid becoming Veii's concubine, but that's not the only reason," Magnes explained. "She also wanted to find her father."

"Did she?" Thessalina asked.

"Yes, she did, but he was not at all what she expected."

"Oh?"

"Just before she, that is, before *we* left, Claudia gave her a signet ring and told her it belonged to her father."

"A signet ring? Then he must be one of their noble-born," Thessalina said.

"You could say that," Magnes chuckled. "The signet turned out to be the family crest of the Onjaras, the rulers of Alasiri."

"Jelena's father is a member of the elven *royal family*?"

"Not just a member, Thess. Her father is *the* Onjara. King Silverlock, himself." Thessalina stared at her brother in shocked silence. "I know how you feel," Magnes continued. "I think I looked the same way you do now when Ashinji told me. Turns out, our cousin is a princess."

"Gods," Thessalina whispered.

"What we call the Portanus Valley the elves call Tono. Thess, if they can't hold it, Alasiri will be overrun. You and I both know what that will mean for them," Magnes said.

"Yes, and there's not a damn thing I can do about it, Brother," Thessalina snapped. "I have my duty to the empress as one of her chief vassals. I can't disobey her orders." Her dark eyes roiled with anger.

"I'm not suggesting you shirk your duty, Sister. I just want you to know what's at stake. Jelena and her child, both of whom are innocent, may not survive."

"I know what's at stake! A lot of innocent people won't survive, Magnes. It's what happens in war, for gods' sake." Thessalina threw up her hands. "I wish things were otherwise, I really do, but I haven't the power to change what's going to happen. We outnumber the elves by at least three to one. They can't defeat us. Portanus will be taken, and if the empress orders us to press forward and take all of the Western Lands, then that's what we'll do!" She lowered her voice and her face softened. "I'm sure that once the elves surrender and they're absorbed into the empire, things won't be so bad for them."

"How can you say that?" Magnes' voice rose to a near shout. "First, they'll never surrender. Second, you know what the average human believes about them. You believed all of that rubbish yourself!"

"Brother, I…" Thessalina began, but Magnes cut her off.

"The empress doesn't want the elves as subjects. She wants them all removed and Alasiri repopulated with humans. This isn't a simple war of conquest, Sister. It's a campaign of extermination!"

Thessalina leaned back in her chair, jaw set. "What would you have me do?"

"Damn it...I don't know!" Magnes cried. Immediately, he regretted his outburst and the anger within him trickled away, leaving a dark stain of sadness in its wake. He cursed the powerlessness that threatened to drown him in despair. In truth, there was nothing either of them could do to stop any of it, just as Thessalina had said.

"I can't come with you," he murmured. "I won't bear arms against the elves."

"I'd be lying if I said I'm surprised," Thessalina sighed. "You'll stay, then, and run Amsara while I'm gone." Her words, for all their softness, still fell upon Magnes with the unmistakable force of command.

"Thank you," he replied. An enormous yawn threatened to break apart his jaw. "Gods, I'm so tired. I've been on the road for over two weeks. I need to go to bed."

Thessalina nodded. "Your old rooms aren't too dusty, I hope. I had standing orders to keep them clean just in case you returned, but two of the chambermaids left service so we've been short-staffed."

"They aren't bad. A little musty, is all," Magnes replied.

"I doubt I'll see my bed much before sunrise," Thessalina said. "There's still so much to do." She reached over and laid a hand atop his. Her fingertips and palm felt as callused as any peasant's. "I'm glad you'll be here to look after Amsara while I'm gone, Brother. Our people have always loved you. They'll feel safe with you here."

"Our people have nothing to fear," Magnes replied quietly.

§

Magnes woke later that night with the sour taste of nightmares on his tongue. Afraid to go back to sleep, he rose, pulled on a tunic and trousers then slipped his feet into a pair of old sandals. A shadow among shadows, he made his way out of the keep and headed across the yard toward the chapel. He paused outside the door, then looked up at the glittering vault of the night sky.

HOUSE OF SHADOWS

Are Jelena and Ashi reunited yet, he wondered. Did they sleep within the comfort of each other's arms beneath this very same sky, their baby cradled between them?

He pushed the heavy wooden door inward and entered the silent chapel. Two brass lamps burned on the altar, filling the room with dim golden light and flickering shadows. A sweet residue of incense hung in the air. With faltering footsteps, Magnes made his way down the center aisle, past the front of the altar painted with representations of the gods, to the staircase leading down to the crypt. An unlocked iron gate barred the entrance. Realizing he had no light, Magnes stepped over to the altar and grabbed a lamp. He thought of the last time he had come here, on that long ago night he and Jelena had fled Amsara.

Now, guilt pricked him as, trembling, he descended to the crypt. In the cool darkness, the departed generations of Preserens, rulers of Amsara for over three hundred years, rested in silence. The tiny pool of light cast by the altar lamp allowed Magnes to find his way through the rows of sarcophagi without stumbling. As the most recent internment, he knew his father's sarcophagus would lie near the front.

He found it alongside the slightly smaller one containing his mother's remains. Both were fashioned of gray marble, topped with lifelike effigies of their respective occupants. Magnes paused to gaze at the carved stone likeness of his mother. The blank eyes stared, unseeing, at the ceiling. The face bore little resemblance to the woman he only barely recalled from childhood memories.

Magnes raised the small lamp higher to illuminate his father's tomb. The unknown artist had done a superb job of coaxing Duke Teodorus' plain, blunt features from the dark stone; it seemed at any moment, the father would awaken from his cold slumber to arise and denounce his treacherous son.

A strangled sob clawed its way past Magnes' clenched teeth; he collapsed to his knees beside the tomb. With shaking hands, he set the lamp atop the carved folds of the effigy's gown.

Tears wet his cheeks as Magnes laid his hands over his father's chilly marble fingers. "I'm sorry Father," he sobbed. "I have no right to ask for your forgiveness. I was always a disappointment to you! I wish with all my heart I could have been the son you wanted. I just couldn't. It was never in me."

He stared into the empty eyes of the effigy, as if by sheer force of will, he could draw a response from the stone. Duke Teodorus remained frozen, implacable, unreachable.

How long he sat slumped beside his father's tomb Magnes didn't know, for he had lost all sense of time in the dark and stillness. Shadows crowded around the tiny pool of light cast by the altar lamp like the spectral presences of his departed progenitors. They surrounded him, accusing, his father's angry spirit standing at the fore.

Staggering to his feet, Magnes snatched the lamp and fled. He slipped on the slick stairs, cracking his left knee on the brutal stone. Groaning, he stumbled up and out of the crypt, then paused just beyond the gate. Breath ragged with agony, he massaged his knee, trying to get some sense of how badly he had injured it. His probing fingers told him nothing.

The chapel's narrow windows glimmered like pearl rectangles within the blackness of the surrounding walls. Dawn was fast approaching. Magnes had been down in the crypt for most of the night. Wearily, he limped toward the front of the chapel, pausing to replace the altar lamp in its rightful spot, then he slipped out through the door to the yard.

Already, he could feel his knee stiffening as he made his way back to the keep. As he passed the kitchen, he heard sounds of activity within. Cook and her staff were always the first ones up and working well before sunrise; the bread had to go into the ovens before anything else.

When Magnes came at last to his rooms, his knee throbbed with such fierceness, he feared he had torn something loose. As bad as it hurt, though, it felt as nothing compared to the pain in his soul. By visiting his father's tomb, he had hoped to ease some of the guilt tormenting him since his return home; instead, he had accomplished the opposite. What peace he had found while living and working with the Eskleipans had been shattered like a dropped mirror into a thousand jagged shards.

You have to find a way to forgive yourself.

Thessalina's words rang mockingly in his head. Magnes groaned aloud.

How can I, when what I've done is so heinous?

Who, in all of Amsara, could help him?

He returned to his bed, but sleep refused to come.

Chapter 7

ON THE BRINK

Four days later, beneath the banner of the Duchy of Amsara—three black lions rampant on an azure field—Thessalina rode out of Amsara Castle at the head of a force numbering some four hundred foot soldiers and a hundred light cavalry.

The ruddy early morning light painted helmets and spearheads with crimson. High atop the castle walls where Magnes stood, the sound of marching boots rumbled like distant thunder. He watched Thessalina's army until it had dwindled to a dark smudge on the horizon, then limped back down the stairs and headed across the yard toward the kitchen. He wasn't really hungry but the part of his mind which could still think rationally reminded him he must eat.

He allowed Cook to serve him a bowl of hot oatmeal, accompanied by a thick slice of bread, fresh from the oven. The look and aroma of the food elicited no response from his body. Each bite became a monumental struggle. Just as he decided to give up and leave his meal unfinished, Claudia appeared at his side, her own breakfast in her hands.

"Are ye leavin' already, young master? Why, ye've hardly touched yer breakfast! Are ye ill?"

Claudia looked a little more stooped, a little less stout, than when he had last seen her, just before his world fell apart on that terrible night all those months ago. Her pale blue eyes had lost none of their sparkle or motherly concern, however. Magnes had not spoken with his old nurse since returning home. He realized upon seeing her now that she knew nothing of Jelena's fate.

"No, Claudia. I'm not ill," he lied. "I hurt my knee and it aches, is all."

Claudia cocked an eyebrow. "Now, young master Magnes, ye never could fib t'me!" She set her bowl and cup on the table and sank to the bench beside him. "Tell yer ol' Claudia what really ails ye." Her voice, so gentle and full of affection nearly caused Magnes to break down and tell her the truth, but he stopped himself.

How can I burden this dear, sweet woman with the poison that festers in my soul? She couldn't possibly understand.

Instead, he changed the subject. "I've news of Jelena."

Claudia's seamed face lit up as bright as a solstice candle. "Oh, Master Magnes, if'n ye mean the news about my baby bein' a princess, then I already know!"

"How did you find out?" Magnes replied, startled.

"Jelena's man told me. Her husband."

"Ashinji was *here*?" Magnes exclaimed. "Here at Amsara? Are you sure, Claudia?"

"Sure I'm sure, young master. I saw him, I did. Spoke to him, even! He told me who he was. He had such a pretty name, but so strange and hard t' get the tongue 'round. Ashee, it was. He told me my baby was expectin' her first baby, theirs t'gether. Oh, Master, I cried, I was so happy!"

"Did my sister's soldiers bring Ashi here?" Magnes asked.

Claudia frowned. "No, sir. They weren't no soldiers! Hard lookin' they was, an' they kept poor Ashee chained to their wagon like a dog." Claudia's voice quivered with sorrow.

The slavers. Of course, Magnes thought.

"I think he was hurt, too, 'cause it looked like his arm was all bound up," Claudia continued. "I prayed every night fer a week, askin' the gods to protect him, even though he weren't human. He was my Jelena's man, an' the father of her child."

"Those men who had Ashi were slavers, Claudia," Magnes explained. "They took him all the way to Darguinia where they sold him to a very wealthy woman. That's where I found him. His mistress used him as a gladiator."

ON THE BRINK

Claudia gasped and pressed her hand to her mouth. "Is he…" Her voice died in her throat before she could finish.

Magnes smiled as he squeezed her forearm. "No. I helped him to escape. He's probably back home with Jelena by now."

"Praise the gods!" the old woman whispered.

"Ashi told you about Jelena's father, then?" Magnes asked.

"Aye, he did, Master. The king of the elves! I always knew my baby was special, an' that her dad was noble-born, but a princess? That I never s'spected." She dabbed her eyes on the hem of her apron. "I guess I'll not see my lamb again, leastways not in this life."

"You never know what fate has in store, Claudia," Magnes replied.

The old nurse nodded, then murmured, "My girl is where she truly belongs now."

Magnes sat with Claudia while she ate her breakfast, answering her questions about Alasiri and the elves. For a time, he managed to forget his pain.

When she had finished her oatmeal and tea, the old nurse said, "Now, if'n you'll excuse me, I must be gettin' this old carcass to the laundry." She rose to her feet, pausing for a few heartbeats with hand pressed to her chest. Her breath rattled alarmingly, then she bent over in a fit of coughing.

Magnes tried to slip his hands beneath her elbows, but she waved him off.

"Claudia, how long have you had that nasty cough?" he inquired after she had recovered enough to stand upright again.

"Ai, 'tis nothing, young master, just a bit 'o the lung fever, is all. I'll be all right. I'm very strong, you know," the old woman insisted.

"That's not what I asked you," Magnes responded patiently. "How long have you been sick?"

She shrugged. "Don't rightly know. Not long, though. I drink me some coltsfoot and licorice tea sweetened with honey and at night I lay a nice onion an' mustard poultice on my chest. Right as rain I am by mornin'!"

Magnes frowned, knowing Claudia made light of her condition.

"When I was in Darguinia, I learned a thing or two about healing," he said. "I trained with the Eskleipans, a very learned order. I'll make you some of their remedies."

"Ach, beggin' yer pardon, young master, but them Esk, Ekslepans sound too foreign t' me," Claudia complained.

"They might not be Soldaran, but they were the only healing order in all of Darguinia who weren't a bunch of charlatans. Do you trust me, Claudia?"

Claudia's eyes widened and her mouth formed an *O* of dismay. "My lord, o'course I trust you! I didna' mean…"

Magnes squeezed her shoulder. "I'll send the medicines up to the servants' hall as soon as I've made them," he said.

Claudia offered a crooked smile. "Thank ye, young master."

She turned to go but Magnes stopped her with a hand upon her forearm. "Claudia, I don't think you should be working so hard," he said gently. "You need to rest so you can get your health back."

"Don't be daft, m'lord!" Claudia scolded. "Me? Not work hard? What good would I be if I couldn't work, eh? I'm still just as strong as th' day I delivered you and laid you squawkin' on yer mam's belly!" Though the top notes of her voice rang with bravado, Magnes heard an unmistakable undertone of resignation. Claudia, like most common-born folk who managed to survive into old age, was a fatalist, and quite prepared to accept whatever came, be it restored good health or death.

"I'll find an easier post for you," Magnes promised. "You've served my family well and faithfully, and you deserve a rest. Let me do this for you."

"It would be nice t' get away from all that heat an' smell," Claudia sighed.

"It's settled, then," Magnes said.

They parted company at the kitchen door, she toward the laundry, he toward the stables. As he stood for a few moments watching his old nurse hobble across the yard, the peace he had enjoyed while sitting with her at breakfast dissolved. Once more, despair slithered up and wrapped him in its clammy embrace.

Got to keep moving, he thought, as he shook himself and continued on. He had no choice; he could stick to the routine of his duties, run the duchy in his sister's absence, or go mad.

On the Brink

&

The days drifted by, one very much like another. Magnes drifted as well, trying not to think too much, and above all, trying not to *feel*. Thinking led to remembering, and remembering led to pain. The duke haunted his dreams again, after leaving him in peace for the last few months. To stave off the nightmares, Magnes drank himself into a stupor each night.

Somehow, he managed to crawl from his bed every morning and attend to his duties, though the effort proved more and more difficult with each passing day. He lost all desire for food; everything he put into his mouth tasted like dust. He ate only because he must in order to stay alive, and increasingly, that was beginning to look like endless torment.

At sunrise, on the twentieth day after Thessalina and her army had left to join the Imperial Army, Magnes stood once again on the battlements, looking down and wondering how long it would take to hit the ground should he decide to jump. Gazing out from the dark, terrible place that had become his prison, death seemed like the perfect choice, if only he had the courage.

He blinked…and found himself on the wall, crouched between two crenellations. He blinked again…and rocked on his heels, fingers caressing the rough stone. He blinked a third time and relaxed into the embrace of the air…only to have unseen hands snatch him backward.

A man's voice, shrill with distress, cried out his name. Strong arms wrapped about him, pinning him against a leather and metal-clad body.

"Gods! Lord Magnes, what're ye doin'? Ye almost fell off'n the wall!"

A shaft of sunlight pierced the veil of clouds that squatted on the horizon, dazzling Magnes' eyes. He lifted a hand to his face and it came back wet with tears.

"I…I don't know what I'm doing," he stammered. "Help me!"

"Just tell me how, milord!" The guardsman released Magnes from his bear hug but stood close, his broad face twisted with confusion.

Magnes started at the man and dredged a name from somewhere deep in his memory. "Talin." he croaked.

"Come down to the yard with me, milord," Talin coaxed. "Please!" As he spoke, the guard inserted himself between Magnes and the wall.

Magnes nodded in acquiescence and allowed Talin to lead him down. At the bottom of the steep stairs, the guardsman touched his forehead in salute, then stood regarding his lord with embarrassed concern. He seemed at a loss as to what to say or do next.

Poor bastard. It isn't every day one's lord attempts to throw himself from the battlements, Magnes thought.

"Thank you, Talin." Magnes couldn't bear to look at the guardsman's face, for fear the pity he had see in the other man's eyes would shatter him completely. What had happened—no, what had *almost* happened—up there on the wall filled him with nearly as much shame and horror as the original act that had precipitated it.

Talin ducked his head and kicked at an imaginary clod of dirt. "Don't need no thanks, milord. Just doin' my duty," he replied. "Will you be all right now, milord?"

Magnes nodded. "You may return to your post," he said.

The guard bowed again and started back up the stairs. Just before rounding the first curve, he turned and glanced over his shoulder at Magnes, shook his head, then disappeared from view. Magnes sighed. By nightfall, the entire castle would be abuzz with the news that the duchess's brother had tried to kill himself.

Magnes had known he teetered on the crumbling edge of a cliff and, sooner or later, he would fall. Perhaps the gods themselves had a hand in his rescue, perhaps not; either way, he knew he had to do something, change *something*, in order to step back from the brink.

Only one person could help him now.

&

Greenwood Town lay a day's ride from Amsara Castle. Magnes' final destination stood on the town's eastern edge, set back from the road down a tree-lined path. He arrived just as the sun touched the crowns of the trees, setting them afire.

A big black dog chuffed up the path to greet him, letting loose a single deep bark, but the effort proved too lackadaisical to cause any alarm. Magnes' horse Storm snorted in equine disdain. A child's piping laughter floated on the warm air, commingling with the happy squeals of an infant. Storm plodded on, escorted by the black dog, and soon the house came into view.

ON THE BRINK

Magnes drew rein at the gate and swung from the saddle. A boy of about seven summers sat cross-legged in the middle of the yard, entertaining a toddler with puppets made of twigs and bits of brightly colored cloth. The boy looked up as Magnes tied Storm to the fence post, then pushed open the gate.

"Ma's out back," the boy announced. He had a narrow, well-sculpted face beneath a shock of black hair, high cheekbones and dark intelligent eyes.

Magnes smiled. "Is your father at home?" he asked. The boy shook his head, quick and sharp as a bird.

"Naw. Da's off with th' duchess, fightin' in the war," he replied.

Of course, Magnes thought. "Will you go and fetch your mother, then?" The boy's brow furrowed as if he were thinking very hard. Abruptly, he nodded, dropped the puppets, climbed to his feet, then swung the baby into his arms. Staggering under his burden, he disappeared around the side of the house. Magnes waited.

After he had counted forty of his own heartbeats, she appeared.

Magnes had always been able to discern her thoughts just by reading the subtle cues of eyes, brow, and mouth, but as the young woman approached, wiping her hands on a clay-stained apron, her face remained unreadable. She stopped an arm's length away and simply looked at him, hands hanging at her sides. The boy came to stand beside her, the baby still in his arms.

"Hello, Livie," Magnes murmured.

Chapter 8

THE MOST PRECIOUS GIFT

I heard you'd disappeared after the duke died," Livie said.

The wind that always came with sunset rattled the tree branches overhead. It lifted the hem of Livie's skirt and blew strands of her raven hair across her brow.

"I went south to Darguinia."

Magnes searched Livie's face in vain for a clue to her thoughts. The toddler, a girl, began to fuss, but before she launched into a full tantrum, Livie scooped her out of the boy's arms.

"Come inside," she said. "It's getting too dark out here." She turned and led the way into the cottage. Once inside, she plopped the baby onto a rug before the hearth, then moved around the room, lighting the lamps with a burning splinter. "Sarian, go fetch me some bacon from the smokehouse," she called out over her shoulder and the boy scampered out the door.

Magnes settled on a stool by the hearth and waited for Livie to finish her task. The baby had found a bit of fluff on the rug and was absorbed in pulling it apart with her chubby fingers. Magnes took a deep breath as he wrestled with his pain and regret, but the feelings proved too strong to be easily vanquished.

This should have been our home and our child, he thought.

"Her name is Rose," Livie said. She pulled a chair up beside him and sat. "She's just past her second birthday."

"She's beautiful," Magnes managed to answer. He feared he would sob if he said any more.

"Sarian is my husband's son by his first wife," Livie explained. "She died giving birth to him. I'm the only mother he's ever known."

They both looked up as the boy burst into the room, out of breath and carrying a chunk of smoked meat. Livie stood up, took the bacon from his hands, and carried it to the table. Sarian followed, licking grease from his fingers. Livie sliced the meat, laying the strips on a platter while the boy watched, shifting from foot to foot.

"C'n I have a piece now, Ma?" he asked.

"Be patient, love," Livie replied gently. "Ma's almost done."

"Sarian," Magnes called out. "Come over here and talk to me." After a final, lingering glance at the food, the boy spun about and flung himself on the floor at Magnes' feet. He looked up, regarding his mother's visitor with all the gravity a seven year old could muster.

"Are you my uncle?" he asked.

"No. I'm an old friend of your ma's," Magnes replied.

"D'you know my da?"

"No. I've never met your father, although I'm certain he's a very good man." Magnes glanced at Livie, but her face was turned away from him.

"That's my sister," the boy said, pointing at the baby. "She can't talk so good now, but she's learnin'. I'm teachin' her."

"That's just what a big brother is supposed to do, Sarian. Teach his little sister everything he knows."

"Supper's ready," Livie announced. The boy jumped to his feet and rushed to the table.

"I'd like to wash my hands first," Magnes said.

"Sarian, show our guest to the basin."

"Awww, Ma, I wanna eat..." Livie's frown cut short the boy's complaint. "C'mon," he huffed, beckoning to Magnes with a wave of his small hand.

Stifling a chuckle, Magnes followed the child outside. Sarian led him around the house to a stone basin filled with water. Magnes rinsed his hands and face, and after a moment's hesitation, Sarian followed suit.

When they returned, Livie had laid out a simple meal of bacon, cheese, bread and apples on the round oak table. A dish of fresh butter and blackberry preserves for the bread, a jug of beer for the grown-ups and milk for the children completed the repast. Magnes took a chair beside Sarian while Livie seated herself opposite, cradling baby Rose on her lap.

She handed Magnes a plate. "Why are you here, Magnes?" she asked, and for the first time since he had arrived, he sensed her emotions.

She's furious but trying hard not to lose control.

Magnes chewed and swallowed a mouthful of bacon before answering. "I needed to talk to someone who knows me better than I know myself," he replied softly.

"And you thought that someone was me?" Livie's biting tone cut him like the jagged edge of a broken mirror, adding to his already prodigious collection of mental wounds.

"Whatever you think I've done, or didn't do, please know I'm so very sorry."

"It's too late for regrets." Livie sighed.

"I can't change the past, but *you* don't know the whole truth." Magnes paused to collect his thoughts before continuing. "My father told me just before...before he died, that he had deliberately lied to you to make you think I'd tossed you aside. *He* did that to us. He thought if I believed I'd lost you, I'd go meekly into a marriage with a girl I loathed. He was wrong, and all of us paid dearly."

Livie's face crumpled as he spoke and tears spilled down her cheeks. "Why are you telling me this now?" she whispered.

"Because I need you to understand what happened. I never abandoned you or stopped loving you."

Livie covered her face with her hands.

Sarian watched, wide-eyed. "Don't be sad, Ma," he said, laying a hand on her forearm. "Da will be home soon."

"Yes, love. I know." Livie wiped her eyes on the hem of her apron, then took a long drink from her beer mug. Magnes remained silent, sensing she needed to just sit for a while.

Finally, Livie spoke. "Sarian, take your sister and go sit by the hearth. Ma needs to talk her friend about grown-up things."

"But I haven't finished supper yet." The boy stuck out his lower lip.

"Take your plate and cup first, then come back for your sister. Go on now." Livie brushed gentle fingers through the child's dark hair. With a huff, the boy did as he was told.

After both children had settled out of earshot, Livie said, "My husband and I have made a good life for ourselves. Our pottery business is thriving. Our children are strong and healthy. When I came to Greenwood to marry Jonus, I swore to myself I'd give my entire heart to him, make the effort to love him as he deserved to be loved, and for the most part, I've kept that vow." She regarded Magnes with eyes grown hard.

"I'm not here to complicate your life, I swear. I've come only because I need your help." He let all the pain and desperation tearing apart his life bleed into his voice.

For an instant, he feared she would refuse him, but then Livie shook her head and her expression softened. "Of course I'll help you, Magnes. Just tell me how."

"I know my father's death was an accident, but I still blame myself and it's destroying me," he murmured. "I nearly jumped off Amsara's wall the other day. The only reason I'm alive now is because a guard stopped me."

Livie's hands flew to her mouth. After a few moments, she relaxed and laid a hand atop his. "I am so thankful that guard was there to stop you. I don't know if I could have borne it if you'd…" Her voice sank to a rough whisper.

"I just want the pain to go away. I thought I'd come to terms with what I'd done, found some peace, but it was an illusion. The monstrous nature of what I did denies me any hope of forgiveness!"

"It's time for you to put this all behind you and get on with living."

Magnes shook his head. "If only it were that easy."

Livie closed her eyes and caught her lower lip between her teeth, a gesture Magnes recognized. She always did that when wrestling with a difficult decision.

Rose's happy squeal broke the stillness. Livie's eyes flew open, all traces of uncertainty gone. She stood, then went to retrieve the baby from the hearth. As she placed Rose on his lap, startled, Magnes looked into Livie's face and saw the truth. "Gods," he whispered.

Livie nodded. "We made her on the last night we were together, just before you left with your cousin. I knew I was pregnant when I came to

Greenwood to marry Jonus." She returned to her chair, then rested her chin in her hand. The anger Magnes had sensed smoldering just below the surface had gone, replaced now by wistful sadness.

"Does your husband know?"

"Yes. I mean, I think he knew all along, but Jonus is the kindest, most decent man I've ever known. He's never said a word of reproach, and he loves Rose with all his heart."

And I love him. Magnes did not need to hear Livie say the words to know they lived in her heart, unspoken but very real.

He laid his cheek against Rose's head and breathed in her sweet aroma. Something shifted within him, and the crushing weight of despair began to ease. He turned Rose so he could look into her face, and within her eyes, he saw his salvation.

"Maaaan," Rose said, pointing a finger at Magnes, and for the first time in what seemed like an eternity, he had no wish to die.

"Your husband is truly blessed to have such a fine family," he murmured. "I understand why you hesitated to tell me about her," he added, indicating the baby with a glance. "You have nothing to worry about. I promise I'll make no claims. Just knowing she's here, that there's a part of me alive outside myself…it's enough."

Tears had started in Livie's eyes again. She reached out and drew him close and they sat together, their child cradled between them. "I wasn't going to tell you," Livie whispered, "but then you asked for my help, and I saw how much pain you were in. I knew the only thing that could save you was your daughter." She laid a hand against Magnes' stubble-roughened cheek. He turned his face to kiss her palm.

"Thank you," he said.

"Ma." Sarian tugged at Livie's sleeve.

"What is it, sweetheart?" She dabbed her eyes and turned to look at the boy.

"May I have some honey cake?"

Magnes noticed a few telltale crumbs sticking to the child's mouth. "Looks like you've already helped yourself, young man," he observed, then laughed at the boy's sheepish expression. It felt good to laugh, after so many bleak, despair-filled weeks.

THE MOST PRECIOUS GIFT

Livie smiled. "Yes, my love, you may have a little *more* honey cake."

"Doooown!" Rose squawked and struggled to get out of Magnes' arms. He obligingly lowered her to the floor and she toddled off after her big brother.

"I should be getting back to Amsara," Magnes said. He didn't relish the all-night ride, but knew he couldn't stay.

Livie nodded in agreement.

Magnes pulled open the cottage door and stepped into warm night. Crickets shrilled in the trees. The big black dog, who had been asleep against the side of the house, woke up with a *whuff* and climbed ponderously to his feet. He ambled over to sniff Magnes' boots. Magnes reached down and scratched behind the dog's floppy ears, receiving a satisfied grunt in reply.

"I know I wasn't very welcoming earlier," Livie began softly, "but it was a shock, seeing you at my gate after…"

"You don't have to explain. I understand."

"It really is good to see you."

Magnes held out his hands and Livie took them without hesitation.

"My sister is an excellent commander. She'll look out for her levies as best she can. Hopefully, this war will be over soon and Jonus will return to you, safe and whole," he said.

"Magnes…" Livie's voice faltered and she hung her head. The darkness hid her tears, but he could taste them on her cheek as he kissed her.

"Thank you for my daughter and my life," he whispered. He turned and crossed the yard with quick steps.

Livie followed and stood beside the gate as he mounted Storm. "Take care of yourself," she said. "Try to find some happiness."

"I'll try. I mean, I will," he replied. He turned Storm's head and urged him forward. The big horse snorted and stepped out smartly, eager to move after standing still for so long. Magnes turned once to look back, but if Livie still watched, the shadows hid her from his sight.

He had wanted to say so much more to her, but mere words could never convey what filled his heart. He fervently hoped she understood just what she had done for him.

I have a daughter and her name is Rose!

He wanted to shout that name from the highest mountaintop.

GRIFFIN'S DESTINY

The moon rode at the top of the tree line, a silver half-disk, shedding just enough light to see by. Storm loped easily along the well-worn path, sure-footed in the dimness. With each hoof beat, Magnes felt a bit more of his depression crack and fall away. His soul had been imprisoned for so long, this new-found joy felt odd and a little frightening. He knew now that the peace he thought he had found while living with the Eskleipans had been nothing more than numbness. The pain had always been there, festering just beneath the surface. His homecoming had merely hastened its inevitable release.

Livie had given him the most precious of gifts—a reason to live. Even knowing his child would be raised by another man did not diminish his gratitude.

Our love made that baby, he thought. *A love that's changed, true enough, but it's still there. Someday, when the time is right, Livie will tell Rose about me.*

Shortly after sunrise, Magnes retired to his bed and for the first time in many weeks, he fell asleep without the aid of drink. He dreamed he danced with a merry little dark-haired girl, and the next morning, he awoke with a smile on his lips.

Chapter 9

REUNITED

*A*shinji dreamed he stood within the hollow heart of a mountain. Sharp spires of rock, some thrusting from the floor, others hanging like swords from the ceiling, hemmed him from all sides. Though total darkness should reign here, a ruddy glow bathed the stones in hues of blood.

How and why he had come to this place, he could not guess. He took a step forward...

...and stumbled across a body lying on the uneven floor. Cautiously, he bent over the prone figure, but a shadow obscured its features.

A voice whispered in his ear. "You must do this, Ashi. There is no other way."

Ashinji started and spun toward the sound.

Gran stepped from behind a pillar, a wickedly curved blade in her hand.

"Gran! What are you doing here?"

"You know what has to be done," the old mage replied, holding out the knife as if she expected him to take it.

"I don't understand, Gran. Please..." Ashinji begged, but his plea died on his lips as a second figure emerged from the darkness.

"Son, take the blade and strike before it is too late! The Nameless One approaches!" Amara pointed to the body lying on the floor.

"You must release the Key now!"

That voice belonged to regal, auburn-haired Princess Taya, who had materialized by his side. An enormous ruby glowed like a baleful red eye at her breast.

Confusion and fear muddled Ashinji's thoughts as a fourth mage joined the circle, a woman of sinister beauty crowned with a mane of flame-red hair. She crouched beside the body at his feet. Tiny red sparks flared within the jade depths of her eyes.

Every instinct within Ashinji cried out in warning. "Sonoe! No, you stay away!"

"I can't. Her fate is sealed. This is the only way." Sonoe's pale hand caressed the unseen face.

"She will not suffer, Son," Amara promised. "Better that it be done by someone she loves."

Ashinji's fingers curved around cold steel. Somehow, the knife had found its way into his hand.

"Do it now! It is almost too late!" Gran urged.

Ashinji stared in mounting horror at the circle of faces surrounding him.

The shadows drew back to reveal the identity of the sacrifice.

He screamed in horror...

...and bolted upright in bed, choking.

When the spasms had subsided and he could breathe again, Ashinji collapsed back onto the bed, shaking like a man in the grip of a fever. Never before had he experienced a vision so powerful, so absolute in its feeling of inescapability.

No! I can't let this happen!

He crawled from the tangle of bedclothes and sat, naked and shivering, by the window of his chamber until the residue of the vision had dissipated. The fading stars heralded the coming dawn; returning to bed now would be pointless.

Besides, the sooner I get dressed and ready, the sooner Gran and I can leave for Sendai, and the sooner I'll be reunited with...

"Jelena," he whispered. The mere sound of her name evoked the feel of her skin, the taste of her lips.

He went to fetch his clothes.

ᘒ

"There's a lot about this ritual you haven't told me, Gran," Ashinji accused, his voice tight with anger. "I want the truth. All of it."

Gran sighed. "Ashi, I withheld certain aspects of the Ritual of Sundering from you because I didn't want to burden you with that knowledge too soon."

"So you thought you'd just spring it on me when the time came, is that it?" Ashinji's voice rose to a near shout. "I'm supposed to kill my own wife! If you think I'll meekly go along with any of this, you are mistaken!"

A light breakfast had been set out for them in the main sitting room of the Sakehera family quarters. Gran sat on Lady Amara's favorite couch, an untouched sweet bun in her hand, while Ashinji paced in a tight circle, body rigid with fury.

"Listen to me," Gran commanded. Ashinji stopped pacing but kept her at his back. "I still believe we can save Jelena, but it will take all of our collective skill as high mages to do so," Gran explained.

Ashinji rounded on her, white-knuckled. "That's supposed to make me feel better?" he spat. "You expect me to plunge a knife into my wife's heart. Her blood will be on *my* hands. Can you give me any assurance that you and my mother and whoever else belongs to this…this Kirian Society, can resurrect her?"

"No," Gran replied, shaking her head. "We tread where none of us has gone before. The forces we will be dealing with, the enemy we face…no mage of our generation has ever been tested thus. What I can tell you is this; only through Jelena's death can we stop the Nameless One."

"No! I won't accept that!" Ashinji collapsed into a chair and buried his face in his hands.

"I am so very sorry, Ashi, but none of us has any choice," Gran murmured. "If the Nameless One prevails, he will bring unspeakable horror and desolation to this world, and all living things will become his slaves, reduced to hideous, twisted imitations of what they once were. Your mother and I, along with our fellow Kirians, have sworn an oath. We are prepared to do whatever it takes to defeat this enemy." Gran emphasized the last words as if to impress upon him the strength of her resolve.

"But why must it be me?" Ashinji looked at the elderly mage with tear-filled eyes. "Why must I strike the blow?"

"The Society is at its lowest ebb in all of our recorded history, for reasons we only partly understand," Gran explained. "To perform a Working of this magnitude, there should be at least twelve trained mages in the circle. When

I left Alasiri, only eight active members of the Society remained, three of whom were much older than I am now. I don't know how many are left, but at the most, it's probably five, counting myself. Five is simply not enough." She paused to let the effect of her words take hold. "You have prodigious Talent, Ashi," she continued. "We need your strength added to ours if we are to succeed. Even though you are untrained, we can direct you. You will act as both an amplifier and a conduit for our magic."

"I still don't understand why I have to strike the blow," he persisted.

"If Jelena knows it is you who will wield the knife, she is less likely to be afraid," Gran replied. "If she dies without fear, the Sundering will go much more smoothly, thereby improving our chances of success."

"And what about bringing her back? If she dies quickly, will it be easier to restore her to life?" Ashinji stared hard into Gran's pale eyes, searching desperately for any shred of hope.

"I give you my word. If it's within our power to do so, we will restore Jelena to life."

If it's within our power...

Ashinji stood and drifted over to a window overlooking a courtyard garden. He leaned against the wall, arms folded, looking down. He had first told Jelena he loved her in that very garden, only to have her run away from him in tears. He had buried the lock of Seijon's hair there, as well, fulfilling his promise to the boy, if only in a symbolic way, to bring him to Alasiri.

Regret tasted so very bitter.

"Does Jelena understand what is to happen?" he asked.

"I don't know," Gran replied. "In truth, it may be better if she doesn't, at least not until it's time."

"If you can't bring her back, then you may as well kill me too," he said in a low voice.

Gran stood behind him now. "You've become very dear to me, Ashi." She laid a hand on his forearm. He turned to face her; the tears upon her cheeks surprised him. "I wish there was some other way to accomplish what we must, but there isn't. I know how much you love your Jelena, and I understand how death might seem preferable to going on without her. I was responsible for the deaths of my entire family, so believe me, *I understand*. But remember. You have a child now, and your child will need a father. Hold that thought close to your heart. Let it keep you strong."

Reunited

"When the time comes, I just don't know if I'll be able to go through with it," Ashinji whispered.

"I have complete faith in you, dear one," Gran replied. "You will not fail us."

Ashinji glanced out the window one last time. "It's getting late. Time we were leaving."

❧

Two days after they rode into Kerala Castle, Ashinji and Gran prepared to ride out again, this time mounted on swift Kerala-bred horses.

The morning of their departure, Gendan and Iruka, Kerala's seneschal, met them at the main gates. Kami came with her husband and she brought along their son.

"I don't know when my parents or my brother will return," Ashinji said, bouncing the little boy in his arms. "You will have to continue to run things as best you can. Kerala is in a perilous position, lying so close to the Soldaran border. You may have to flee at a moment's notice."

"We'll do whatever we have to, my lord," Gendan answered. He reached out to caress his son's wheaten head. "Don't forget the troops that fought at the Saihama fords last fall are still billeted here."

"Thessalina Preseren has no doubt taken her forces west to Tono to join the main Imperial Army," Ashinji said. "I'm still worried, though. The Soldarans could still decide to march a division east to attack through Kerala as well."

"You can rest assured we won't allow Kerala to be taken by the humans, not while there's one of us left standing and hale enough to hold a weapon," Gendan vowed.

"My main concern is for the safety of Kerala's folk," Ashinji responded. "Protect them first, Gendan, even if it means abandoning Kerala to the Soldarans. If the worst happens, we have to survive as a people if we're to win back our land some day." He gently kissed the child's cheek and returned him to his mother.

A small crowd of castle folk turned out to see them off. Many wept, some coming forward to clutch at Ashinji's hand so they might press it to their foreheads in obeisance. He realized they were afraid, yet Ashinji could see their collective resolve in their faces. He knew that if they had to, his people would master their fear to defend themselves.

He and Gran climbed aboard their mounts then rode through the gates, Gendan, Kami, and Iruka keeping pace beside them.

At the far side of the bridge linking the castle to the mainland, Ashinji drew rein and turned to look back at the whitewashed walls of his birthplace. He wondered if he would ever see it again.

Gendan, his young son in his arms, Kami by his side, and Iruka stood in the shade beneath the guardhouse, watching. Ashinji raised a hand in farewell and Gendan raised his in salute. High overhead, a pair of hawks soared in the early summer sky, black shapes against azure. Their mating screams drifted on the warm air; the sound struck a melancholy chord in Ashinji's heart.

When this summer is over and the hawks' chicks have fledged, will my home still stand, or will it lie in ruins?

He sighed and pointed his horse's head west toward Sendai.

&

"Did you reach her? Did you speak to my mother?" Ashinji burned with impatience.

Gran's eyes fluttered open and she took a deep breath before answering. "Yes, Ashi, and I'm quite surprised I was able to. At such a distance, mindspeech without an amplifier is very difficult. We are still at least a week's ride from Sendai, after all."

After pushing their mounts hard for most of the day, the two travelers had stopped for the night at a small manor house set atop a low hill, surrounded by tidy parklands. The manor had been left in the care of its steward; the lord and his adult children had ridden south with the main army while the lady had fled north with her little ones. When Ashinji and Gran had arrived and introduced themselves, the steward willingly extended the hospitality of the manor in the name of his absent master. After serving them a meal of poached fish and salad in the sitting room, the steward had left them to themselves.

"Naturally, your mother was shocked to hear from me after so many years." Gran relaxed into the comfortable embrace of the yellow silk-upholstered couch that served as the centerpiece of the room. "I couldn't hold the link for very long," she continued, "but I did manage to tell her I was on my way to Sendai and that you were with me."

"Now that she knows I'm alive…she'll…she'll tell Jelena…" Ashinji's voice trailed off as he swallowed a sudden spate of tears.

I should be delirious with joy, he thought. *My wife knows I'm not dead! And yet…*

"I'm sorry for your pain, my son," Gran murmured.

Weariness bent his shoulders and dragged at his eyelids. "I'm going to bed," he announced. He departed the sitting room, leaving Gran alone with her thoughts.

&

"Captain Sakehera! You sure look good for a dead man," the city guardsman observed.

"I've heard that a lot, lately." Ashinji and Gran had just been admitted into the city through the smallest of its four gates and now found themselves surrounded by a clutch of curious guards. Ashinji's gelding snorted, prancing in place, tail lashing. He patted the animal's neck to calm it, but his own anxiety only fueled its fractiousness.

"A lot's happened since you've been gone, sir," the guard said. "The army's already marched south."

"I expected as much." Near desperate to ride on toward the castle, Ashinji had to force himself not to scream for the guards to get out of his way. "Please. I need to go to my wife now."

"The king's deathly ill, Captain." The other guards nodded in somber confirmation. "We hear it's the plague. The princess has hardly left his side for days."

"Ai, Goddess," Gran sighed. "This is a catastrophe."

"We must go now. Please let us through!" Fear turned Ashinji's request into a harsh command. The guards melted aside. Ashinji drummed his heels against his horse's flanks and the gelding broke into a ground-eating lope. With Gran's mount close behind, the horse pounded up the avenue toward Sendai Castle.

GRIFFIN'S DESTINY

An eerie stillness reigned over a city that had once bustled with sound and motion. Only the clatter of hoofbeats broke the quiet. Shop fronts turned blank, shuttered faces to the street; the few people abroad in the lanes and alleys scurried like scared rabbits seeking sanctuary. All of Sendai had battened down, as if awaiting the arrival of a massive storm.

At the summit of the avenue, as its feet touched the sand of the parade ground, Ashinji whipped the horse into a gallop then bent low over its neck as the gelding hurtled straight for the open gates.

When the horse barreled through, scattering the guards who had come to investigate, Ashinji paid no heed to their cries. He fixed his gaze on the massive iron-banded doors, and like a thrown knife, the horse shot toward them. Gran's mare had fallen far behind, but Ashinji remained heedless to all but his goal.

A heartbeat shy of disaster, he hauled back on the reins and the gelding slid to a stop amid a shower of gravel, tossing its head in distress. Ashinji vaulted from the saddle as the horse pirouetted away with a snort, then sprinted toward the broad, shallow steps leading up to the entrance.

Close, so close!

He called to her, with his voice and with mindspeech.

She answered…

…and he saw her running toward him, arms outstretched, crying his name.

She fell into his arms, sobbing.

His own tears mingled with hers as he covered her face and throat with kisses, whispering her name each time his lips touched her skin.

Nothing else mattered, except her.

PART II

Chapter 10

THE LIE IS REVEALED

A shi, is it really you?" Jelena whispered.

"Yes, it's really me. I've come back to you, my love." He clung to her with such strength, she could barely breathe, and yet she wished he could hold her even closer.

Cries of astonishment echoed against the whitewashed stone façade of the castle as a small crowd of guards formed about them.

"Ashinji! My son!" The guards fell back, bowing in respect, as Amara swept through them. Jelena shifted in Ashinji's arms so he could see his mother. For a few heartbeats, mother and son gazed at each other, and then Jelena relinquished her hold so Ashinji might go to her.

"My child," Amara sighed as she pulled him against her breast. "My son is returned to me."

"I've missed you so much," Ashinji whispered. He laid his head on his mother's shoulder and wept as Jelena looked on, her heart full to bursting. Amara murmured words of comfort, stroking Ashinji's face and hair until he regained control of his emotions. As he stepped out of her embrace, Amara gasped.

"Son, your Talent…" Her hand lifted to her mouth, then fluttered back to her side. "You are no longer blocked! How is this possible?"

Ashinji shook his head. "Never mind about that now, Mother."

"Greetings, Amara. It is good to see you again."

An elderly woman stepped from the circle of onlookers. She carried herself with the unmistakable air of an aristocrat, and yet Jelena sensed no arrogance in her. She wore a simple blue cotton robe and split leather riding skirt, her silver-blond hair held back by a braided leather cord.

"It is good to see you as well, Chiana," Amara replied, smiling. "The news of your return is already the talk of Sendai's magical community. We are in sore need of your help." The two women clasped hands and stared into each other's eyes. They stood thus for several heartbeats, then both nodded and released their hold.

Ashinji had taken Jelena back into his arms again. "Jelena, this is Lady Chiana Hiraino, my friend and companion," he said. "If not for her, I wouldn't be here now."

"Then I owe you a debt of gratitude that can never be repaid, Lady Chiana," Jelena said.

"Please, child, call me Gran," the old woman instructed, "and you owe me nothing." She turned to Ashinji. "She is every bit as beautiful as you've described, Ashi." Jelena ducked her head, blushing with embarrassment, still uncomfortable with high praise, even now. "Look at me, Jelena," Gran commanded softly. Jelena raised her eyes to meet the other woman's. They were ice-pale, yet they shone with warmth and kindness. "Your husband says that were it not for me, he wouldn't be here now, but he's wrong. *You* are the reason Ashi fought so hard to survive."

Gran turned to Amara. "We have much to discuss," she stated.

Amara nodded. "Yes, but all that can wait. You must be exhausted from your long journey."

"We came as quickly as we could," Gran replied. "Right now, I'd love a cup of tea and a nap."

"I'll see to it you get both," Jelena promised. A familiar touch, light as a cobweb, brushed her mind. Hatora had awakened and wanted her mother.

"There's someone you need to meet, love," Jelena said, squeezing Ashinji's forearm. A tiny needle of pain stabbed her heart as she noticed the network of fine white scars lacing his skin, scars that had not been there before he had gone away. Fresh tears blurred her vision.

"Come with me to my...to our quarters," she urged.

Two guards stepped forward and saluted, presenting themselves as escorts. Jelena took Ashinji's hand and, together with Amara and Gran, they followed the guards into the castle.

Eikko waited in the entryway to Jelena's apartments, little Hatora riding her ample hip. When the baby saw her mother, she burbled with delight.

Jelena plucked the child from the hikui girl's arms. "Here is your daughter," she said.

Ashinji stood gazing at the baby as if trying to memorize every detail of her, then gathered Hatora into his arms and laid his cheek against her tawny curls. The baby settled into her father's embrace, relaxed and calm, as if she already knew who held her.

When Ashinji could finally speak, his voice emerged in a hoarse and broken whisper. "She…she's…beautiful!"

Jelena took Ashinji's arm and gently steered him into the sitting room toward the couch, where he sat, clinging to Hatora as if he feared to let her go. Jelena stood for a moment just watching. She wanted to etch this memory indelibly in her mind, so that she could recall it with perfect clarity in the years to come.

I've always believed our daughter had more of Ashi's looks than mine, she thought. *I'm so glad I was right!*

Father and daughter each stared into the eyes of the other. In a sudden flash of understanding, Jelena realized their minds had joined in a link.

"You see, Ashi? I told you so," Gran said.

Smiling, the baby reached out and laid a finger on Ashinji's chin. "Gran told me that as soon as I saw my child, it would be as if we had been together from the beginning," he explained in response to Jelena's questioning look. Hatora continued to stare at him, as if at this moment, no one else existed in her universe except her father.

After a few more heartbeats, Jelena sat on the couch beside her husband and daughter while Amara and Gran settled into chairs opposite. Eikko brought in a tray and poured tea.

For a time, no one spoke. So many questions clamored, demanding answers, but Ashinji needed to gather his strength first. Jelena waited patiently, content just to have him close to her again. She thought back to that day a week ago, when Sonoe had come to her with the news. She had not believed it at first, thinking someone or something—the Nameless One, perhaps—

aimed to perpetrate a monstrous hoax upon all of them as a distraction, but when Amara had confirmed it, she had collapsed in shock.

The last few days had passed in a fog of exquisite torture. Jelena suffered through emotional swings that left her exhausted and feeling like a twisted rag. Delirious with joy one moment, she had been wracked with guilt the next, for had not she given Ashi up for dead, abandoned him, sought comfort in another man's arms?

How could she be a real wife to Ashinji again with such a stain of betrayal on her soul?

And what of that other man? Loyal, kind, steadfast Mai?

Mai had been there to give her comfort, support, friendship and love. His courtship of her had been gentle, patient, and above all, considerate of her grief. He had offered marriage and the promise to raise Hatora as his own, even though he knew the woman who had claimed his heart did not feel the same way about him.

Jelena gazed at Ashinji's profile and felt the heat of desire warm her body, a unique fire only he could kindle in her. She had felt desire for Mai, yes, but it had never been the deep, flesh-searing passion she had felt for Ashinji.

I do love Mai, she thought, *but Ashi is the love of my life. I just hope that both of them can forgive me!*

"There's so much to tell," Ashinji began, at long last breaking the silence. Hatora lay in his arms in perfect contentment, sucking her tiny fist.

"It all began at the battle of the Saihama Fords," he continued. "The human army lay across the river, but they sent raiding parties to fire the meadow where our army camped. It was a stupid mistake for us to be caught like that! Within moments, the fire had us hemmed in on three sides. I managed to break through and I rode toward the river, hoping to stop anything else from happening." He shook his head.

"It was a foolish thing to do, riding out alone like that. My sergeant tried to stop me, but I wouldn't listen. I rode straight into an ambush. One of the raiding parties lay in wait on the riverbank. They gutted my horse and when I fell to the ground, they attacked me." Ashinji fell silent and closed his eyes, hands clinched into fists.

"Ashi, what's wrong?" Jelena whispered.

"What is it, my son?" Amara leaned forward in her chair.

THE LIE IS REVEALED

Ashinji drew in a deep, shaky breath. "There were too many of them for me to have any chance," he continued. "I knew I was going to die, but still…I tried. I fought as hard as I could and just when I thought it was finished, I saw someone, an elven horseman, riding toward me. I called out for help, but he just stopped and…and watched."

"One of our people refused to help you?" Jelena exclaimed. "I don't understand! How could an elf stand by and watch a gang of humans kill another elf?"

"I didn't understand either, not at first." Ashinji's voice began to fade. "Not until I caught a glimpse of the man's armor did I realize his identity." Now, he spoke in a whisper. "It…*he*…was…" Ashinji's head dropped and his voice failed.

Amara stiffened as if beneath an unseen blow and her hands flew to her mouth. "No," she moaned.

"Who was that man?" Jelena gripped Ashinji's arm and squeezed it.

He looked at her with haunted eyes. "Sadaiyo," he replied.

&

The hazy afternoon sunlight had given way to evening's purple shadows by the time Ashinji had finished his tale. Eikko ghosted around the sitting room, lighting the lamps. The warm glow cast by their tiny flames beat back the encroaching darkness. Hatora sprawled in her father's lap, sleeping.

"Your father and I failed you, Son."

Amara had listened in silence to Ashinji's narrative, a soft shimmer of tears in her eyes the only clue to her inner turmoil. "We failed both you and your brother," she whispered. "It caused your father such anguish that he could not love Sadaiyo as he loved…loves you, Ashi," she continued. "Both of us were guilty of turning a blind eye to Sadaiyo's jealousy, and by doing so, we ultimately set this terrible thing in motion."

"No, Mother. I beg you, do not blame yourself or Father for any of this," Ashinji pleaded. "My brother made his choice long ago. What I don't understand is how he hid the truth from you, of all people."

Amara dropped her face in her hands, and after a moment's hesitation, Jelena stood and put her arms around her mother-in-law.

"He most certainly had magical help," Gran said. "Some kind of memory-altering spell. Such magic doesn't come cheap."

Amara looked up and nodded. "Sadaiyo has the financial means to purchase such a spell." She pulled a small square of yellow silk from her sleeve and dried her eyes. "I will find out exactly how he did it." The grim look on her face made Jelena shiver.

Hatora stirred and whimpered, catching her thumb in her mouth. Sucking contentedly, she lapsed back into sleep. Ashinji's face lit with joy, but then he sighed and the light faded.

"Sadaiyo is with Father, of course. Eventually, I must ride south to join the army…" He paused to look into his mother's eyes. "How am I going to tell Father about all this?" Pain infused his every word.

Amara did not answer at first. Instead, she stared at her upturned palms, as if by studying the intricate tattoos marked into her skin she could somehow divine a way to deflect the sorrow that lay in store for her family.

Finally, she spoke. "There are other things that are more important to think about right now, Son, but when the time comes, both of us together will find the strength to help your father deal with this." She rose to her feet and held out her arms. "Chiana and I will leave you two alone now. I will look after the baby tonight."

After kissing Hatora several times on the forehead, Ashinji relinquished his daughter to her grandmother.

"Would you like to sleep with cousin Sentashi tonight, my sweet?" Amara cooed. The baby scrubbed her eyes with her fists, then fell back into a doze.

Sadaiyo and Misune had placed their son, Sentashi, in Amara's care when they had ridden south with Lord Sen and the army. Jelena had to struggle not to hold the boy's parentage against him; allowing Hatora to spend time with her cousin had helped.

"Shall we come to you early tomorrow morning?" Jelena asked. "We have so much more to talk about."

For many long months, now, Jelena had studied and honed what Talent she had to its sharpest edge, all in preparation for the greatest trial of her life—completion of the Ritual of Sundering. She had long suspected the Kirians—Amara, Princess Taya, Sonoe, and now Gran—had withheld certain aspects of the Ritual from her, perhaps fearing that if she knew the entire truth, she would not willingly participate.

THE LIE IS REVEALED

The Kirians were wrong. Jelena understood full well the very existence of the material world hung in the balance, and she would to do whatever it took to safeguard her daughter's future.

"Your husband has just come home to you, Daughter. Things are not so dire that they can't wait one more day. We will see you after dinner tomorrow," Amara replied. She and Gran glanced at each other in the knowing way of partners sharing a difficult task. Eikko leapt from her seat on the floor near the window then started toward the door, but Amara held up a hand. "No, girl. See to your mistress. We'll let ourselves out."

"Yes, my lady," Eikko said, bowing her head.

After Amara and Gran had left with the baby, Eikko inquired if she should have food sent up.

"No. I'm not hungry," Ashinji said.

"Yes, Eikko, please. Ashi, you need to eat," Jelena insisted. "You're far too thin!" Exhaustion darkened the skin beneath his eyes, and it seemed to her a heavy burden of worry weighted his brow.

He's afraid, and I think I know why.

"Did Gran speak to you of the Ritual of Sundering?" She snuggled into Ashinji's arms as he reclined on the couch.

"She did," he murmured.

"Don't be afraid. The Kirians have been preparing me for months. The Key must be released from me and safeguarded in an inanimate vessel. It's the only way they'll be able to defeat the Nameless One." She brushed the side of his neck with her lips and felt a shiver course through his body.

"I can't help it. I'm terrified, my love," Ashinji replied. Jelena sensed he wanted to say more, but something made him hesitate.

"I know there's a chance I could die," she acknowledged, "but I'm not afraid, especially now that I have you back." Ashinji did not answer, only squeezed her tighter. Jelena pulled his face to hers and they kissed, gently at first, then with growing heat. "Forget the food," she sighed. "We've been apart too long, Husband!"

Pulling Ashinji up by his hands, Jelena led him toward the bedchamber. His weariness seemed to fall away with each step.

When the food arrived, Eikko covered everything with cloths and laid the tray on the hearth. She knew when the princess and her husband eventually emerged from the bedchamber, they would want to eat.

Making love is hungry work! she thought, a tiny giggle escaping her lips. After a while, she helped herself to a meat pie and a glass of the crisp, pale wine the princess loved so much, knowing her mistress wouldn't mind.

Settling down on a cushion beneath the open window, she munched on the pie and breathed in the warm, fragrant night breeze. Somewhere in the distance, voices shouted in raucous song. An owl hooted, patrolling the dark sky on silent wings. From behind the closed doors of the bedchamber, muffled cries of passion drifted.

Eikko sighed and squirmed a little with longing. She allowed herself a brief flight of fancy then pushed all such improper thoughts from her mind.

A fine okui man like Captain Sakehera is far, far beyond the reach of a girl like me!

She would have to content herself with Tori, the gardener's assistant who'd been courting her these last two months. Drowsy with the comfort of a full belly, Eikko closed her eyes and lay down on the floor. Within a few heartbeats, she had fallen asleep.

Chapter 11

NO MORE SECRETS

Jelena closed the bedchamber door and turned to face her husband. Ashinji stood by the bed, awash in a stream of moonlight.

Slowly, she approached, savoring the anticipation of what was to come. When she reached him, he gathered her into his arms and bent to touch his lips to hers. A stray breeze from the open window, sweet with the perfume of honeysuckle, blew a loose strand of his hair against her cheek. The gossamer sensation made syrup of her limbs.

With trembling fingers, they relieved each other of their clothes. The whip of guilt that had scored Jelena for so many days disappeared as she and Ashinji clung to each other, skin to skin, their hearts beating in sync. She laid her head on his chest and kissed the irregular scar left by the arrow which had almost taken his life. The mere thought of him alone and suffering in the war camp of her cousin Thessalina caused hot tears to spill from her eyes.

"Why are you crying, love?" Ashinji whispered. Jelena shook her head, unable to answer with words. Instead, she squeezed him tighter and allowed the warmth of his body to soothe her. Her hands wandered across his chest and belly, then downward to caress his swelling manhood. Ashinji gasped and shivered. Scooping her into his arms, he carried her to the bed and laid her atop the silken coverlets.

"When I was a slave in Darguinia, the one thing, the one *hope*, that kept me alive, was the dream of seeing you again, my love," Ashinji whispered as he lay down beside her.

"Ashi…" The whip had returned, stinging her again with relentless ferocity. "Even after Sadaiyo told me you were dead, I didn't believe him… not for a long time. I never *felt* your death. It just seemed like you were far away from me. But, in time, I let everyone convince me you really were dead, and…and…" Her throat clogged with tears, allowing no more words to pass.

"Hush, love, don't cry," Ashinji murmured, stroking her hair. "I know what happened. You moved on with your life, found someone else…" She could feel how it hurt him to speak those words.

"I'm sorry. I should have waited. I should have known…"

Ashinji said nothing. Jelena reached out to touch his mind and what she saw tore at her heart.

You didn't love me enough to wait for me.

"Gods, gods, Ashi, no!" she moaned in Soldaran. "I never stopped loving you, never! You must believe that." *Look into my heart, love. The truth is there!*

Like a river in flood, Ashinji's pent-up emotions overflowed Jelena's consciousness, nearly sweeping her away.

Forgive me, forgive me for hurting you. I know you never stopped loving me. I hate myself for thinking those terrible things. How could I ever think you'd stop loving me…

He rocked her in his arms until the torrent of remorse had spent itself. "I, of all men, have no right to reproach you!" He took a deep breath and his next words came out in a rush. "In Darguinia, in Mistress de Guera's yard, there was another slave, a woman. In a moment of desperation, I…"

"Stop, Ashi," Jelena shook her head. "I don't want to know. Whatever you did, it doesn't matter now."

"But it does. I betrayed you, and even though I did it to escape my captivity, it still tears me up inside! No. I have no right…" He fell silent, his face suffused with pain. After a few heartbeats, he whispered, "I don't blame you…or him, I swear. You believed me lost to you forever. And if I really were dead, I would want you to move on and find love again."

"Ashi, you are the only man…"

"*Shhh*…my love. Just hold me."

"Ashi…"

"*Shhhh*," Ashinji breathed against her neck. Jelena could once again feel the heat of his arousal, and her own body's powerful response. The words she wanted so much to say evaporated in the fire of their rising passion.

All guilt fell away as they lost themselves within each other. Their bodies had not forgotten, despite the long, cruel separation.

At the moment of climax, when her consciousness at last merged with his, Jelena's mind cried out in wonder as the full light of Ashinji's Talent lay revealed to her. When she had last seen it, it had looked wan and pale, like a candle flame at dawn.Something profound had occurred during the time of their separation, for now it shimmered with a multihued complexity that defied description. Jelena did not question the change, not yet, for her mind and body still rode the wave of sexual union.

Afterward, they rested, still joined in mindlink, savoring the rekindled flame of their love. Eventually, the sweet lassitude that comes after lovemaking ushered them both into sleep.

Sometime later, Jelena awoke from a dream in which she looked down upon Ashinji cradling her body in his arms, weeping. She shivered with dread and shifted to look at her husband sleeping beside her. He lay on his stomach and she noted the pale puckered scar above his right hip marking the place where another slave's knife had nearly taken his life yet again.

Thank all the gods Magnes was there to save him that time!

She reached out to touch him, a little afraid he would disappear, chimera-like, into thin air, leaving her alone and heartbroken once again. When her fingers met warm flesh, she sighed with relief.

Ashinji awoke to her touch, almost as if he had not been asleep at all, but rather, waiting for her to stir. He rolled onto his side and pulled her close, his lips seeking hers for a drowsy kiss. She inhaled deeply, filling her nostrils with his unique scent, letting the feel of his body lull her back to sleep.

The raucous chatter of a pair of jays scolding each other below the bedroom window woke Jelena the next morning. She indulged in a full body stretch, luxuriating in the delicious comfort of the soft, warm bed. Shifting her head on the pillow, she gazed at Ashinji, snoring softly beside her.

Pressing her lips to his ear, she whispered, "Wake up, Husband. Your wife needs you." Ashinji's breath caught in his throat; he stopped snoring but remained asleep. "Wake up, Husband," she whispered, louder this time. Ashinji's eyes fluttered open and he smiled.

"Good morning, Wife. I still can't quite believe I'm home in bed with you." He caressed her cheek.

"You are home...in bed...with me." She threw her leg over and straddled him, a wicked grin on her lips. "And now, I intend to make love to you until you beg for mercy."

"That'll never happen," he growled as he twisted his fingers into her hair and pulled her down.

Later, as they lay dozing in each other's arms, Jelena remembered what she had seen when her mind and Ashinji's had joined last night.

"Ashi, your Talent, it's changed," she said. "It's so much stronger now. How is that possible? I thought the amount of Talent an elf is born with is all he or she gets. A little or a lot...it doesn't change. Was I wrong?"

"No, not really," Ashinji replied. "The strength of my Talent hasn't changed. It is as it's always been, it's just not blocked anymore."

Jelena stared at him in confusion. "Someone blocked your Talent? I don't understand. Who would do such a thing?"

"My mother." Jelena both heard and felt her husband's anger.

Why would Amara purposefully deny her son his birthright?

Jelena propped herself on an elbow and Ashinji followed suit. "How did you discover the block and how did you manage to overcome it?" she asked. "Your mother is a very powerful sorceress."

"Gran discovered it and told me, but my mother did such a good job, not even Gran could break it." Ashinji paused, as if remembering something painful. "I broke through on my own. It happened when I saw that slave catcher kill Seijon, the hikui boy we brought out of Darguinia with us. My rage was so great, it just blew through the barrier. I killed two of the slavers before I even had time to think."

"I'm so sorry about Seijon, and I'm sorry it happened the way it did, but I'm glad you've regained what's rightfully yours." Jelena shook her head. "Why would your mother deny you something so important?"

"I asked her once why every second-born Sakehera was always pledged to the sovereign's service," Ashinji replied. "She said it was tradition. It had always been so, and it would always be thus. She advised me to learn acceptance. Ai, Goddess! I was so angry and frustrated." He paused, and Jelena remained silent, waiting.

No More Secrets

"My mother knew how much I wanted a different life," Ashinji continued, "but she also knew my father would never break with his family's tradition, nor she with hers. She would have known, even before I was born, the strength of my Talent, but only the females of her line are trained in high magic. So, she did the only thing she thought she could. I understand that now, though it doesn't make me any less angry."

Not until now did Jelena truly understand just what the block placed on Ashinji's Talent in childhood had deprived him of. Her soul rejoiced at its unbinding.

They both lay back down and for a time, neither one spoke. At last, Jelena broke the silence.

"Ashi, how much do you know about the Ritual of Sundering?"

Ashinji frowned and propped himself up again to look at her. "Are you sure you wish to talk about this now, love?" His green eyes had grown somber.

Jelena nodded. "Yes, I'm sure. Tell me what you know."

"The magical energy you harbor must be released from you in a controlled manner and recaptured into a new vessel, and the only way to release it is to…" He fell silent and turned his face away from her.

"To what, Ashi?" Jelena had never known Ashinji to lie, but she could sense he wanted very much to keep something from her. "What, Ashi?" she repeated. She grabbed his chin and pulled until he had to look at her.

"Did the Kirians not tell you?" he asked softly.

"Tell me what?" Jelena searched his eyes, then said, "If you mean about the danger to my life…yes, they told me, but I've been preparing for months! My Talent's strong, or as strong as it can be." She kissed him. "Your mother and the other Kirians will protect me."

Ashinji sighed and fixed his gaze on the whitewashed ceiling. Jelena rested her head against his shoulder.

There's something else he knows and isn't telling me, she thought, *something he's terrified of. Gods, what could it be?*

For now, she felt unwilling to push him.

Now is our time to just be together, as husband and wife.

She traced a lazy trail down his torso with a finger, hoping to lift his mood. It worked.

"Goddess' tits, but you're insatiable! Is there no end to your lust, woman?" Ashinji grinned in anticipation as her head disappeared beneath the coverlets.

When Jelena reached her destination, she set to work.

§

They did not leave their bed until mid-morning. After a leisurely bath and a quiet breakfast, Ashinji announced he wished to see his sisters.

The Sakehera family still resided in guest quarters in the west wing of the castle, a fair distance to walk from the royal apartments.

Hand in hand, Jelena and Ashinji traversed the castle complex along a series of gravel paths meandering through gardens and courtyards, past gurgling fountains and reflecting ponds. Within an alley of blossoming cherry trees, they paused to share a kiss. Petals swirled around them like pink snow, dusting their hair and clothes. Here, within the peaceful confines of her father's stronghold, Jelena could almost forget the threats to their lives and their world.

Almost.

The enemy is near and my father lies stricken, perhaps on his deathbed, she thought. *Are the elven people doomed?*

She reached out to trail a finger across Ashinji's cheek. He caught her hand in his and kissed her palm.

"What are you thinking, love?" He kissed the back of her hand this time.

Is our daughter's future to be blighted by suffering, slavery, and death? Does my own future hold victory over this…this terrible evil the Kirians call The Nameless One? Or is there naught but catastrophe awaiting all of us?

She had no answers, only questions upon questions.

The only thing I'm certain of, that I know will survive any calamity, is my love for this man standing before me now.

"I'm thinking about how much I love you," she murmured.

They lingered awhile longer among the cherry trees, allowing the serenity of the place to seep into their bones. Such beauty could not be allowed to pass from the world without a fight. By the time they left the alley, Jelena felt more determined than ever to prevail.

No More Secrets

Mariso and Jena shrieked in unison upon seeing their brother alive. They rushed Ashinji as he stepped through the front door of the apartment, flinging themselves into his open arms, nearly knocking him off his feet. They wiggled in his embrace like joyous puppies as he kissed their upturned faces again and again.

"Goddess, but you two have gotten so big!" he exclaimed. "Where are my little monkeys, eh?"

"We never believed you were dead, Ashi!" Jena spoke first.

"Never, never, never!" Mariso shook her head with each word.

"Promise you'll never leave again, Ashi!"

"Promise!"

Ashinji laughed but Jelena thought she heard a note of pain in it. "I promise I'll never leave you again, my dear, not-so-little monkeys," he swore.

"Welcome home, Brother!" Lani appeared in the inner doorway leading to the sitting room, her customarily cool demeanor abandoned. Ashinji set the twins on their feet then rushed to embrace his eldest sister. He lifted Lani and spun her around before setting her down and kissing her cheeks and forehead.

She pulled away from him, eyes widening in surprise. "Ashi, your Talent!" she whispered. "What...How...?"

Ashinji shook his head. "It's a long story, Sister," he replied. "Right now, I just want to be with you and not have to think too hard about anything."

Lani nodded and linked her arm with his. "Hatora can't wait to see you," she said, looking first at her brother, then Jelena. "She already loves her father, even though she's only known him for a day." Jelena reached out with her mind to touch her daughter's and found Hatora's baby thoughts to be totally focused on Ashinji.

Amazing, she thought. *The two of them formed such a powerful bond, almost upon the instant they first saw each other...*

"Let's not keep your daughter waiting, Husband" Jelena urged.

"Gaaaaa!" Hatora squealed when Ashinji entered the sitting room. She strained against Amara's arms, in a frantic effort to reach her father. Ashinji laughed and plucked her from his mother's embrace. He cuddled the baby close and pressed his face to hers.

"Come, you two, and sit," Amara directed. "The others should be here shortly. We have much to talk about." Jelena did not need to be told who they awaited or what needed to be discussed. She looked at her husband and child and a wave of sorrow swept over her.

We've had so little time together! It's not fair! What if I don't survive this? What will you do, my love? Can you go on without me? For Hatora's sake, you must!

Ashinji looked into her eyes and the love she saw there bolstered her courage.

"Sonoe won't leave the king's side until the last possible moment, so she may be late," Amara said. "Chiana and Taya should be...oh, here they are, now." A heartbeat later, they heard both the princess and Gran in the outer chamber. Taya entered the sitting room first, carrying a large book bound in black, pebbly leather. Gran followed close behind, a smaller, red leather-bound volume in her hands.

"Good. You both are here," Taya said, nodding toward Jelena and Ashinji. "I see we must wait on Sonoe, as usual." She cast a hard glance at Gran.

Taya sat in the room's best chair, smoothing her clothes before resting the sinister black book upon her knees. The princess wore an unadorned blue silk robe bound with a red sash; Jelena surmised that, at least for this meeting, her aunt had put aside royal rank and acted now as the head of the Kirian Society.

Feeling the need to defend her friend, Jelena said, "Sonoe tends my father, Aunt. I'm sure she'll be here very soon."

Taya's eyes flashed, but her voice remained calm. "Yes. We will wait, of course."

"How are you feeling, Ashi?" Gran asked, smiling at Hatora.

"Much better, now that I've had a chance to rest and be with my wife," Ashinji replied. He laid a hand on Jelena's knee.

"Lani, please take the children down to that little garden with the dolphin fountain so they can get some fresh air," Amara directed.

"Yes, Mother." If Ashinji's sister resented being sent off like a child to play while the adults discussed important things, she gave no sign. "May I take the twins to the king's stables instead? There's a newborn foal. I think they'd enjoy petting it."

Amara nodded.

The twins could not leave without first bestowing multiple kisses on the faces of both their brother and their infant niece. When Lani had at last shepherded them out the door, Gran asked, "When are you sending that one to the Kan Onji?"

Amara sighed. "My eldest daughter is a stubborn one. Despite the strength of her Talent, she has no interest in formal magical training. She has her eye on other things." She glanced at Taya and the princess responded with a near imperceptible nod.

"Perhaps my sister is the one who will find the courage to break with tradition," Ashinji commented. He kept his eyes focused on Hatora's face as he spoke.

A tiny crease formed in Amara's brow, then smoothed as she regarded her son. "There are reasons for maintaining tradition, my son," she replied.

"Not all of them good," Ashinji shot back. His face had gone hard and cold. Jelena laid her hand over his and it seemed to soothe him, for his expression relaxed and the tight set of his mouth softened. Amara sighed again, as if she recognized that a confrontation had been averted, but only for now.

"Ah, Sonoe has arrived at last," Taya announced.

"Forgive me," Sonoe begged as she entered the room.

Jelena rose to her feet and went to greet her friend. "How is he?" she asked as they exchanged kisses.

"No change, which I suppose is good news. Each day Keizo still breathes is an occasion for hope. Your father is extraordinarily strong. He holds fast to life as fiercely as a bear-dog holds on to its quarry. He may yet overcome this thing."

Jelena nodded, relieved.

My father is strong. He will continue to fight with all that he has, for his family and for the people of Alasiri.

"Now that we're all present, we can get down to business," Taya said as Jelena and Sonoe settled into their places. She propped the heavy book up on her lap. "Niece, this is the first volume of *Kashegi's Notebooks.*" She tapped the black volume's brass-inlaid cover. "It contains the only known written description of the Ritual of Sundering. Master Kashegi was the immediate successor to Iku Azarasha. He headed the Society for some one hundred years after the death of Master Iku, and it was he that transcribed much of the great Azarasha's notes into workable texts."

Taya caressed the rough leather as she would a living, breathing creature. "This is perhaps the single most precious book the Society possesses. It is bound in black dragon's hide, an animal that has not walked this land in over a thousand years. If you were to open this book, Jelena, to your eyes, the pages would appear to be just blank parchment. Only a mage—and one of sufficiently high training, mind you—can discern the writing upon the pages, and only one who has attained the skill necessary to gain admittance into the Kirian Society can make sense of the words."

Taya looked at each one of them in turn. "The very fate of the material world rests upon everyone in this room," she intoned. "Jelena, for many months now, I and my colleagues have schooled you in the use of your Talent. We've strived to prepare you as best we can for the ordeal we must all undergo. Now, please just listen to what I'm about to say, and hold onto your courage."

Jelena felt her insides go cold. She gripped Ashinji's fingers so hard, he winced.

"For very important reasons, we've withheld the entire truth from you, Niece, but now that the time is at hand, you must know everything." Taya paused and fixed Jelena with a look both compassionate and resolute.

"I suspected as much, Aunt," Jelena replied. "I'm ready for whatever must be done. I'm not afraid."

Taya nodded, as if satisfied with her answer. "In order for the Ritual to be successful, we must separate the Key from the essential energy that is your life force."

The princess paused, then said, "The only way to accomplish this is to kill you."

Chapter 12

NO LOOSE ENDS

So. My death is a certainty?"

Now that the words had been said, Jelena realized she had known the truth all along, but beside that knowledge had nested the stubborn hope that she might somehow avoid her fate.

"Is there no other way?" she whispered.

Gran's voice was gentle. "No, child, there is not."

"You promised me there's a chance to bring her back afterward," Ashinji interjected. He turned uncompromising eyes on each of the mages, lingering the longest on his mother's face. Her own gaze did not waver.

"We won't conceal the truth from either of you anymore," Gran replied. "When the psychic cord binding a soul to the body has been severed, it is extremely difficult and dangerous to retrieve that soul, for both the soul and the magician who is attempting the retrieval. Some call it 'resurrection' while others call it 'necromancy'. By either name, many consider it an abomination. No modern Kirian has ever attempted a resurrection, though all of us know the spell. It is one of the Great Workings." Gran heaved a sigh and smoothed back a stray lock of silver-blond hair.

"Are you saying you won't attempt it, then?" Ashinji shot back. Hatora began to whimper. Jelena tried to coax the baby onto her own lap, but she refused, clinging to Ashinji like a mussel to a rock, impossible to shift.

She feels her father's anguish, and is responding the only way she knows how.

Jelena's eyebrows shot up as she recognized Amara's mindspeech. Her mother-in-law's eyes, as green as her son's, sparkled with unshed tears.

"We will attempt to retrieve Jelena's soul, Ashi, but we can't promise success," Gran continued. "There are a lot of *ifs* we must deal with. *If* we have the necessary strength left between us, *if* Jelena will even want to return…"

If any of us are still alive…

That thought remained unvoiced but it haunted the room, nonetheless.

"Why would I not wish to return?" Jelena's gaze lingered on Ashinji and Hatora. "Why would I choose death over life with my husband and child?"

"We elves believe that when we die, we go to dwell in Paradise, gathered to the bosom of the One Goddess. The afterlife is beautiful, peaceful…" Ashinji paused and raised a hand to cover his eyes. He sat very still for several heartbeats, then turned to her, his face filled with such despair, Jelena's breath stopped.

"After I plunge the knife into your heart, you may not want to come back to me," he said.

"What do you mean?" Jelena could feel all sensation trickling from her limbs, leaving them numb, immovable.

"The Kirians need someone to strike the killing blow at precisely the right moment," Ashinji whispered in a torn voice. "I am to wield the knife, my love."

Jelena swallowed hard. The room tilted, then righted itself, then tilted again. For a few heartbeats, blackness closed in on her and a foul, freezing wind tore through her. She heard a fearsome sound, as if from a great distance—the grinding squeal of metal scraping against metal. A sickening wave of savage emotion hit her—rage, arousal, anticipation, hunger…

He is coming! He is coming for me!

I am coming for you!

Jelena awoke with a scream. She looked up to see Ashinji's face floating above her, stricken. She felt the scratch of woven mats upon her back through the fine cotton of her tunic. Her mouth tasted of metal.

Somehow, she had ended up on the floor.

"Jelena! What happened?"

Jelena had never heard such fear in Ashinji's voice. She pushed herself up to a sitting position.

No Loose Ends

"I'm all right," she mumbled. She coughed and wiped her streaming eyes and nose on her sleeve. "I...I think I just had some kind of...of vision."

"Goddess' tits," Ashinji muttered as he helped her back to her seat on the couch. Hatora wailed and thrashed in her grandmother's arms.

"Jelena, tell us what you saw," Taya commanded over the screeching baby.

Hattie, please! Mama's not hurt! Jelena called to her daughter in mindspeech. The child's wails subsided to whimpers.

"Whatever you saw, it obviously terrified you, pet," Sonoe said. She sat beside Jelena and clasped her hands. "You've gone completely white!"

Jelena frowned, trying to recapture the essence of the vision. "I heard an awful sound, like metal ripping," she whispered She paused and her nose wrinkled. "There was a smell like the stink from a garbage pit. I think...no, I'm certain it was the Nameless One. He knows I'm here and he knows what we're doing, what we're going to try to do. He's certain he will defeat us." She looked at Sonoe. "How did he find me? We've been so careful! I thought all of you were shielding me from him."

"We have been, pet," Sonoe replied, her pretty mouth twisted in a frown, "but the Nameless One has known of our plans from the beginning. He's been awaiting the return of the Key since the time of his imprisonment. He knew when the Key returned, the Kirians would have no choice but to perform the Sundering. What we've done up 'til now is conceal your exact location and the time and place of the Ritual, in order to catch him off-guard. Our greatest hope of success lies with surprise, though perhaps we've lost that now."

"Sonoe is right," Taya confirmed.

"Gods, my head is throbbing!" Jelena muttered in Soldaran. She rubbed her temples, wishing she could crawl into bed, curl up in Ashi's arms, and forget everything.

"This vision of Jelena's means we can wait no longer," Amara said.

"I agree," Gran responded. "We've run out of time. We must perform the Ritual now."

"What? Do you mean now as in right *now*?" Ashinji rose to his feet, and Jelena heard the note of panic in his voice. "You can't be serious! I've just...we've only just..."

"Son!" Amara snapped. "The Nameless One knows Jelena's whereabouts. We can no longer delay!"

Why is all this happening, Jelena thought. *Why can't Ashi and I just live our lives in peace with our daughter? Why was I chosen for this sacrifice?*

Even as she asked herself those questions, she already knew the answers. The weak and powerless often served as tools of the powerful precisely because they could do nothing else. The accident of her blood had made of her a perfect tool and pawn of mighty forces. She had no choice but to accept her destiny.

"Ashi, if the Kirians say we must do this now, then we must." She stood and the others rose with her.

If my death will save the world, then for my daughter's sake, I must embrace it, she thought.

"I'm ready," she said and clasped Ashinji's hand.

&

Jelena bent to kiss her father's brow in farewell, then allowed Ashinji to lead her from the bedchamber. Her eyes were dry for she had no more tears left. She had shed the last ones while saying goodbye to Hatora.

The sweet smell of her body, the softness of her skin; these memories of her baby, along with that of Ashinji's touch, were the things Jelena most wanted to carry with her into death. When at last she could bring herself to let go, she had relinquished the child to Eikko's waiting arms.

"Look after my daughter, Eikko, until my husband and my mother-in-law return," she had instructed with as little emotion in her voice as she could manage. The hikui servant girl knew nothing specific, but she was no fool. As soon as she had taken Hatora into her arms, she gulped and shuddered as fat tears rolled from her brown eyes.

"Hush, Eikko, please!" Jelena had admonished gently. "You'll upset the baby even more than she already is." As she turned from her daughter for the last time, she heard in her mind the bird-like sound of Hatora calling to her. She had not dared to respond, for fear she would lose all courage.

The hard parts are done. Now, all that's left is to die, she thought.

No, that's not true. I still have to say goodbye to Ashi.

He strode alongside her now, his arm linked with hers. The *scuff scuff* of his boots on the stone floor kept time with the beating of her heart. Ahead of them walked Taya, carrying *Kashegi's Notebooks*. The Eye of Lajdala, ancient badge of office for the masters of the Kirian Society, shone like a red lantern on her breast. The fire of its magic blazed in response to the princess' Talent, casting a blood-red glow on the walls, ceiling, and floor.

Behind them walked Gran and Amara, each woman carrying a cloth-wrapped bundle in her arms. Sonoe had stayed behind for a few extra moments alone with the king, but had promised to catch up. She would bring the White Griffin Ring.

Taya led them at a brisk pace along a series of hallways and down two flights of stairs before stopping in front of a set of doors carved with the likenesses of figures from elven mythology.

"The library?" Jelena asked.

Aren't big, important rituals supposed to take place in tower rooms or stone chambers deep within the earth?

"Your question will soon be answered," Taya replied, as if she had heard Jelena's thoughts. She pushed the left door open and after they had all passed through, shut it behind them then led the way to an alcove in the rearmost chamber.

"We'll wait here for Sonoe," the princess stated. "I checked on the portal just last week. The magic is holding firm. We should all be able to teleport together."

Jelena and Ashinji looked at each other in confusion.

"Are we leaving the castle?" Ashinji asked.

"Yes, Son," Amara answered and pointed to what appeared to be a plain wooden panel. "Behind this door is a teleportal, a device created by our Society many ages ago. It allowed the Kirians of old to travel great distances in the blink of an eye, saving much time and effort. The magic used to create new portals has long been lost to us, but we modern Kirians have retained the knowledge needed to maintain the existing ones."

"At least the ones we know about," added Gran.

Taya nodded. "Quite true," she said. "The Ritual will take place many hundreds of leagues from here, in an ancient fortress that once served as the stronghold of the Society. No Kirian has traveled to the Black Tower for quite some time now. We're not even sure it still stands."

"Then why are we going there?" Jelena asked.

"Because we know the portal beneath the fortress is still activated, which means at least part of the underground complex is still intact," Amara explained. "At the very heart of the complex lies the main Spell Chamber, the strongest, most protected part of the fortress. It was built to withstand the most powerful of magical energies. We believe, based on writings of Kirians who survived the original battle with the Nameless One, that the Spell Chamber escaped destruction."

"The Spell Chamber will be the safest place for us to conduct the Ritual," Gran continued. "Also, it is near to where the Nameless One lies imprisoned. According to our chronicles, his prison vault lies directly below."

Jelena shuddered and pressed closer to Ashinji, who tightened his embrace in response.

"Now is the time to ask about anything you still don't understand," Taya said, addressing Jelena. Her voice, usually so stern and commanding, softened. "I know you are afraid, Niece. You need feel no shame about it, not now. We all know the courage of your heart."

"I understand what my part is, but why does Ashi need to do this?" Jelena demanded. All the bitter anger she had kept hidden, until now, rushed to the surface. She rounded on Amara, eyes flashing. "Pardon my insolence, Mother-in-law, but you deliberately denied your son his birthright, but now, you have no trouble using him when it suits you!"

"Jelena, leave it be," Ashinji whispered.

"No, I won't, Ashi!"

Amara held up her hand. "No, Son. Your wife is right to be angry with me. I did deny you what is yours, and for that, I am sorry, though at the time, I believed I was saving you from a lifetime of frustration and heartache. The Kirians have been woefully shortsighted and neglectful of our sworn duty. We never should have let our numbers dwindle to so dangerous a level. Now, we must rely on your raw Talent to provide the necessary boost to our power. Without your Talent, Ashi, we simply are too weak to defeat the Nameless One."

"Our minds must all be linked within the Working. Since Ashinji is untrained, he can't participate directly in the creation of the Spell," Gran explained. "We four Kirians must concentrate on maintaining the integrity of the Working. Ashi, therefore, will be free to perform the most vital part of the ritual. We will draw down his energy and direct it through the blade as he strikes to sunder the Key from your body."

Jelena closed her eyes and rested her head against Ashinji's chest. The surge of anger had passed, leaving her drained. If she let go, she could fall asleep right here and now, lulled by the steady beat of Ashi's heart.

They all fell silent, waiting.

"Where is Sonoe?" Taya hissed, breaking the silence and tapping her foot in a staccato rhythm. "She knows we have very little time!"

"She'll be here soon, Aunt," Jelena replied in a low voice. "She hates leaving…"

At that moment, something tore loose in her mind and vanished. She pushed away from Ashinji and took a step backward, hand to her mouth.

"What? What is it, love?" Ashinji reached out a hand to steady her.

"I'm not sure…" She shook her head, then realized with a start what had changed.

"I can't feel my father anymore."

৶

Sonoe stood at the king's bedside, gazing down at his still form.

The time is at hand, dear heart! My plan has been worked out to the last detail. The others think they know what will happen. They are mistaken!

She touched a fingertip to the stone pendant that served as her link to the Nameless One. It rested between her pale breasts like a drop of crystallized darkness.

No loose ends, my love.

She kissed Keizo tenderly on the lips for the last time, then pressed a silk-covered pillow hard against his slack face. There was no struggle, no pain. Keizo's soul quit his wasted flesh with ease.

It is done.

She smoothed the bedclothes and rearranged the pillows then allowed herself a few moments to grieve. Keizo Onjara had been her companion and lover for many years, after all. To a casual observer, nothing would seem amiss.

GRIFFIN'S DESTINY

The two guards outside the entrance to the king's apartments remained at their posts, ensorcelled, their minds sponged clean of all conscious thought and recollection of her presence. If approached, they would respond, but only as automatons until the enchantment binding them dissipated. The king's lifeless body should lie undiscovered for many hours.

Before she departed, she removed the White Griffin from the king's finger then carefully folded his hands upon his breast. The ring felt heavy and cold against the skin of her palm, almost as if by removing it from its rightful owner, it had lost the ability to absorb body heat.

Sonoe raised the ring to eye level. With her mage sight, she could see the magical energy binding the very substance of the ring together.

So much power…so much potential…but useless without the Key!

A tiny smile crept across her sensuous mouth.

I shall have to get this sized to fit my finger.

The only task she had left to do now was to secure the Key for herself, but to accomplish this, she must first subjugate the Nameless One.

I am ready. I, alone, know his true name, and just when he reaches out to seize victory, I'll snatch it from him and make him my slave!

She giggled a little, flushed with excitement. The other Kirians—fools all—would assist her, unwittingly, of course. She had not counted on Chiana Hiraino's inconvenient return, though that should not present a real problem. The old woman's powers had greatly diminished since her time as Mistress of the Society so many years ago, but she could still pose a threat if Sonoe didn't act quickly to stop her.

Even weakened, the old cow is still the most Talented of the Society…except for me.

A log collapsed in the fireplace, sending a shower of sparks whirling up the chimney like a cloud of manic fireflies. The large, overheated room smelled of sickness, but Sonoe felt reluctant to leave just yet. She let her eyes roam, taking in every last detail so she would remember them later—the intricate murals of woodland scenes adorning the walls, the finely woven mats cushioning the stone floor, the figurine of a mare and foal, carved from a whale's tooth, resting on her dressing table.

I'll miss all of this so much!

Her gaze settled on the big bed with its mounds of pillows and sumptuously embroidered coverlets where the king lay unmoving.

120

No Loose Ends

Has it really been almost twenty years since Keizo first made love to me in this very bed?

Sonoe sighed, and a bittersweet twinge of desire and loss stirred the place below her belly.

A soft whimper distracted her from her musing. She looked down to see her little dog Jewel sprawled at her feet. The animal squirmed and presented its flank for petting.

In her intense focus on the endgame, Sonoe had forgotten all about Jewel. She scooped the dog into her arms, laughing as it ecstatically licked her face.

"My poor little poppet," Sonoe murmured. "I wish I could take you with me, I really do." She cuddled the quivering dog against her breast and stroked its silky fur. "I love you, pet," she crooned, then with a quick twist of her hands, she snapped the animal's neck and dropped the carcass to the floor, where it landed in a little heap, twitching.

The time had come. She must leave now, for the others would be waiting. At the bedchamber door, she paused to look back one final time. Despite the ravages of the plague upon his body, Keizo looked remarkably well in death—peaceful, handsome, and above all, kingly.

Sonoe's heart skipped a beat. "Goodbye, my darling," she whispered and fled.

Chapter 13

THE BLACK TOWER

What do you mean, you can't feel your father?" Ashinji saw fresh distress in his wife's eyes.

"I can't sense his mind anymore. It's as if he's disappeared! Ashi, I think he's…he's…"

Jelena's face blanched as her voice stuttered to a halt. Ashinji could only hold her as she stared blankly past his shoulder.

"Sonoe should have been here by now," Taya muttered through clenched teeth. "Whatever is taking her so long?"

"Patience, I beg you, Sister," Amara soothed. "Sonoe knows what's at stake. A few moments to say goodbye to her beloved, is not too much to ask for…"

"It is when she puts all of us in jeopardy." the princess shot back. She glared at Amara for a moment, then abruptly turned away and said, "At last!"

Ashinji heard the sound of rapid footfalls approaching. A heartbeat later, Sonoe rushed into the room, breathing hard as if she had just run a great distance. Instinctively, Ashinji moved to put himself between the red-haired sorceress and Jelena, but his wife pushed past him and went to her friend.

"Sonoe, I can't feel my father in my mind anymore!" Jelena cried. "Is he…"

Sonoe flung her arms around Jelena, and Ashinji had to resist the urge to pull her away. "My dear friend," she murmured. "Your father still lives, but he is very weak. Perhaps that's why you can no longer sense him."

She's lying!

Ashinji opened his mouth to speak but the accusation froze on his lips.

She's afraid if Jelena knows the truth, her grief might jeopardize the Sundering! She's right, Goddess damn her!

Jelena sighed and nodded. "Yes, of course. That must be it. Thank you for taking such good care of him, Sonoe. I'm truly grateful." With a final squeeze, she broke their embrace, and added, "I wish now I'd insisted my father marry you."

"Oh, pet." Sonoe's voice caught and as tears filled her jade eyes, Ashinji felt a wave of uneasiness wash over him.

I have no proof she's anything other than what she seems to be, he thought. *All I've got is the message of my visions…Sonoe, surrounded by shadows and a cloud of menace. Though if she were truly evil, surely the others would have sensed it and never allowed her so close to Jelena.*

"Now that you are finally here, we can go." Taya snapped. "Give me the ring." She thrust out her hand. Sonoe froze, and for an instant, Ashinji thought she might refuse, but then, she reached into a pouch at her waist and withdrew the White Griffin. She dropped it onto Taya's palm without comment.

The princess tucked the ring into a fold of her sash, then turned toward the wall. Ashinji could not see how she did it, but a moment later, the panel swung open to reveal a short passageway of dressed stone and a steep staircase leading down. An exhalation of cold, musty air flowed around them. With a flick of her fingers, Taya conjured an orb of magelight and sent the glowing sphere bobbing ahead. Without looking back, she strode through the door to the staircase and started down.

"Quickly, children," Amara urged as she followed after the princess.

Jelena clasped Ashinji's hand and led him forward. "Come, Husband," she said. "We have work to do."

Taya, Amara, and the magelight had already disappeared around the first turn of the staircase. Gran and Sonoe stepped through onto the landing and the eldest Kirian closed the panel behind them, plunging the passage into darkness.

Ashinji could feel Sonoe's presence at his back; while not exactly menacing, nonetheless, an uncomfortable tingle pricked the nape of his neck. He squeezed Jelena's hand and felt her squeeze back as she started down, pulling him along in her wake.

The stairs spiraled through three turns and ended in another passage, this one made of rough-hewn stone. Taya and Amara already stood at the far end before a plain wooden door. As the others caught up, Taya whispered a single word and tapped the door with a forefinger. It swung open to reveal a small circular chamber. An elaborate pattern of lines had been carved into the hard-packed clay floor. Taya stood aside and indicated with a wave of her hand that they should all enter ahead of her. When everyone had gathered inside the little room, the princess spoke another word and the door shut with a soft thud. She then clapped her hands once and Ashinji started in surprise as a backwash of magical energy blew over him, setting every nerve afire for an instant.

"The door is now sealed against anyone or anything without the proper password," Taya explained as she looked first at Jelena, then Ashinji. In the silvery glow of the magelight, the planes of her face stood out in sharp relief. "Before we go," she continued, "I want to describe what we will encounter on the other side. Or, I should say, what I *think* we will encounter, for none of us here knows for sure."

She glanced at her fellow Kirians before continuing.

"This portal is linked with at least two others we know of within the Black Tower. The one we seek lies closest to the center of the fortress. Nearby, we hope to find the main Spell Chamber—the place where the ancient Kirians worked their greatest magic—intact. This room is the safest place to perform the Ritual, though if we can't reach it, or if it's been destroyed, we can work anywhere within the fortress. Once we reach our destination, there is no turning back. We must either accomplish our task, or die trying."

"We won't fail, Aunt," Jelena stated. She lifted her chin and added, "My daughter's future depends on us."

She looks so brave and determined, Ashinji thought. *She's not the least bit afraid, not anymore...Goddess, I'm the one who's terrified! How am I going to do this? How will I make myself kill the woman I love?*

The princess gestured to the center of the room. "Jelena, Ashinji, stand there in the middle of the sigil. We will position ourselves around you and I'll take us through. It will feel like you are falling. Remain calm. The sensation won't last long."

As everyone took their places, Ashinji brushed Jelena's consciousness with his, communicating not with words, but with the direct force of his love. She returned the mental caress, but did not look at him.

Taya spoke a single Word and the chamber vanished.

Ashinji's stomach lurched as the floor dropped from under him. He stifled a yell as his body plunged through nothingness. A heartbeat later, he found himself fighting to keep his balance on an uneven surface, all the while struggling to hang onto Jelena. Total darkness surrounded them and the cold, like a quick punch to the gut, took his breath away, despite his heavy fur-lined coat and quilted breeches.

Amara cried out in pain and Ashinji's heart slammed against his ribs. "Mother, what's wrong?" he shouted.

Someone muttered an incantation, and an orb of magelight flared to life, revealing a confusing jumble. It took several heartbeats of staring before Ashinji could make sense of things.

The group had materialized on a slope of shattered rock, cascading from an unseen source above. It flowed through a ragged hole to a buckled floor of flagstones below. Amara had slipped and fallen, and now crouched in the loose scree, clutching her ankle.

"Mother!" Ashinji cried in alarm.

"It's all right, Son!" Amara gasped. "I twisted my ankle, that's all." Her face looked ghost-pale in the silver light, wreathed about with the steam of her breath.

"Go help your mother, Ashi." Jelena nodded and patted his arm.

"Can you walk, Sister?" Sonoe asked.

Is that genuine concern I hear in her voice, Ashinji wondered, as he scrambled to help Amara, slipping his arm through hers and gently lifting her to her feet.

Amara grimaced as she put her full weight upon her injured ankle. "I'll do well enough," she declared. "Let's just go."

"The main Spell Chamber is supposed to lie at the end of a wide corridor, to the east of this portal," Taya said, peering into the gloom. "The portal itself must be buried beneath all this rubble. That it still functions is a testament to the strength of the ancient Kirians."

Ashinji took in their surroundings with horrified awe.

*The amount of energy that had to have been unleashed to do such damage...*he thought. *I wouldn't believe it if I weren't standing here looking at this!*

Ashinji pointed at the hole leading to the corridor below. "We'll have to climb down there," he said. "Do you think that's the way to the Spell Chamber?"

"I believe so," Taya replied.

"I'll go first." Ashinji looked over his shoulder at Gran. "I'll need to borrow your magelight."

"You can conjure your own magelight, Ashi," Gran replied. "Just think about it, *will* it to be, and your Talent will transform your thought into substance."

"This is no time for a magic lesson!" Sonoe snapped.

"Sonoe is right, Chiana," Taya agreed, but before she could say any more, Ashinji had a small orb of light glowing on his palm. Neither as large nor as bright as those of the Kirians, it was magelight nonetheless, and he had done it just as Gran had said he could.

He cupped his hand and tossed the orb away from him as he would a game ball. It described a graceful arc and came to rest, hovering, just above the hole in the floor.

Despite the heavy layers of wool, leather, and fur between his skin and the air, Ashinji felt the bitter cold seeping into his flesh. He reached into the sleeve of his coat, withdrew a pair of thick leather gloves then pulled them on over fingers already numb with cold.

"Don't come down until I say so," he said as he carefully picked his way along the jumbled surface of broken slabs and loose debris.

Frost glittered like a crust of diamonds on the stones beneath his boots, but despite the treacherous footing, he made it to the corridor below without mishap. With a flick of his hand, he sent the tiny sphere of magelight spinning down the passage. The way appeared unobstructed, at least as far as the magelight could travel.

Cupping his hands to his mouth, he called up through the hole. "The passage is clear. Be careful where you put your feet. The stones are very slippery!" Sonoe scrambled through first, followed closely by Jelena. Gran came next, with Taya and Amara, who leaned heavily on the princess for support, bringing up the rear.

Ashinji stepped up to take his mother's arm, but she waved him off.

"I don't need your help, Son. I can walk on my own. Look to your wife."

She's deliberately downplaying her condition to reassure me, but what can I do?

His mother seemed determined to not add her own pain to the burdens her son already carried. With a sigh of resignation, Ashinji turned away and went to stand beside Jelena.

"Come sisters, we must hurry," Taya urged. "Time is running short."

"Yes, I can feel it, too," Gran responded. She sent her own magelight bobbing down the corridor after Ashinji's smaller one.

Ashinji met Jelena's gaze. "Feel what?" he asked, though he already knew the answer.

"The Nameless One," Sonoe replied. "He knows we are here."

Ashinji glanced at the youngest Kirian, and for an instant, he thought he saw a tiny smile twitch her sensuous mouth. All of his instinct for danger raced along every nerve and without conscious thought, he had his dagger in his hand and leveled at her before he realized it.

Sonoe's eyes gleamed in the semi-darkness. "What are you doing?" she whispered, taking a step backward.

Ashinji looked at the knife and then back at Sonoe. Slowly, he re-sheathed the weapon. "I'm sorry. I don't know what got into me."

"Apology accepted." Sonoe licked her lips, then added, "I know you're afraid. We all are." Despite her soothing tone, Ashinji still could not banish his unease. He found it impossible to erase from his mind the memory of that terrible vision he had, back when he had been a slave in Darguinia, of Sonoe reaching into Jelena's throat and removing something.

"Follow me!" Taya commanded. She set off down the corridor at a brisk pace. Ashinji took Jelena's hand and fell in behind the princess. Sonoe, Gran, and Amara walked abreast at their heels. The corridor stretched ahead of them, arrow straight. The floor had buckled in places and deep cracks scored the walls and ceiling, but the structural integrity of this part of the fortress appeared to have survived the monumental forces that had torn the rest of the complex apart.

They hurried along in silence with only the scuff of their boots on the flagstones to break the stillness. Ahead, Ashinji could see the magelights had stopped before what looked like a wall of blackness. As the group drew closer, the wall resolved itself into a massive stone doorframe. The twisted remnants of iron hinges hung in jagged shards from the sides. The doorway itself gaped like an empty black maw.

"The main Spell Chamber should be through this doorway. Pray that it's still intact," Taya said. The group approached with caution, but before Taya could step through the gap, Ashinji laid a hand on her arm to stop her.

"No, Princess. Let me go first." Taya hesitated for a heartbeat, then nodded and stepped aside, allowing Ashinji to step over the threshold, his little magelight floating ahead.

He found himself standing in an eight-sided chamber, empty save for a large platform in its exact center. The chamber appeared to be fashioned of black stone. Deep cracks fissured the walls and rubble-strewn floor. Part of the ceiling had caved in, creating a pile of broken stone near the platform. A thick, unbroken layer of dust covered the floor and the top surface of the platform. Ashinji took a step forward and kicked up such a choking cloud, he had to fall back through the opening to the corridor outside.

"The...room's pretty much...intact," he gasped, then succumbed to a sneezing fit. Eyes watering, throat burning, he struggled to clear his lungs of the irritating dust.

Taya stepped forward to peer into the room. She withdrew, clicking her tongue in dismay. "We'll need to clear out all that dust first, or none of us will be able to breathe."

"I'll do it," Gran volunteered. The elder Kirian raised her right hand.

"Ashi, Jelena, stand away from the doors," Amara instructed. Gran spoke three words and Ashinji felt the air around him beginning to stir. He pressed his back against the chilly stone, one arm looped protectively around Jelena's waist.

A ghostly veil of dust swirled through the gap between the doors and flowed, serpentine-like, past Gran and down the corridor, disappearing into the darkness behind her. When she lowered her hand a few heartbeats later, Taya once more peered into the room, then looked over her shoulder at the others and nodded.

THE BLACK TOWER

The princess slipped through the gap and crossed the chamber to the central platform. Gran's spell had scoured the chamber clean. Not a speck of dust remained to dull the polished floor—black as the night sky during a new moon—beneath Ashinji's boots.

Gran and Amara followed Taya to the platform, where they laid down their bundles, then opened them to reveal an assortment of magical paraphernalia: a small thurible, a chalice, beeswax tapers, a glass rod. Ashinji realized the slab must be an altar. Sonoe pulled a small pouch from her sash and paced clockwise around the altar, sprinkling the contents of the pouch on the floor to form a circular space whose boundaries consisted of a crystalline white powder.

"When we begin the Ritual, you can't step outside this circle," Sonoe instructed, looking pointedly at Ashinji. "It will be very dangerous for you if you do." She tucked the now empty pouch back in her sash and brushed her hands together. Amara and Gran busied themselves with setting up the altar, while Taya moved to the periphery of the room and paced through each corner, her eyes trained on the featureless black walls as if searching for something.

"Jelena, pet, how are you?" Sonoe inquired, caressing Jelena's cheek, and though he tried otherwise, Ashinji could detect nothing but genuine concern in her voice.

"I'm better than I thought I would be." Jelena looked at Ashinji and smiled. "It helps that my husband is here. I don't think I'd be nearly so calm without him."

"You are the bravest of all of us," Sonoe murmured, and pulled Jelena close, kissing her forehead. "I love you, my dear friend."

"And I you," Jelena replied. Ashinji struggled to control his unease, but every nerve thrummed with alarm. As the two women held each other, his agitation grew, until he could no longer contain it. Gripping Jelena's shoulders, he pulled her out of Sonoe's arms, eliciting a gasp of surprise from both women. Jelena turned on him, her eyes demanding an explanation.

"Sonoe has to...to prepare for the Ritual now, love, and I want these last moments with you all to myself," he offered, realizing his reason must sound awkward, but not caring.

"Your husband is right, pet," Sonoe responded. If she had taken offense to Ashinji's action, she gave no sign. "You two need do nothing now. We'll call you when it's time."

"Young man, keep watch at the doors until we are ready." Taya had finished her circuit of the room; frustration swirled about her like thunderclouds .

"Of course, Princess," Ashinji replied.

"There are spells of protection woven into the walls and floor of this chamber, but I can't find a way to activate them!" The chief Kirian seemed to be giving voice to her thoughts rather than addressing anyone in particular.

Sonoe moved over to stand beside the princess. "Perhaps if we tried..." she began.

Ashinji took Jelena's hand and led her toward the doors, out of earshot of Sonoe's suggestion. They sat down and Jelena snuggled against him, laying her head on his shoulder. Ashinji could feel his backside going numb with cold, but he ignored the petty discomfort.

They sat in silence for a time, concealed by the darkness, their arms locked about each other. At last, Ashinji spoke. "You don't know how much I want to get up and run as fast as I can from this place, get you away from here to somewhere safe." All of the anger, pain, sorrow, and fear he had, until this very moment, managed to keep in check, now clamored to break free.

"I do know, my love," Jelena replied, almost too softly to hear. "But we both know we can't. We have to do this, for our daughter, so she can live."

Ashinji removed a glove so he might caress Jelena's face and feel the softness of her cheek. A rush of desire, so powerful it made him dizzy, swept through him. He pressed his lips hard against hers, feeling as though he would drown in the sweet ecstasy of her taste. "I want to make love to you so badly right now," he whispered.

"Then do," she replied then wiggled onto his lap. Freeing her hands of her own gloves, she began pulling at the laces of his trousers.

"No, wait!" he gasped, grabbing her fingers. "We can't!" His body shivered with swelling passion.

"Why not?" Jelena breathed into his ear.

"Because there's not enough time!"

Jelena looked over her shoulder toward the altar where the four mages worked, then back at Ashinji. "They'll just have to wait for us, then," she declared, smiling.

With a groan, Ashinji surrendered.

THE BLACK TOWER

Amara found them sitting by the doors, arms around each other, heads together, eyes closed. Regret, sharp as a serpent's strike, stung her heart.

They look so innocent and beautiful, like two children asleep, she thought. For a moment, she wondered if she could somehow spare them the agonies to come.

No.

The sweet smell of incense tickled her nostrils.

All is prepared.

She felt a subtle shift in the energy of the room, a growing heaviness in the atmosphere, seeping up from below.

He knows, Goddess help us!

"Ashi…Jelena." Ashinji's eyes snapped open as if he had been waiting for her summons. He rubbed Jelena's hands and kissed her eyelids until she woke. Amara waited until they had both gained their feet. She glanced at the altar where her fellow mages waited, then looked back at her son and daughter-in-law.

"It is time," she said.

Chapter 14

THE SUNDERING

A rm in arm, they approached the altar where the other Kirians waited.
The last time Jelena and I stood before an altar was on our wedding day.

Ashinji felt himself losing his grip on his emotions; fiercely, he struggled to regain control.

I must not falter, not now!

Jelena walked with a firm, purposeful tread. Without hesitation or help, she stepped up to the polished black stone slab and lay down. Gran stood ready with a small cushion for her head. Ashinji took his place, standing at her side.

Jelena reached up and clasped his hand. "Don't hesitate, Ashi," she whispered.

He nodded, half-blinded by tears. She let go of his hand, undid the ties of her heavy jacket, and pushed the quilted wool aside. Loosening the laces at the neck of her tunic, she pulled down the thick fabric to expose the bare skin above her left breast.

The fog of their breath, mingled with incense smoke, wreathed the Kirians' forms in a bluish haze. The mages looked like a quartet of spirits, called up from some otherworldly plane to perform an unfathomable, arcane task. They formed a circle around the altar, and Ashinji could feel their combined Talents enclosing them in a wall of protective energy.

The floor shuddered. Ashinji looked around apprehensively. "What was that?" he whispered.

THE SUNDERING

"We must start now," Taya said, ignoring him. She picked up a plain leather sheath and withdrew a knife, a double hand-span in length with a slight curve to the blade. Ashinji could tell, even without holding it, that the knife was very fine, well balanced and razor-sharp. The princess reversed the blade to lie along her forearm, then offered it to him, hilt-first. After a moment's hesitation, he took it from her. At any other time, he would have appreciated the feel of such a finely crafted weapon, but now, he just wanted to hurl it away.

"Sonoe, activate the circle," Taya directed. Sonoe turned and muttered a single word. The crystalline powder on the floor flared and burned with a white flame for several heartbeats. When the fire flickered out, a glowing, circular trace remained, like a thread of light carved into the stone itself. A shimmering haze sprang up from the trace and arched over their heads, enclosing them within a dome of magical energy.

The floor shook again. Ignoring the tremor, Taya looked down at Jelena and said in a commanding voice, "Open your mind to us now, Niece." The great ruby hanging at her breast glowed like a blood-red star. She laid her hand on her niece's forehead and Jelena's eyelids drooped. Taya glanced at the other Kirians. "Follow me in," she instructed. All four women closed their eyes.

Wracked with shivers, Ashinji could do naught but wait. The knife felt cold in his hand, and his mouth had gone so dry, he doubted he could speak beyond a croak if called upon.

Grab Jelena and run! Get out of here, now! his panicked, inner voice screamed, but the part of him that recognized duty and responsibility prevailed.

No, I can't. I must see this through.

Impulsively, he sent his consciousness plunging in after the Kirians.

Jelena's mind lay open, without any protective barriers to slow his entry. He dropped like a stone through water, pushing toward the blue light pulsing with each beat of her heart, nestled there at the center of her being.

It's always been so beautiful, he thought, remembering when he had first seen the Key, in his earliest visions of Jelena, before he knew she truly existed in the flesh.

The four Kirians hovered over the Key like fireflies near a lamp. Ashinji moved closer, straining to discern their thoughts.

Ashi, get out at once! We need you to keep watch!

Amara's mental command stung him like a whip. Ashinji considered defying his mother, then conceded that she was right. Reluctantly, he withdrew. He opened his eyes and sucked in the smoky air. The mages stood unmoving, hands at their sides, eyes shut. Ashinji had no choice but to wait.

He began to count.

When he had reached one hundred and fifty seven, all four Kirians opened their eyes simultaneously. Jelena stirred and moaned his name. Ashinji crouched so his lips could touch her ear.

"I'm right here, my love," he whispered.

Her hand fluttered up to his cheek and she sighed, "Almost done now." Ashinji looked up at Amara, a question in his eyes.

"We've soothed her, just enough so she won't feel the full pain of the knife," Amara explained. "We need her to be partially aware, so she can help to expel the Key from her body. She knows what she has to do."

With gentle strokes, Ashinji ran his fingers through Jelena's coiled locks.

I brushed your beautiful hair just this morning, brushed it free of tangles, like I always do…

"Listen to me, Wife," he said, struggling to get the words past the lump in his throat. "You *fight,* with all your strength, to come back to me. Don't forget I love you, and I need you, and our daughter needs her mother. You fight!" His voice broke as tears blinded him. "Don't leave me." he sobbed.

"I…promise…I'll…try," Jelena replied, her words a mere thread of sound.

"Young Sakehera, are you ready?" A note of sympathy softened Taya's clipped question.

Ashinji dashed the tears from his face and drew himself up to his full height. He nodded once. "I am ready."

The princess removed the glowing ruby pendant from her neck and placed it on the altar beside the White Griffin ring. "The Key shall remain safe in our keeping from this day forth," she intoned. "Ensconced in the Eye of Lajdala, it will become the sacred duty of all those who wear this symbol of office to guard it with their lives." She raised her hands and the other Kirians followed suit. "Wait for my signal," the princess said, looking at

THE SUNDERING

Ashinji. "It is vitally important the old vessel be broken at the exact instant the new one is ready."

This isn't just an inanimate object to be broken, this is my wife!

Ashinji felt himself drowning in despair.

Taya began to chant.

☙

At long last! The moment of my release is at hand! She has brought them, just as she said she would, and most importantly, they have brought the Key!

Pathetic bitches! I will make them all grovel before me, and after I've taken my pleasure from their puny bodies, I will slaughter them and paint the walls with their blood. But first, I must secure the Key, the only thing that really matters!

How infuriating, this need to wait on her, but I've no choice. Only through the use of her body can I ultimately make my escape. The red bitch thinks she's so very clever! Did she really believe she could conceal her innermost thoughts from me? Oh, but I have a very nasty surprise for her!

I can feel the force of their magic, building...When they shatter the vessel and release the Key, she will open the way for me and I will come roaring through, wielding my vengeance like a scourge! I will utterly destroy the Kirians, once and for all!

The sound of tearing metal rent the air.

☙

Ashinji stifled a cry of pain as the Kirians began drawing down the energy of his Talent. Simultaneously, they sent the combined flows of their own power coursing through him.

This is what it must feel like to be burned alive!

Sweat rolled down his sides beneath the layers of his heavy clothing, and dripped from his brow to sting his eyes. His senses began to fragment.

Hold on, Son! We're almost there!

Taya picked up one of Jelena's limp hands, and with a shard of white quartz she pricked Jelena's thumb and squeezed out a single crimson drop. Next, she pressed the White Griffin to the bleeding wound and nodded as the ring's magic flared to life in response.

Jelena, can you hear me?

Ashinji heard Taya in his head as well as Jelena's reply.

Yes, Aunt.

Reach down inside now, and touch the Key. Can you feel it?

Yes…yes! It…it's cold, Aunt…so cold.

Push it out now, Jelena! Push very hard! Ashinji Sakehera, strike now!

Ashinji stared hard at the gleaming blade in his hand, poised above the tender skin of Jelena's breast. His vision swam, creating overlapping images that twisted crazily before his eyes. He raised the knife.

You must strike now, before it's too late!

Don't hesitate, Ashi!

Why do I have this feeling something is not right? Ashinji swayed, the knife point wavering over its target.

"Hurry, Ashi! Do it now!"

Jelena gazed up at him with no trace of fear in her hazel eyes.

"You're awake! Ai, Goddess," he whispered, horrified. "I can't do this, not now!"

"Listen to me, beloved. Yes, you can. We both can," she replied, her voice calm. "You know there's no other way. I won't feel any pain, I promise. My death will be as easy as falling asleep in your arms. When it's all over, we'll be together." She smiled, and it felt like the sunrise after a long, harrowing night. "Remember how much I love you."

"I love you, too."

Son, strike now!

Ashinji snapped back to consciousness. He looked down at Jelena, who lay unmoving on the altar slab, slack-jawed, eyes closed.

I've been entranced, and she's been asleep all along, he realized. *She reached out to me, in a vision, to give me the strength to do what I must.*

Sobbing aloud, he brought the knife down in one smooth motion.

Jelena's body arched then fell back as the knife bit deep. A bright stain of red, like a rose opening to the morning sun, bubbled around the blade buried in her breast. Ashinji fell to his knees, his hands pressed to the wound. He felt like his body was being torn apart as the magic of the Kirians flowed through the conduit of his mind. He sensed Jelena's life ebbing away, but he felt something else happening as well.

THE SUNDERING

Taya spoke a Word of Power and Ashinji screamed as a thunderbolt detonated in his head. He looked up, senses swimming, to see, hovering a handspan above Jelena's body, a dazzling sphere of blue light.

The Key!

Gran spoke a second Word, and Ashinji groaned as the backwash seared his already flayed nerves. The Key sparked like an ember beneath the bellows of a forge. Ashinji braced himself.

Sonoe spoke a Word and without warning, the protective circle collapsed and the flow of magic ceased. At the same instant, the red-haired mage stepped backward and threw something to the floor.

A geyser of darkness erupted from the stone to form a swirling column of black.

"Come, Master, come!" Sonoe screamed. "The way is open!"

Taya's howl of fury mingled with Gran's and Amara's cries of horror.

Instinctively, Ashinji threw himself across Jelena's body. He stared at his mother in confusion. "What's happening!" he shouted.

"Treachery!" Amara cried.

The black column coalesced into the rough shape of a man. Ashinji could only stare, helpless, as the other Kirians raced to complete the Ritual. As Taya held aloft the Eye of Lajdala and began to intone the final incantations, a bolt of dark energy shot from the shadow figure and struck the Eye from her hand. Taya spun about and launched a fireball from her fingertips. It flew straight for Sonoe but the younger mage easily deflected it.

"Give it up, fools!" Sonoe cried, her voice ringing with triumphant glee. "You can't win! The Key is mine!"

Wrong, slave-bitch! The Key belongs to me! It always has!

The voice of the Nameless One rolled over them, deep and grinding. Ashinji felt more than heard it, and shuddered at the slimy residue it left in its wake.

Sonoe whirled, laughing, to face what she had freed. "The tables are turned, truly, *Master!*" she hissed. "I command you, *Shiiiieee...*"

Before she could finish, Sonoe's voice shredded into an unrecognizable croak, as if an unseen force had ripped her tongue from her mouth. She clapped her hands to her throat, eyes bulging.

"Sisters!" Taya cried. "We must secure the Key! Quickly now, while the spirit is distracted!"

"The Eye has been destroyed!" Gran pointed to the congealed lump of scorched metal and shattered stone that had once been the symbol of office for the leaders of the Society. "We have no other suitable vessel!"

"Yes, we do!" Taya replied. "We will use the White Griffin."

"We cannot!" Amara objected. "The Key must not reside within the same vessel as the spell that opens the Void! It's too dangerous!"

"We have no choice," Taya shot back.

"Taya is right," Gran said. "If we all survive, then we can separate the two later."

An agonized shriek tore the air, causing them all to start.

"Great Goddess!" Amara whispered.

Slowly, Ashinji turned his head and if, at that moment, he had been given the choice to be struck blind, he would have gladly surrendered his eyesight rather than witness what he saw next.

The Nameless One hovered over Sonoe, who lay face-down on the unyielding stones, her body pressed to the floor as if pinned by a great weight. Her clothes had been torn away and scattered. Ugly welts striped her naked back and buttocks, starkly red against the whiteness of her skin. As Ashinji watched in horror, the spirit flowed between her legs, forcing them apart. Like a black snake crawling into its burrow, it began to push its way into her body. Sonoe thrashed and shrieked, a hideous high-pitched keening, like a tortured animal. Relentlessly, the spirit pushed until it had inserted its entire substance within the struggling woman.

Ashinji turned his head and retched.

The screaming stopped.

Ashinji dared to look again and the sight of Sonoe's lifeless body, contorted from her death throes, made him wish he had not.

"Ashinji!" His head snapped around at the sound of his name. "Get ready! We are going to need your energy again!" Taya called out. She held the White Griffin between her thumb and forefinger, seemingly unaffected by the gruesome death of her erstwhile colleague. "Now, sisters!" she cried.

Ashinji braced himself, but even though he expected it, the pain still proved almost unbearable. He thought about what Gran had told him, about how to control his Talent, and imagined a filter between himself and the full power of the remaining three Kirians, a barrier of sorts that would lessen the pain while still allowing his own energy to flow.

THE SUNDERING

It seemed to help, for the pain eased. He could concentrate now on what the Kirians were doing. All three mages chanted in unison, their eyes fixed on the ring, which rested on Taya's palm. The Key hovered just above, and its light pulsed to the rhythm of the incantation. Slowly, Taya raised her free hand until she had both the Key and the ring cupped between both palms. The Kirians fell silent.

Ashinji looked down at Jelena's face. Her lips had already begun to lose their color in the chilly air. The terrifying rush of blood from the wound in her chest had slowed to a trickle. Even though he knew it would do no good, he couldn't make himself stop pressing his hands against her stilled heart.

Ai, Goddess! My beautiful wife, my love, my Jelena!

A whisper of sound from behind made him turn his head.

Too late, he saw a blur of white rushing toward him, swinging. He shouted a warning just as Sonoe's fist smashed into the side of his head with the force of a war hammer. He slumped to the floor, consciousness shattered.

For a time, he drifted, lost amid a whirlwind of confusion. Shouts, screams, Words of Power—all swirled around him in a deafening cacophony. An explosion shook the floor beneath his cold-numbed body. He heard someone crying his name. Struggling against the dark that fettered his senses, he managed to wrench himself free and regain full consciousness.

He lay sprawled on the floor, in total darkness. After a few heartbeats, he groped his way into a sitting position, afraid to move much farther.

"Mother?" he croaked.

Silence.

"Gran...Princess!"

He heard a soft moan to his left. As quickly as he dared, Ashinji slithered across the slick floor toward the thread of sound. His questing fingers soon touched cloth and worked their way along the unseen form until they found skin. A voice whispered his name. "Yes, Gran, it's me," he replied.

"Can you conjure a light?" Gran rasped.

"I think so." Conjuring magelight proved much simpler now that he had done it already. A silvery orb flared to life on his palm—small, but much brighter than his first attempt.

The sight of Gran's blood-covered face made him curse in dismay. "What happened, Gran?" he whispered as he slipped his arms beneath the elder mage's shoulders and helped her to sit up. She sucked in a sharp breath and her hand flew to her side. "Are you badly hurt?" Ashinji's chest tightened in alarm. "Tell me how to help you!"

Gran shook her head. "I'm not important right now."

Ashinji looked into her pale eyes and saw the terrible truth.

"No!"

Gran nodded, her face grim. "The Nameless One has possessed the corpse of Sonoe and escaped." She pressed a shaking hand to her forehead. "I was such a fool, Ashi! I should have trusted my instincts and your Talent! All those months ago when we were slaves in the de Guera Yard...you asked me about the red-haired woman you'd seen in your visions, the one surrounded by shadow. Why did I not *see*?"

"Please, Gran," Ashinji pleaded. "You mustn't blame yourself."

"Who else, then?"

"There must be some way to stop it...stop *her*!" Ashinji's skin crawled with revulsion.

"Help me up, Ashi. We must see to the others."

Ashinji held steady while Gran pulled herself to her feet. The blood on her face had dripped from a cut on her forehead. It looked shallow, but it extended past her hairline.

"Your mother and Taya are still alive, but they were both rendered unconscious in the struggle," she said. Ashinji breathed a sigh of relief. Together, they limped to where Amara and the princess lay sprawled on the stones, loose as rag dolls.

"Does the Nameless One have the White Griffin?" Ashinji asked. He crouched beside his mother and stroked her face. She moaned, her head rolling from side to side.

"He does," Gran replied. She eased herself down on the altar beside Jelena's body. "Poor, child," she murmured, gazing at Jelena's bloodless face. "We failed you."

"If we don't get that ring back, my wife will have died for nothing!" Ashinji felt he would choke on his despair. Just as he started to lift his mother's head to his lap, she stirred and sat up.

"Son..." she mumbled, a swollen and bruised lower lip slurring her speech.

140

"There is a way to retrieve the ring, but you are the only one who can do it, Ashi," Gran replied.

"No!" Amara cried. "He's not trained! He can't possibly..."

"He can, Sister, and he must!" Gran insisted. "The Kirians have failed! Your son is the only one left standing with the necessary Talent."

"Chiana is right," Taya added in a rough whisper, awake now. The princess climbed laboriously to her feet and shuffled over to the altar where Gran now sat. "We must send young Sakehera and there's no time to lose."

"What are you all talking about?" Ashinji asked, confused.

"You must go after The Nameless One and stop him from executing the spell that will open the Void," Taya answered. Ashinji stared at the three mages in turn.

"But how?"

"I've never trusted Sonoe, and with good reason, as it turns out, but even I never dreamed her capable of such duplicity!" The princess paused to wipe a thin trickle of blood from her mouth. "I kept watch upon her mind during the Ritual," she continued. "I have the skill to monitor others undetected— but I now realize, to my everlasting sorrow, that I grossly underestimated her."

A tiny, bitter smile touched Taya's lips. "Before Sonoe turned on us, she let slip a very important piece of information. I suppose the anticipation of her victory made her careless. She did not know I gleaned from her mind the one thing that can save us."

"What, Sister? Tell us," Amara said.

The princess replied, "I now know the true name of the Nameless One."

Chapter 15

AFTERMATH

Ashinji sat on the edge of the altar and lifted Jelena's hand to his face. "You're so cold, already, my love," he sighed, pressing his cheek to her palm.

Though he had wielded the knife, her death had not seemed real to him, until now. The agonizing realization struck him like a spear of ice through his heart. "Jelena," he sobbed. "I've killed you. Ai Goddess! They made me kill you!" He slipped his arms beneath Jelena's shoulders and raised her so he could cradle her limp body against his chest.

"Ashi, my son." Ashinji felt his mother's hand on his shoulder and viciously, he slapped it away.

"Leave us alone!" he snarled. "Just leave us alone…" His voice dissolved in a flood of tears.

"Ashinji Sakehera, listen to me!" Taya's voice sliced through the haze of his grief. "You must put aside your pain, at least for now, for the fate of the material world hangs in the balance!"

Ashinji raised his head.

"Are you listening?"

"Yes, damn you!"

"The spirit's true name is the one weapon you'll have that can prevail against him." Taya looked at Gran, who nodded in agreement.

"Even if I do know its true name, how am I supposed to defeat something powerful enough to toss aside three of the most skilled mages in Alasiri?"

AFTERMATH

Ashinji stared at the princess, incredulous. "Goddess' tits! I'm not a mage! I'm a soldier!"

"You won't need any training, Ashi," Gran said. "Your lack of it will work to your advantage. The Nameless One won't view you as a threat; in fact, he'll dismiss you out of hand. This will allow you to get close enough to spring the trap we will prepare."

"You wish my son to capture the Nameless One in the spirit box," Amara stated, her voice sharp with fear.

"He can do it, Sister," Gran insisted. "You are well aware of the strength of your son's Talent."

"Yes, I am."

Ashinji looked in his mother's eyes and caught a glimpse of the guilt that haunted her. He also saw reluctant consensus.

They all believe I'm the only one who can defeat this thing! They must be truly desperate!

"Tell me what I must do, then." He continued to hold Jelena in his arms, rocking her as if she merely slept. His tears had ceased, but the pain still ripped at his heart.

Taya bent to pick up a small wooden casket that had tumbled to the floor. She held it out so Ashinji could see the intricate glyphs carved into the lid and sides.

"This is a spirit box," Taya spoke quickly now. "It's designed to capture and hold any type of non-corporeal being, but it's meant to be a temporary receptacle only. Eventually, the entity within must be transferred to a permanent containment vessel. All that's necessary for the capture is to get within a few paces of the spirit and speak the appropriate incantation."

"Its true name," Ashinji said.

"Yes. That's the surest way of capturing the spirit, though there are other ways," Taya replied. "We had prepared another incantation, but that one won't be needed now."

"Do you know where Sonoe, I mean, the Nameless One, has gone?" Ashinji stared at the box, and blinking in surprise, realized the glyphs were crawling along the wood like fantastically shaped insects.

"Not precisely, but you can track her by using your Talent," Gran said.

"I think I may know," Ashinji replied, still staring with near hypnotic fascination at the animated glyphs. "It's common sense, really. Sonoe, the Nameless One, I mean, intends to subjugate first Alasiri, then the rest of the known world. In order to do that, he must kill everyone standing in his way. He'll start with all of the surviving Onjaras."

Including my daughter.

With some difficulty, Ashinji finally looked away from the box back to the three mages.

"He'll return to Sendai first, in order to finish off the king," he added, "but I suspect Sonoe's already done that. If so, then he'll head south to where the army lies and kill Prince Raidan and his sons."

"Of course," Taya murmured. "He'll no doubt seek out the mages assisting the army with the defense of Tono. He needs the power of at least three other trained sorcerers in order to perform the Great Working that opens the Void. As great as his own strength is, he still can't do it alone."

"He'll have to take their power by force. No sane mage would ever willingly assist in such an evil act," Gran interjected.

"Ashi, what about Hatora?" Amara's voice shook and her face, already pale in the semi-darkness, blanched even more.

"My daughter still lives. The connection I have with her is very strong, even over so great a distance. Either the Nameless One hasn't found her yet, or he's passed her by for now."

"Then you must go, immediately!" Gran urged.

Ashinji shook his head. "No."

"You must!" Taya snapped. "We have no time for…"

"I'm not doing anything else for you until you bring my wife back!"

Ashinji glared at the three women. They looked at each other, then back at him. Their combined energies pushed at him, but he refused to budge, not until he heard from their lips that they intended to resurrect Jelena.

"We will try," Taya replied, but her voice held no promises.

"You must do more than try," he insisted.

"Ashi, we…" Amara began, but Ashinji cut her off with a shout.

"Bring my wife back! You promised!"

His whole body shook with fury.

"*You* demanded this sacrifice of us! *You*…insisted it was the only way to defeat our enemy! And now, my lover, my best friend, the mother of my child is…is *dead*…and *still*, the task isn't done! You owe this to her! To both of us!"

Ashinji gazed into Jelena's face, and marveled at how beautiful it still looked. A fresh flow of tears wet his cheeks. Tenderly, he lowered her head back to the altar's surface. His hand brushed the hilt of the knife still protruding from her chest, and with a gasp of dismay, he jerked away, as if Jelena could still feel the pain of that cruel blade.

"Swear you'll bring her back. Please," he whispered.

Amara wept in silence behind shaking hands. Taya turned her face away and sighed. Gran came forward and touched Ashinji's shoulder. He flinched, but did not pull away.

"Ashi, I swear."

Ashinji looked into Gran's eyes, and the calm determination he saw there cooled his anger. He knew the elder Kirian would keep her word.

After a few moments of silence, he rose to his feet and faced Taya. "I'm ready now," he stated.

"Then I will send you back through the portal to Sendai," the princess said. "When you pick up his trail, be very careful. The Nameless One is more dangerous than you can possibly imagine, and he will have absorbed all of Sonoe's essence, including her magical abilities. They will only serve to enhance his already formidable skills. He will mimic her flawlessly, and so will be able to gain easy access to my husband and his council." The princess pressed the spirit box into Ashinji's hands. "When you get close enough, simply open the lid and speak his name. And now you must go!"

Ashinji tucked the box inside his jacket and knelt once more beside the altar stone. Fighting back still more tears, he leaned over and kissed Jelena's cold lips. His eyes never left her face as he spoke. "I can't imagine going on without you, love, but I suppose I must." His voice caught and for an instant, he wished the stones beneath his knees would turn to sand and suck him down.

I would welcome death now, if it meant reunion with you!

He took a deep breath and rose to his feet. "Let's go," he said, and started for the door.

He didn't look back as he followed the princess from the chamber. They hurried down the dark corridor toward the portal, Taya's magelight swooping ahead of them. When they reached the base of the rubble slope, Taya sent the magelight up through the breach and set it to hovering. Together, they began to climb.

When Ashinji reached the place where the magelight bobbed, he paused and tried to feel the magic of the portal.

Yes, there it is, and there's the trigger!

He felt a rush of excitement. "Princess, I think I can activate the portal myself," he declared.

"You can feel the trigger?" Taya sounded a little dubious.

Ashinji nodded. "I just form a picture in my mind of the place I want to go and…"

"It's not quite that simple, young Sakehera," Taya snapped. "If you don't have a perfect mental picture of the locator glyph, you could end up materializing inside of solid stone!"

They climbed the remainder of the way in silence. At the top of the slope, Ashinji paused to catch his breath, then demanded, "Show me the glyph." An image formed before his mind's eye like ink-strokes on paper. He nodded sharply. "Got it."

"Everything depends on you now." Taya said. "Go quickly, and may the One keep you safe."

"Keep your promise to me, Princess," Ashinji replied.

Before he reached with his mind to trigger the portal, Ashinji called out, "Princess Taya, you haven't told me the name of the spirit!"

"Shiura Onjara." Taya's brow creased as if the appellation left a bitter residue in her mouth.

"If we all survive this, I'll meet you back in Sendai." Ashinji triggered the portal and darkness engulfed him.

❧

"Poor child." Amara sat on the altar, stroking Jelena's cold cheek. "The day my son first brought you to me, I knew you would change all our lives. I just didn't know how." She dabbed her eyes with the hem of her sleeve. "I will carry the burden of this day to my grave," she sighed.

"Jelena understood the necessity of what we all had to do, Amara." Gran squeezed her friend's shoulder. "She possessed remarkable courage, and so does your son. He won't fail us, just as Jelena did not."

"How will we do what we promised, Chiana?" Amara continued to stroke her daughter-in-law's cheek. "We haven't the strength left for another major Working. A resurrection must be attempted within the first hour of death. Any later, and the risk of failure is all but certain. By the time our strength is restored, it will be too late."

"There is a way," Gran replied softly. "I can give up my life energy to complete the spell."

Amara stared at her friend. "Chiana...you would do this for my son and daughter-in-law?"

"My life, my *true* life, ended when I destroyed everything I loved in a mad quest for power. Exchanging my life for hers," Gran continued, glancing at Jelena then back at Amara, "won't bring my husband and children back, I know, but perhaps, just perhaps, the One will show mercy and reunite me with them on the other side."

Amara looked away, too overcome to speak.

"You and Taya will need to act without delay. Jelena's body is gravely injured. She's lost a great deal of blood, and could die again if she's not attended to properly."

"Yes. I had thought of that," Amara said. "We should first draw out the knife and bind the wound." She looked around, then slid off the altar and strode across the chamber to gather the remnants of Sonoe's clothing. "These should do nicely for bandages," she said dryly.

Taya returned to find them wrapping strips of cloth around Jelena's chest. "What are you doing?" she asked.

"Preparing Jelena for resurrection," Gran replied.

"Sister, we haven't the strength..."

Gran raised her hand and Taya fell silent. "I'm giving Jelena my life force," the elder Kirian said.

If Taya felt shock, dismay, or any emotion at all, she gave no sign. Stone-faced, she stood with arms folded, watching as Gran and Amara finished their task.

"These rags are poor bandages, but they'll have to do," Gran muttered.

"I'm no doctor," Taya said, "but I haven't spent forty years married to one without learning a thing or two. She's lost too much blood to live. Your sacrifice will be for naught."

You grieve for her, Amara. I grieve as well, though I may not show it. You and I are made differently that way.

Yes, I know…You didn't love her as I learned to, but I saw how you came to respect her. Chiana is…

I'm willing…more than willing, to do this.

"I think Jelena will fight to live," Gran said aloud. "Her love for her husband and child will give her the strength." She sighed and wiped her bloodied hands on the tops of her breeches. "Once this is done, just go. Don't stop to see to my body." Her pale eyes wandered around the chamber before settling on Taya's face. "This will be a far better resting place for me than I deserve."

She rose to her feet and said, "Sisters, the Society must never fall into such a state again. The one who can bring us back to our full power has just left to perform the task, on his own, that the three of us could not. If he succeeds, he is the future of the Society." She looked at Amara.

"Traditions must at times give way to necessity. Amara, send your son to the Kan Onji. His life is wasted as a mere soldier. He needs the proper training so he can fulfill his true destiny."

Amara nodded, tears once again filling her eyes.

"You were our leader once, Chiana," Taya said quietly. "I've never doubted your wisdom or insight. If you say young Sakehera is the future of the Society, then so be it. I'll supervise his training myself…if he succeeds."

"He will." Gran replied. "And now, I must fulfill my promise. Help me, please."

The three mages linked hands and Gran completed the connection by taking up Jelena's.

They began to chant.

Chapter 16

THE PURSUIT COMMENCES

Ashinji stumbled as he landed on the hard packed earth of the portal chamber. The lamps they had left behind, though still burning, flickered close to exhaustion. Snatching one up, he bounded to the door and tried to throw it open. It wouldn't budge. He stared at the door in confusion for a few tense heartbeats until he remembered that Taya had secured it with a locking spell. He reached out with his mind. The energy of the spell had a definite structure; if he could study it long enough, he would be able figure out how to unravel it. He did not have that kind of time. He simply cut through the spell, flung open the door, and ran up the corridor toward the stairs.

It did not occur to him to wonder at the ease with which he destroyed the spell; his mind remained focused on reaching his daughter. He would have time enough for exploring the limits of his newly unbound Talent only if he could stop the thing that now wore Sonoe's body. *If* he could find it in time. *If* he could stop it from killing Prince Raidan *If* he could prevent it from opening the Void...

If, if, if! Too many ifs! I've got to get to Hatora first!

He felt the familiar tug of the link binding his daughter to him, a link stronger, even, than the one that had bound him to Jelena. Hatora's energy felt calm and unafraid. For the moment, she seemed to be in no danger. That could mean one of two things: The Nameless One had passed her by and was no longer in the castle, or the spirit lay in wait, ready to ambush him when he came for his daughter. Whatever the case, he had no choice but to go to her, and his fears would not be allayed until he had seen for himself that Hatora remained truly safe.

When he reached the secret door that opened into the library, Ashinji did not stop to check if anyone might be on the other side; it didn't matter anymore that the portal remain a secret. The library lay deserted; he pelted through the empty rooms and out into the corridor, running at full speed toward the apartments where Hatora waited. Sweating profusely beneath his heavy clothes and growing light-headed from the trapped heat, Ashinji paused to shed his coat before continuing.

He pulled up outside the apartments where Jelena had lived as his widow for the last year, breathing hard. Eikko let out a shriek as he burst through the doors, then cried "Captain Sakehera, it's you!" A heartbeat later, her face blanched with fear. "My lord, your hands are all bloody!" she gasped.

"Where is my daughter?" Ashinji softened his tone as the girl cringed. "Eikko, I'm sorry." Looking down at his hands, he added, "I didn't mean to frighten you." He had been so intent on reaching the baby, he had not noticed just how much of Jelena's blood stained his skin. No wonder Eikko had screamed. "Has anyone come here while we've been gone?" he asked.

The girl gulped and ducked her head. "Uh, no Captain, no one."

"Lady Sonoe didn't come here?"

"N…no, my lord. Was she supposed to?" Eikko looked scared and bewildered, as if she thought she may have made a mistake, but didn't know exactly what she had done wrong. "If she did come by, I swear I didn't hear her knock…"

"Never mind." Ashinji pushed past the flustered maid and rushed toward the bedchamber. Despite what his magical sense told him, he had to see with his own eyes that Hatora lived.

The baby lay on her back in the center of the big bed, sleeping.

Thank the Goddess! Ashinji blinked back tears of relief as he eased himself down beside her.

"My little bird, my sweet little baby," he whispered, stroking her shock of wheaten curls. "Eikko," he called out, never taking his eyes from Hatora's face.

"Yes, Captain," The hikui girl peered around the door.

THE PURSUIT COMMENCES

"Where are my sisters?"

"Lady Lani took the little ones down to the bath house, my lord. They should all be back very soon." Eikko smiled at the sleeping child. "She's such a good baby, my lord, hardly any trouble at all. Always grinning and burbling."

"Gather whatever you'll need for the baby and yourself. I'm taking you both to a place where you'll be safe...safer, anyway...until I can come back for you."

And if I don't come back...if Hatora disappears, perhaps Shiura Onjara won't bother to look for her.

He could see fear spark in the hikui girl's eyes, but that couldn't be helped. To her credit, she asked no questions; within a short time, she announced she was ready to go.

"What about Lady Lani and the twins, my lord? Shouldn't we wait for them?"

Ashinji shook his head. "No time. Besides, my mother will be returning soon." Hopefully, Lani wouldn't panic when she and the twins came back to an empty apartment. "Do you know where the weaver Sateyuka lives?" he asked.

"Yes, my lord. I've been there once with Princess Jelena," Eikko answered. "I think I can find my way."

"Good. Then I'll need you to lead us there." He scooped the still-sleeping baby into his arms and settled her against his chest. "Come."

Without another word, he left the apartment with a confused but trusting Eikko in tow, a rucksack slung over her round shoulder. They encountered no one; Sendai Castle appeared deserted, though Ashinji's magical sense told him otherwise. He felt the energies of those left behind whose jobs were to make sure the castle continued to function, albeit at a very low level, while most of the court was away.

When they reached the broad corridor that led to the king's apartments, Eikko balked. "Lord Ashinji," she squeaked. "I'm not allowed up here! I'll be punished if I'm caught!" A sheen of moisture glistened on her brow.

"You won't be punished, Eikko, I promise," Ashinji reassured her. "You're with me." The hikui girl wrung her hands, but followed at his heels as Ashinji approached the tall, ornate double doors.

Two soldiers of the King's Guard stood rigid at their posts; nothing looked out of place but Ashinji's newly heightened magical sense jangled in alarm. The energy residue of a powerful enchantment clung to both men like a pall of smoke.

Cautiously, he extended his mind toward the guards.

His consciousness rebounded off slick walls of black ice.

Those are not normal mental shields. This is very bad.

Ashinji looked at Eikko, who stared at the guards with wary eyes. "They're bound by some sort of enchantment," he said. "They don't even know we're here. Follow me."

Taking care not to jostle the baby, Ashinji pushed open one door then entered the darkened anteroom. Neither guard moved. He closed the door on their stiff backs then carefully transferred Hatora into Eikko's arms. "Wait here," he said.

Swiftly he crossed the room to pause before the smaller set of double doors leading to the king's bedchamber. No King's Guard stood watch here, yet another bad sign. Once again, Ashinji extended his senses to quest through the doors into the room beyond. He detected no enchantments and no telltale warmth of a living, shielded mind.

He pushed the doors open and slipped inside.

The room appeared exactly as he had seen it last, when he and Jelena had come to bid goodbye to her father. His eyes darted to the bed where Keizo lay unmoving, hands folded atop his chest. He took a step forward and felt something soft crunch beneath his boot. In the dim light, he could just make out the shape of Jewel, Sonoe's dog, sprawled lifeless upon the mats.

With a soft curse, Ashinji sidestepped the tiny corpse. He approached the big, silk-draped bed and peered down at the king's waxen face. No residual magical energy lingered and he saw no telltale physical clues that could lead to any conclusion other than Keizo had died from his illness. Nevertheless, Ashinji knew with unshakable certainty that Sonoe had murdered him, perhaps even before they had all left for the Black Fortress. The ensorcelled guards at the outer doors and the slain dog all stood as proof.

"My lord?" Ashinji looked up to see Eikko peeking through the open doorway. When she caught sight of the king's corpse, her eyes grew huge.

"I thought I told you to wait for me by the outer door!" Ashinji moved away from the bed, grabbed the girl's shoulders then ushered her—Hatora still sound asleep in her arms—out of the bedroom and back across the dark antechamber.

"I'm sorry, Lord Ashinji, but I got scared," the girl whimpered, fat tears rolling down her florid cheeks. "I thought I heard something!"

Ashinji's annoyance fizzled. "I'm sorry I snapped at you," he said in a kindlier tone.

"The king. He's dead, isn't he?" The girl sniffed and scrubbed at her dripping nose with the hem of her sleeve.

"He is," Ashinji replied. "I don't think anyone but us knows it yet, though." He steered Eikko through the doorway back out into the hall and shut the heavy panel behind him, then paused to think.

I'll need to wash my hands and change clothes, get a horse from the stables…

Princess Taya's warning about his quarry sprang to his weary and traumatized mind.

The Nameless One is more dangerous than you can possibly imagine.

He glanced at the frozen guards, then at Eikko, hoping she had not seen him shiver. "Come," he said. Wordlessly, Eikko followed.

&

"This is it, my lord, right here," Eikko said, pointing to a tidy, mid-sized house nestled between two smaller ones. Lamplight spilled out onto the dark street through a beautifully carved wooden window screen, forming a complicated pattern on the beaten earth. The street itself was quiet, but all around him, Ashinji heard the muffled sounds of people in their homes preparing the evening meal, laughing with their spouses, playing with children, arguing with one another. He reined in the horse then waited while Eikko slid to the ground before carefully dismounting.

Loosening the knotted ends of the blanket he had used to bind Hatora securely to his back, Ashinji allowed Eikko to take his daughter into her arms. The baby, awake now, sucked contentedly on a dimpled fist.

"Shall I go knock?" Eikko asked.

"No, I'll do it." He retrieved Eikko's rucksack from the back of the saddle then pulled the horse's reins over its head and dropped them to the ground. Passing the sack to the girl, he then stepped up to the door and knocked.

A few moments passed with no response, so he tried again. This time, a woman's voice called out through the door, "Yes, who is it?"

"Mistress Sateyuka, it's Ashinji Sakehera. Jelena's husband."

The door flew open to reveal a dark-haired hikui woman in early middle age. "I know who you are, my lord!" She stared at him in shock. "Everyone thought you were dead!"

"May we come in?" Ashinji asked.

"Of course, my lord!" She stepped aside to let Ashinji, Eikko, and the baby enter. "Does Jelena know you're alive?" Sateyuka then caught sight of Hatora. "Yes, she must because you have Hatora. Why are you here, Captain Sakehera?"

Sateyuka was a handsome woman, with clear, intelligent eyes and the no-nonsense demeanor of someone used to giving orders. Ashinji knew right away his decision had been a sound one. "I've come to ask a very great favor of you," he said quietly. "I've no time to explain. I must leave Sendai immediately and I need someone trustworthy to care for my daughter."

"What has happened to Jelena, my lord?" Sateyuka asked.

Ashinji sensed the strength of the hikui woman's Talent, but felt only mild surprise. She was doing an excellent job of shielding her thoughts but she could not hide her emotions quite so well; Ashinji felt her alarm like a burst of heat on his skin.

"It's too complicated. Please Sateyuka. Time is running out. Will you shelter my child?"

On impulse, Ashinji mindspoke.

You are Jelena's dear friend. She trusted...trusts you, so I will, too. We both need you to do this for us. I promise, when I return, everything will be explained to you.

Sateyuka's face blanched. She stared hard at Ashinji for a few heartbeats, then gazed at Hatora, still calmly sucking her fist as Eikko bounced her in her arms.

Yes, Captain, of course I'll look after your daughter! After all, I was there when she took her first breath. I love Hatora because she's Jelena's.

"You are the first okui who has ever mindspoken to me," Sateyuka added aloud. She reached out to stroke the baby's cheek. "I'll keep her for as long as you need me to."

THE PURSUIT COMMENCES

"What about me?" Eikko asked in a tiny voice. "Am I to stay here as well?"

"The mistress will need your help with my daughter," Ashinji replied.

Sateyuka cocked her head. "You look strong and capable, girl. I think I can find something for you to do in my shop when little Hatora doesn't need you. Can you read?"

"Yes, Mistress," Eikko replied, then added, "I can do figures also."

"Sateyuka, I really must go." Ashinji swung Hatora from Eikko's arms and held her close. "I've a very long ride ahead of me." The baby squirmed as he kissed her cheeks and forehead. He knew her thoughts, even though her mind could not yet form words to articulate them.

She knows I'm leaving her and that I have no idea when I'll return.

Hatora's face crumpled and she let out a wail.

"Please, baby," Ashinji whispered, unable to hold back his own tears. "Don't cry!" For a while, he could do nothing but weep, and when at last he felt strong enough, he handed his still bawling child over to Sateyuka and departed.

With Hatora's cries ringing in his ears and her mental anguish piercing him like a flight of arrows, he flung himself onto his horse and took off into the night.

Chapter 17

A SIMPLE DEFENSE

Sen Sakehera peered through his spyglass, humming tunelessly to himself. He swept the glass from left to right, scanning the valley below. Off in the distance, nearly lost in bluish haze, the twin towers of Tono Castle stabbed defiantly skyward. The big bay stallion beneath him snorted and stamped at the rocky ground, tail thrashing with impatience.

Prince Raidan maneuvered his own mount alongside that of his co-general. The two stallions glared at each other, ears flattened.

"By the One, I think we've beaten 'em," Sen announced. "The valley looks quiet and Odata's colors still fly over the castle." He lowered the spyglass and closed it with a snap.

"I'm expecting a scout in shortly," Raidan responded. "We'll know more then." The two men sat their horses atop a ridge overlooking the broad expanse of the valley; below, grasslands rolled away in a series of gentle folds to merge with the rich farmland of the valley floor. Behind them massed the combined elven forces, some twenty thousand strong, consisting of the professional army at its core, augmented by the levies of Alasiri's great lords.

The elves would face a human army estimated at between forty and fifty thousand professional, well-seasoned troops. Though not quite as outnumbered as they had feared, nevertheless, both elven generals knew their only chance for survival lay with superior tactics and magic.

A SIMPLE DEFENSE

Raidan gazed toward a dark smudge in the distance, almost directly opposite their current position—the high ridgeline pierced by the Tono Pass. The pass provided the only way for the Soldaran army to gain entry into the valley from the south; it was the key to the elves' entire defensive strategy.

"I pray there's been no more plague," Sen muttered. He twisted in his saddle, first one way and then the other. "Where is that son of mine?" he grumbled. "I need him."

"If we push, we can make the castle before nightfall," Raidan said.

Sen scratched his chin and scowled. "Let's hope that scout gets here soon," he said. "We need to know how much time we've got. I'll see you at the castle." He wheeled his mount away from Raidan's, then trotted off along the ridge toward where his Kerala troops waited.

Raidan raised his hand and his own aides, who had been hanging back at a discreet distance, now urged their mounts forward. "Give the order to march," he commanded and they dispersed to their duties. The prince did not move off right away, but stayed awhile longer on the ridge, pondering the enormity of the task at hand.

The elves had devised a deceptively simple defense plan. The valley was shaped like a wineskin; at its narrowest point, the pass acted like a spout. That spout would be defended by a small elite force, which would serve to delay the Soldarans, and at the same time, trick them into believing they faced sparse resistance.

At a specified time, the elves would turn and flee toward the castle. Emboldened by the apparent weakness of their opposition, the humans would rush into the narrow neck of the valley.

Unbeknownst to the Soldarans, the bulk of the elven army, along with most of the mages, would be positioned behind the rocky ridgelines above the valley floor. They would sweep down in a pincer movement, catching the humans by surprise and surrounding them before they realized their mistake. As the final piece of the trap, the remainder of the elven forces, bolstered by their most powerful mages, would sally forth from the castle to meet the charging Soldarans head on.

In theory, the plan should work.

If only we had about ten thousand more troops, Raidan thought.

"The army is ready to move, my lord Prince!" an aide called out. Raidan waved his hand in acknowledgment, then turned his mount's head toward the steep path that led down off the ridge into the valley.

&

"Isn't this exciting, Little Brother?" Raidu crowed, a savage grin twisting his mouth. "Soon we'll be real warriors, with the blood of dozens of humans on our blades!"

Raidan frowned, disturbed by his eldest son's eagerness to kill.

"I'll be glad when all of this is over," Kaisik murmured in reply.

The prince had convened a final council in the great hall of Tono Castle. All of his war leaders, along with their senior staffs, were present, as well as the contingent of mages, led by a dour-faced old man whose name Raidan couldn't remember. A generous meal had been laid out, and for the first hour or so, there had been no talk of the coming fight.

"Look after your brother, Prince Raidu," Sadaiyo Sakehera spoke up. "I made the mistake of not looking after mine, much to my sorrow."

Raidan's eyes narrowed as he studied the Heir of Kerala. He heard no genuine sorrow in the younger Sakehera's voice; rather, Raidan thought he could detect a subtle smugness in the other man's tone. If Sen Sakehera noticed, he gave no sign.

When the servants had cleared away the last of the dishes, Raidan raised his hand to gain everyone's attention. "Our scouts report the Soldarans are less than three days' march south of the pass," he began. "That should give us enough time to get our forces into position. Everyone here in this hall knows the gravity of our situation. If we fail to turn back the Soldarans here at Tono, they will charge north to take Sendai and there'd be no stopping them. It would mean the end of Alasiri as a free nation."

Silence hung over the room like a shroud.

"Do we have a contingency plan, in case this one proves unsuccessful?" Odata asked.

The ever-practical mistress of understatement, Raidan thought.

"Fall back with whatever forces we have left and retreat to Sendai, where we'll make a final stand," he replied. He scrutinized the faces before him and saw a range of emotions—calm resignation, fierce determination, naked worry. He measured his next words very carefully.

"The king lies ill with the plague, as you all know. When I last saw him, he hovered very close to death. His daughter remains by his side." Raidan paused to gauge the reaction of the assembly to the mention of Keizo's hikui daughter. The group remained quiet and attentive, but he could feel a dangerous undercurrent tugging at the edges of his senses. He forged on. "None of us can ignore the possibility that my brother may die, and that I and both my sons may fall in the coming battle. If that happens, the elves will need to put aside their long-held prejudices and embrace the only Onjara who will be capable of leading them…my niece Jelena."

Angry shouts erupted around the room.

Morio of Ayame stood, his face florid. "Your Highness, I don't understand this sudden change in attitude! You can't possibly expect us to elevate a *hikui* to the throne!" Morio's eyes blazed with accusation, but he was too clever to let slip anything that would reveal his participation in Raidan's previous conspiracy.

"My brother-in-law's right!" Coronji of Tohru shouted. "My lord Prince, it doesn't matter that she's Keizo's daughter. The elven people would never accept her!"

"You're both fools. Jelena is a true Onjara!" Sen Sakehera retorted. "Would you rather our people have no one to lead them?"

"We can serve as a regents' council for the prince's next oldest child," Morio shot back. "Why put a hikui bastard on the throne when we still have legitimate Onjara heirs?"

Sen Sakehera leapt from his chair. "The prince's other children are babies! Why elevate a baby when we have the king's own *legitimized* daughter, a grown woman, who is fit to be our queen?"

"Of course you would take her side, Sakehera!" Morio snarled. "After all, you allowed her into your family and now your bloodline is sullied…"

"How dare you!" Sen's face purpled with fury. Raidan had never seen him in such a state before.

Stung a little himself by Morio's insults, the prince shouted, *"Enough!"*

Both men subsided, but by the look on his face, Raidan knew Sen had been deeply offended by Morio's words.

"My lords, we can't afford to let dissent divide us like this, not now," the prince admonished. "It's clear some of you have strong objections to the inclusion of my niece into the order of succession, but I am telling you all now...put aside your prejudices for the sake of Alasiri!" He paused, but no one spoke up. "It took a long time for me to accept Jelena as a part of my family, but I have," he stated. "She has shown herself to be intelligent, brave, and worthy of our name. I need to know that all of Alasiri's great lords will stand behind her if the worst happens."

"I will stand behind her," Sen declared.

"As will I," Odata added, after a pause.

No one else spoke. The silence of the gathering gave clear testimony to the stubbornness of long-held bigotry. The prince understood the ugliness of the emotion all too well. He let his face settle into a mask of calm determination, and waited.

Finally, a voice broke the stillness.

"I, too, will stand behind the daughter of our king," Kaita of Arrisae pledged. The youngest of Alasiri's great lords, she had just come into her title upon the death of her mother, less than a year ago. Raidan nodded in acknowledgment.

Kaita's declaration broke the barrier, and one by one, the other lords stood and offered their support, even Coronji, who had never before broken ranks with his brother-in-law, Morio. Only Morio remained in his seat, silent and stone-faced. When at last all had stood, every face turned toward the Lord of Ayame, who kept his eyes focused on Raidan.

The assembly held its collective breath, waiting for the explosion...

...which never came.

Morio's eyes remained hard, but his expression softened a little. "I can't pledge my support to the hikui, Highness, but neither will I openly oppose her. That is the best I can offer. I beg you not to ask any more of me."

Raidan felt some of the tension in his body drain away. "I will accept that," he replied, then addressed the entire assembly. "Make no mistake, my lords and ladies," he intoned. "I have no plans to give up my life or my throne, should it come to me through my brother's death. My niece has made it clear she has no desire to be queen, and will assume that burden only if forced to by necessity. But know this. I have the utmost faith in her ability to lead the elven people."

Morio had one final shot. "I pray to the One she is never put to that test," he said.

A Simple Defense

&

"Such grand words of support for my hikui cousin, Father," Raidu commented. "If only you had the same confidence in me."

The mildness of Raidan's tone stood in sharp contrast to the irritation he felt. "I have always supported you, even when you've given me ample reason not to," he replied.

After the war council, Raidan had retired to the chamber he shared with Raidu and Kaisik to prepare himself for bed. Both his sons had accompanied him, but while Kaisik seemed eager to seek his pallet, Raidu remained alert and restless.

"Morio was right, Father. The people won't accept Jelena as queen, even if there's no one else for the job. Besides, she'll never get the chance. We're going to win this fight and you'll take your rightful place as king." Raidu's smile reminded his father of a young wolf's toothy snarl.

"Our uncle's not dead yet. Stop talking about him as if he were!" Kaisik snapped. He had already undressed and now lay on his pallet, a light blanket pulled up to his chin. He glared at his older brother, his brown eyes uncharacteristically stern.

"Easy, Little Brother," Raidu soothed. "I meant no disrespect to our uncle." He turned to look at Raidan. "I can't sleep now, Father," he announced. "I'm going out." He strode to the door and departed before Raidan had a chance to object.

The elder prince sighed in annoyance. Raidu was a grown man, no longer bound by the strict rules governing his younger brother. He could come and go as he pleased.

No doubt he's spotted a comely servant girl and has gone off to find her. A quick tryst in a corner somewhere and then he'll return...

Raidan, still dressed in his dusty undertunic and breeches, removed his boots and lay down on the big bed. He doubted he would get much sleep this night.

The prince turned his head to stare at his younger son's face. The boy's eyes were closed, as if he had already fallen asleep. The prince thought about the stark differences between his two sons, and about what he believed their relationship to be like.

Raidu had always been protective of Kaisik, and yet, they seemed more like master and servant than brothers. Raidu commanded, Kaisik obeyed; most folk would agree that this was the proper way of things. Still, it pleased Raidan to see Kaisik speak up to scold his brother.

Raidan made the decision to work harder to encourage his younger son's independence.

"Kaisik," he called out softly.

The boy's eyes popped open. He had not been asleep after all. "Yes, Father?"

"Tomorrow, I want you to ride out with the scouts to reconnoiter the pass," the elder prince said.

"But, Father, Raidu is going up to the west ridgeline. He'll want me to go with him."

"I don't care. It's time you had some experience on your own. Raidu can do without you for one day. He'll just have to fetch and carry his own gear, now won't he?"

"Yes, Father," Kaisik murmured, but Raidan couldn't tell if he heard relief or worry in the boy's voice.

A sudden noise broke the quiet. Someone pounded on the outer chamber door, shouting with great urgency. Kaisik sat up on his pallet, eyes wide with alarm. Raidan jumped up and reached the door in three quick strides. He jerked it open to reveal a man dressed in castle livery, standing at the threshold.

"My lord Prince, come quickly! There's plague in the castle! My lady needs you now!" the man cried. His fear stung Raidan like a cloud of angry hornets.

The prince rushed to pull his boots back on. "Stay put!" he growled, jabbing his finger at Kaisik, then turning back to the servant he ordered, "Take me to your mistress!"

The servant led the way through a series of darkened back corridors into the part of the castle frequented only by the staff. Muttering about "the end times" and wringing his hands, he kept glancing over his shoulder as if to assure himself Raidan still followed.

The two men rushed through the castle's cavernous kitchen, lit only by the crimson glow of banked fires, and came to a hallway lined with wooden doors, most of them thrown open to reveal plain, serviceable furniture. At the far end, a whispering, weeping clutch of castle folk clogged one of the doorways.

"Step aside!" cried Raidan's guide. "Step aside for his Highness!" The servants melted against the walls, their heads bowed. The air thrummed with their fright. Raidan stepped into the room, and Odata greeted him with a curse and a question.

"Goddess' tits! What are we going to do now?"

Chapter 18

A PRINCE NO MORE

This is not good, not good at all," muttered Sen Sakehera. He paced the length of Odata's small study in quick, jerky strides. "You're the physician, Raidan. Is there anything we can do to stop this from spreading?"

"Yes, but it'll make defending Tono nearly impossible," the prince replied. "We'd have to seal up the castle."

In total, three castle dwellers had already fallen ill: a housemaid, a kitchen drudge, and the guardsman Raidan had been called out to examine.

"What if we isolate the sick and anyone who came in contact with them?" Odata suggested.

Raidan nodded, impressed with the lady's grasp of the basic scientific principle of quarantine. "Yes, that would be ideal, but there's no way to know how many people may have been exposed, since we still don't know exactly how this disease is spread. It would mean losing most of your kitchen staff and at least half of the castle guard. No, it's just not practical."

"What if all the lords and their staffs move out and set up camp outside the walls," Sen said. "That way, at least, we'll lessen the risk to the most vital among us."

"I agree," Raidan replied. "The castle guard will stay inside, of course, as will most of your serving staff, Odata. The only persons allowed to go in and out will be us three."

"Then let's get started," Sen said.

A Prince No More

&

The evacuation of the castle proceeded without any problems. The large tent Raidan shared with Raidu and Kaisik became the new command center.

After he had settled in, the prince's first order of business was to survey all the captains about any unusual sickness they may have observed among their units. Fortunately, none had anything out of the ordinary to report, but this did little to ease Raidan's mind. The exact nature of the contagion remained a mystery; despite the many hours the prince had spent trying to unlock its secrets, he found himself no closer to understanding when and why the plague would strike. He had to assume the entire army stood at risk, even though, so far, no soldier had actually fallen ill.

As the sun dipped below the horizon, submerging the valley in muggy darkness, small groups of scouts assigned to the high ridges moved out of camp, winding their way across empty fields that should have been sown weeks ago. Even if the elves prevailed, hunger would stalk the land like a gaunt specter, for there would be no harvest come summer's end.

In the royal pavilion, Raidan, Sen, young Kaisik, and Sen's son Sadaiyo sat down to a cold dinner of roasted duck and apples. Several of the prince's aides had also been invited, including Mai Nohe. The day had been long and hot, and all were weary, none more so than the prince himself. So many tasks remained to be done. One last war council had be convened and all the lords given their final orders; a fresh source of fodder for the army's horses had to be found; there were dispatches to be written and sent back to Sendai— Raidan feared he would never sleep again.

"I've made my choice of who is to command the diversionary force at the pass," the prince announced after everyone had filled their plates. He turned to look at Sen.

"It has to be you, old friend," the prince said. "Only you have the necessary experience and instinct to pull this off convincingly. The Soldarans must believe the ruse and follow you into the valley. Otherwise, our entire plan will fail."

Sen took a gulp of wine, wiped his mouth with the back of his hand, and glanced at his son. "We'll make sure the Soldarans run straight into our trap like rabbits to the snare."

Sadaiyo Sakehera's eyes gleamed and a tiny smile curled his lips.

"Our scouts have started for the ridges, Highness," Mai Nohe reported. "They should all be in position by midnight."

If the Soldaran generals were canny, and Raidan had no doubt they were, he knew they had sent their own scouts to reconnoiter the ridges as well.

"For our plan to remain viable, the Soldaran scouts will have to be allowed to report back that there's only a small garrison here to defend the valley," Raidan said.

"Every one of our scouts is mage-trained in detection and memory alteration," Sen responded. "All the humans will remember seeing is a whole lot of dark and a few torches on the castle walls."

"Mai, I believe you have a report on the state of the provisions," Raidan prompted as he refilled his wine goblet.

"Yes, Highness," Mai Nohe replied. He wiped his hands on his breeches then pulled a scroll from the leather satchel at his feet. Unrolling the paper, he scanned it for a heartbeat, then cleared his throat and spoke. "We have enough grain, meat, and…"

"Father, a human scout's been captured!"

Everyone turned to look at Raidu as he burst into the tent, flushed and out of breath.

At the same moment, a commotion erupted outside. Someone cried, "Make way for the lady!" and a female voice, calm and perfectly audible above the racket, commanded, "I am here to see Prince Raidan. Let me pass."

Raidan found himself on his feet with no memory of having left his chair.

Goddess' tits, what's she doing here?

The tent flap lifted and the King's Companion swept in, trailing an agitated clot of guards and fellow mages in her wake. "My lord Prince," she murmured and sank into a deep bow.

"Lady Sonoe…I confess, I'm surprised to see you," Raidan responded. "Why have you left my brother's side?"

Something feels wrong here, Raidan thought. He took a step forward and offered a hand to assist the sorceress as she rose to her feet. As his fingers closed about hers, a wave of vertigo struck him. He staggered a little, then shook his head like a man ridding himself of the last vestiges of a dream.

"Is something wrong, Raidan?" Sen inquired.

"No, no. I'm fine," Raidan replied. Perplexed by what he had just experienced but having no ready explanation, he dismissed it from his mind. He stared into Sonoe's face, and saw written there the very thing he feared most to hear.

"My brother is dead," he murmured.

Sonoe's eyes shone like luminous disks of jade in her pale, heart-shaped face. Something flickered within their depths, a glow the prince had never seen before.

Her chin lifted before she spoke to confirm what Raidan had already stated. "Yes," she whispered.

Even though he knew it might happen and he believed himself prepared, the reality of Keizo's death still struck Raidan like an axe blow. For a few terrible moments, he couldn't breathe.

"The One have mercy on us." Sen murmured, then asked, "What of my daughter-in-law?"

Sonoe turned her unsettling gaze on the Lord of Kerala. "She is devastated," the mage replied. "She has sunk into a despair so deep, I fear she may never emerge."

Raidan's lips twisted into a frown. "Jelena is strong. She knows what's at stake. She will recover." He framed his words as a statement, for to do otherwise would be to admit his uncertainty.

"Highness, I have ridden practically without pause to reach you. May I sit?" Sonoe asked.

"Yes, of course." He gestured for one of the servants to bring a stool, and the sorceress sank onto it with a grateful sigh. Her fellow mages remained standing in the background, their faces masks of consternation and worry. Even the dour old man whom Raidan had presumed to be their leader remained on his feet, as if he had already ceded his authority to the Companion.

Sonoe's next words confirmed her new office. "I'm here to take command of the mages, your Highness," she stated. "I can't help the king...I mean, I can't help Keizo any longer, but as a First Mage of the Kan Onji, I'm the most powerful practitioner in Alasiri after your wife. The princess herself ordered me to come."

"Father," Raidu interrupted. He stood at the tent flap, holding it open with one hand. "The scouts have brought the human. They're outside with him now."

"Have him brought in," Raidan ordered. "Sonoe, we must talk, but I need to question this human."

Too much is happening at once, Raidan thought. He felt oddly unbalanced, as if some unseen force sucked at him, draining him of vitality.

"Yes, my lord Prince," Sonoe answered, inclining her head in submission. Raidan stared for a few heartbeats at the Companion, trying to fathom why she seemed *different*, somehow, then ascribed it to grief and fatigue, both his own and hers. He turned his attention to the commotion at the pavilion entrance.

Two scouts pushed their way through the flap, dragging a struggling figure between them. They hauled their captive to the center of the room and shoved him hard, sending him sprawling to the mats. Both scouts bowed, then readied themselves to pounce should the human try to make an escape.

"Your Highness, we captured this human on the east ridge," one of the scouts stated.

"Stand up," Raidan ordered in Soldaran. The man, who'd been crouching on the floor, unmoving, looked up sharply. His thin, ugly face bore a look of such astonishment that Raidan had to laugh. "I said, stand up," he repeated, "or is my Soldaran so bad that you do not understand?"

The man unfolded his lanky frame and stood, though his shoulders remained stooped, as if he expected a killing blow to fall at any moment. "I understan' ye well enough, tink," the man muttered. His brown eyes burned with sullen defiance. It was difficult to tell his age; humans did not weather the passage of time very well, but Raidan thought he might be just past his youth.

"I am a merciful man," Raidan said. "Tell me what I need to know and I will spare your life."

The human sniffed, then with cool deliberateness, spat on Raidan's boot.

Everyone in the room froze.

Like a hound unleashed, Raidu sprang to attack. He felled the captive with a brutal punch to the man's face, then began kicking him in the ribs. The prince's guards, after a moment's hesitation, joined in. The sound of their boots made a meaty, thudding accompaniment to the man's screams. Raidan heard the unmistakable wet crunch of breaking bone.

"What are you doing!" Sen Sakehera shouted.

"Stop this at once!" Raidan roared. The guards fell back immediately, but Raidu, face alight with savage glee, aimed a final kick at the human's head. The man convulsed, then lay still, blood and vomit leaking from his nose and mouth. Raidu spat in his face, then backed off.

Raidan stared at the broken, bleeding human, too consumed with rage to speak. Everyone in the tent shrank back against the walls except Sen, Raidu and Sonoe. Sen clutched the sides of his head and uttered a string of curses. Raidu insolently held his ground while Sonoe crouched and carefully laid a hand on the human's forehead. She remained thus for many heartbeats, a living statue, eyes closed.

The air in the room, saturated with violence and horror, shimmered on the verge of ignition.

"We...are not...barbarians," Raidan finally managed to croak through jaws clenched so tight, they ached. *"We do not kick prisoners to death!"* He whirled around to glare at the guards, who all fell to their knees like wheat beneath the scythe, heads bowed. Out of the corner of his eye, Raidan saw Kaisik staring at his brother, whey-faced. The boy pressed a hand to his mouth, stumbled over to the wall then vomited against the canvas.

"Sorry, Father, but the cur had it coming," Raidu drawled. "He dared to insult an elven prince."

Raidan lowered his head and focused for a moment on his dusty, spittle-stained boots, reining in his anger so he could respond to his son without howling.

"I needed the information that man could have provided," he said. "Something he knew may have spared the lives of many of our troops. Did you even...*for an instant*...consider that?" He looked into Raidu's eyes, hoping to find the tiniest scrap of remorse, but he saw none. His son merely shrugged.

"Your Highness," Sonoe spoke up softly. "I've scanned the dead man's mind and retrieved some images. They might be of use."

If a trained mage scanned a person's mind immediately after death, the deceased's last thoughts, impressions, and memories could sometimes be recovered.

Perhaps Sonoe has been able to salvage something useful out of this debacle, Raidan thought.

"I commend you on your quick thinking, my lady," he replied, then snapped to the guards, "Get this body out of here!"

The guards scrambled to obey, dragging the dead human out of the tent, leaving a bloody trail in their wake.

"You," Sen gestured to the two scouts, both of whom had jumped out of the way the moment Raidu had attacked. "Could you tell whether or not the Soldaran had a partner?"

The pair stepped forward, shaking their heads in unison. "No, my lord," the older man answered. "He was alone. Neither of us sensed any others nearby."

"Tell us what you learned," Sen ordered, turning to Sonoe.

"He did have a partner, Highness," she answered. "But I got no sense that they were together when your scouts discovered this man. The other one may very well still be up on the ridge, or he may have already returned to the main body of the Soldaran army. This man felt certain, though, that the Soldarans will have no difficulty retaking the valley."

"Very good," Sen commented.

"You see, Father?" Raidu interjected. "Questioning that creature would have been useless, so there's really no harm done..."

"Be silent!" Raidan barked. He glared at his son. "At this moment, I can barely stand to look at you, much less listen to any opinions you might have." Raidu's lips twisted into a petulant bow and for an instant, Raidan thought his son might actually defy him, but the younger prince evidently thought better of it and held his tongue.

Before Raidan could speak again, Lady Odata strode into the pavilion. "I came as soon as I heard, your Highness. Where is the prisoner?" Odata wore a look of high expectation on her face but she stopped short in obvious confusion when she saw the grim expressions confronting her. "What is it? What has happened?" She looked first at Raidan, then at Sen.

"The prisoner is dead," Sen replied.

"What? How?" Odata exclaimed in dismay.

"It doesn't matter," Raidan stated. "He didn't know anything useful." Odata glanced at the blood on the mats and her eyes narrowed, but she didn't press the issue.

"I'm glad you're here now, Odata. I need to speak with you." Raidan took a deep breath and forced himself to sit. With that simple act, he banished enough tension in the room to allow everyone else to relax.

"Guardsmen and scouts, you are all dismissed," the prince ordered. "Mages as well. Lady Sonoe, you and your second, please stay." He waited until all the guards, the two scouts, and the rest of the mages had filed out before he spoke again. "Tell me about my brother."

"He died in my arms," Sonoe answered in a rough whisper. "In the end, he was at peace and in no pain. I saw to that myself."

"Thank you," Raidan tried to say, but a strange lassitude had begun to creep over him, turning his body into an unwieldy sack of stones and his mind into treacle. Sonoe's eyes expanded before his sight, merging into a single, whirling jade pool. He felt it sucking him down, and he struggled to break free. Just as he thought he might be pulled in, he was released.

"Ai, Goddess!" he gasped. "What just happened?" He shook his head and pressed a palm to his brow.

"What do you mean, my lord? Is something wrong?" Sonoe murmured.

"Did you try to scan me just now?" Raidan regarded the sorceress with growing suspicion.

Sonoe's face lost all color. "No, your, Highness!" she replied, bowing her head. "I would never presume to enter your mind without your permission. I apologize if my own grief somehow disturbed you. The king's death has affected me very deeply." Her beautiful mouth trembled.

A sharp pang of remorse stung Raidan's already aching heart. "Of course. Of course it has. I know how you felt about my brother, Sonoe," he said softly, "and your love and loyalty won't go unrewarded."

"I don't want any reward, your Highness. All I want is to have my soulmate back, but that's not possible." She turned her face away, but not before the prince glimpsed the sparkle of tears on her cheeks.

"The other lords must be informed of the king's death, Raidan," Sen said in a low voice.

Raidan raised his hand and Mai Nohe materialized at his shoulder. "See to it that runners are sent to all the other lords. I want them here right away," he ordered.

"Yes, my lord Prince," Mai answered and strode out of the tent.

Sen crouched by Raidan's stool and murmured, too softly for anyone else to hear, "Raidan, you are king of Alasiri now."

Raidan sighed. Ever since the day when Keizo had ascended the throne and had named him Heir, the prince had prepared for this moment, but now that it had come, he felt nothing but sorrow and desolation.

This is not how I wanted to be made king!

"Yes, I realize that." he replied aloud. "All too well."

Raidan rose from his stool and looked around the room. Sen remained kneeling, and the prince saw that everyone else in the pavilion had knelt as well, including Raidu, who for once seemed beyond insolence.

"Please, all of you, get up," he commanded wearily. "News of my brother's death must not leave this tent."

"But why, your Majesty?" Sen exclaimed as he hauled himself to his feet. "The other lords and the army have a right to know!"

"The army, as do the rest of the elven people, love Keizo with a fervor they have yet to feel for me. No, old friend," Raidan held up a hand to silence Sen's protest. "Please don't patronize me. I'm far too sensible to delude myself on that account. The troops need their unconditional love for my brother. It's what's sustaining their courage. If they learn of his death, it will break their hearts and take away the edge we need to win this fight."

Sen nodded in reluctant agreement. "Perhaps, you're right, but I think you're selling yourself short, Majesty."

"Please, remember…all of you must still think of me as I was, not as who I will become if, *when*, we drive out the Soldarans," Raidan admonished.

A heartbeat later, Mai Nohe returned. "My lord Prince, the other lords are on their way," he announced.

"Good," Raidan said. "All of you…pour yourselves more wine and get comfortable. We have a long night ahead of us."

Chapter 19

BATTLE DAWN

The rest of the lords agreed that Sen Sakehera, as Raidan's most experienced commander, should lead the force that would first engage the enemy and hold them at the pass.

Sen rode out well before dawn, his son Sadaiyo beside him, at the head of a force just over eight hundred strong—large enough to be an effective barrier for a time, yet small enough to, hopefully, fool the Soldarans into believing they would have little trouble taking back the valley. With Sakehera in place, the plan would be set and the elves as ready as they could possibly be.

Raidan witnessed Sen's departure from atop the battlements of Tono Castle, an agitated Odata at his side. From the heights, the army looked like a slim column of ants marching out across the valley floor. The valley itself lay empty as part of the deception. The bulk of the elven forces were in place, positioned among the rocky crags that ringed the valley like dragon's teeth.

Behind the fortress—hidden by its sturdy walls—awaited the cream of Alasiri's army. These units were composed of the toughest, most seasoned warriors, men and women who'd been battle-tested through years of border defense on the eastern and northern frontiers.

One hundred and fifty years of peace with the Soldarans had not meant any respite for Alasiri's armed forces. In the east, they battled nomadic tribes from the windy steppes, whose warlords decorated their battle standards with the severed heads of their enemies. In the north, bearded, pale-haired warriors attacked by sea in dragon-prowed longships. Alasiri had always been a beleaguered nation, surrounded on all sides by humankind who coveted the elves' fertile land and resources.

Raidan sighed and rubbed his aching eyes. He couldn't remember when he had last slept. "How many more have fallen sick?"

Odata drummed her gloved fingers on the stone parapet. "Seven, at last count, all among the household staff. So far, our luck appears to be holding. No more guards have gotten sick, and I've heard no reports of anything unusual among the army."

"It's science, Odata, far more than luck, that's prevented this plague from spreading," Raidan commented.

The Lady of Tono sniffed. "Respectfully, my lord Prince, I believe in luck and the One who bestows it. You speak of science and how it has the power to explain everything, yet you still have no idea what causes this sickness." She paused to wet her lips before continuing. "I believe the Goddess has sent this plague and this war to us as a sign. People have been turning away from Her, turning their backs on She who created us! The temples are empty, the priesthood is dwindling…There are some holy days where I and my family are the only ones attending worship in our village."

Raidan regarded Odata thoughtfully, one eyebrow raised. "My lady, I had no idea you were so…pious." He nearly said zealous but thought better of it.

Odata returned his look with a frown. "If the elven people hadn't been so shamefully negligent in their duty to Her, then none of this would be happening."

Raidan said nothing; instead, he pushed off from the wall and walked along the rampart toward the stairs. Odata stalked along beside him in silence. Guards stationed at regular intervals along the parapets saluted as he passed; they saluted their commander and prince, not their king, for Raidan's orders had been obeyed and no one outside the small group who'd been present at Sonoe's arrival knew of Keizo's death.

Raidan felt a twinge of unease as he thought of his brother's Companion. She seemed undeniably different somehow, yet changed in a way too subtle for him to articulate. He had initially ascribed it to grief, but now he was not so sure.

She had taken charge of the other mages competently enough, and they had all seemed content to let her, even the cranky old man who had been in command. She had even improved upon their magical strategy, and had volunteered to ride out with Sakehera's force.

"I have a few showy tricks I can use…Nothing too lethal," she had explained. "It will make them think our vaunted magical reputation is mostly myth, so when my mages hit them with the real thing, it will be that much more demoralizing. Also, I can direct the magical attacks much more efficiently if I'm on the battlefield."

Sen Sakehera had agreed, and so Sonoe had taken two other mages and together, they had ridden out with the Lord of Kerala. For no reason he could explain, Raidan felt relieved to see her go.

"I expect Sakehera to engage the enemy shortly after sunrise," he said to Odata. The Lady of Tono had turned out in full battle dress, a graceful willow tree motif decorating both breast and back plates. Raidan knew her to be a competent commander and a decent swordswoman, but he also knew it had been years since she had last swung a weapon in battle. He hoped she would do the sensible thing and stay behind Tono's walls, letting her eldest son lead her troops onto the field when the fight came to the gates of the castle.

"I'm going to my private chapel to pray, Highness," Odata said as the two of them descended into the inner yard. "You are welcome to join me, of course."

Raidan shook his head. "Thank you, but no, my lady," he replied.

"As you wish, my lord Prince." Odata inclined her head and left him standing alone by the stairs.

Taya, how I wish you were here! The sudden ache of longing caught Raidan by surprise. *We've been separated by duty before, but this time, it's different. Yes, my life has been at risk, but never have the stakes been so high! If we fail here, I will probably never see you again, my love, for it will mean the end of everything.*

The prince went in search of his sons.

He found both young men back at the royal pavilion. Kaisik assisted his older brother with the elaborately painted armor Raidu had commissioned just for this day.

"Father!" Raidu called out as Raidan entered. "Your Heir and your spare are ready. It's killing time!" He pumped his fist in the air, face stretched in a savage grin.

"You would do well to shed some of that arrogance," Raidan shot back. "This is no game, Raidu. If you don't keep your wits about you, if your concentration flags for even an instant…"

"My concentration will be perfect, Father, and so will Kaisik's" he said, looking down at his brother, who crouched on the floor, fighting with a stubborn strap at Raidu's ankle.

"Kaisik!" Raidan snapped, then instantly regretted his irritable tone as his younger son flinched. "You don't need to do that," he said in a gentler voice. It had never bothered him before, but now he hated to see Kaisik in so servile a posture. "You've not yet armed yourself, Son. Call for a servant to help you get ready. I need to speak with your brother."

"Yes, Father," Kaisik answered as he scrambled to his feet. "Father, am I to ride out with you and Raidu today?" Raidan needed no Talent to sense his younger son's mood.

The boy is afraid, and yet…

The prince saw determination in Kaisik's sea-green eyes.

He wants to conquer his fear and acquit himself well today.

Raidan felt a newfound pride in the boy that he had not felt before. "I can't risk both of you unless it's absolutely necessary, so no, Kaisik, you will stay behind and help defend the castle from the ramparts," he said, then added to lessen the sting, "Don't think I haven't noticed what a good shot you've become, Son."

The boy looked down at his feet for a moment, then nodded. "You know what's best, Father, but I would rather be with you and my brother," he replied. Without another word, he brushed by them and left the tent.

"Why won't you let Kaisik come with us? He's got to prove himself sometime, you know."

Raidan glared at his eldest son. "He'll never be able to prove himself as long as you keep treating him like your manservant."

"That's not fair, Father," Raidu shot back. "I've always looked out for him, always protected him…"

"Be quiet, Son," Raidan commanded. "This is not the time for us to talk about your relationship with your brother. I need to discuss what will happen should I fall in battle today."

Raidu swallowed hard and his body tensed.

That got his attention!

"If I die, you will be king. Do you realize what that means?" Raidan stared into his son's eyes.

"Of course I do, and I'll be ready, but you're not going to die today, Father," Raidu insisted, frowning. He had a way of tilting down one eyebrow that instantly transformed his face into a masculine version of Taya's.

Again, Raidan felt longing for his wife, like a shard of glass, pierce his heart. "Denial won't change things, Son. I may die today, and I won't feel easy unless I know you understand what must be done if I do." He held up his hand to forestall the protest forming on Raidu's lips. "Just listen! If Sen Sakehera survives the initial battle, and I don't, then he will be in complete charge of the army. You follow his directions without question. He will be Alasiri's last hope to avoid total conquest."

Raidan paused to gauge his son's reaction. Raidu had grown somber, with not the slightest hint of insolence in his eyes. "If the worst should happen and Sakehera also falls, then you must take whatever forces we have left, abandon the valley and retreat to Sendai."

"And what if we can't hold Sendai, Father?"

"Then your first duty is to survive and to ensure the survival of the elves as a people. If that means," he had to force his next words past tense lips, "surrender and submission, then so be it. The elves can't liberate themselves if they're all dead. Our people will need a living Onjara as well, to eventually lead them back to freedom."

Raidu lifted his chin and clenched both fists. "I have no intention of ever surrendering to the humans, Father," he said. "I would rather die, and so should every okui. We'll slaughter as many of them as we can until they kill the last of us. Then, they can have the hikui dregs for their slaves!"

"Goddess' tits!" Raidan shouted. Raidu flinched and stepped back. "Son," the prince continued, struggling to keep himself in check. "The elves as a people *must survive*. That is the most important...no, the *only* thing that matters. Swear to me...*swear*, Raidu, that you will obey my orders should the battle not go our way!"

The younger prince's gaze remained unwavering, but the slight drop of his shoulders told Raidan his son had yielded.

"Yes, Father. I swear."

Raidan regarded his son, who stood before him brimming with such vitality and youthful arrogance, and his heart ached with sadness.

If only my children could be spared this calamity, he thought. He sighed and turned away. "When you're ready, meet me at the castle gates," he said over his shoulder as he left the tent.

❧

The predawn darkness roiled with the sounds of an army readying itself for battle. Men and women shouted, horses neighed, armor clanked and harness jingled. The smells of wood smoke, dry grass, and horse manure permeated the air. High on the castle battlements, a bell rang the hour.

Raidan made his way through the controlled maelstrom, cursorily acknowledging the salutes of his troops. When he reached the outer gates, he found Odata and Morio waiting for him. The contingent of mages assigned to help with the frontal defense waited there as well.

The old man whom Sonoe had supplanted had charge of them. He stepped up to Raidan and sketched a bow. "My lord Prince, we will need an area up on the walls where we can view the entire battlefield so we might effectively aim our attacks. The captains up there won't let us position ourselves in front. They say we will interfere with the archers!"

"Master..."

"Katram, my lord."

"Master Katram, you and your fellow mages can position yourselves against the western tower. You should have a clear view of the valley and you'll have the archers on the tower to cover you."

"We require no additional protection, my lord Prince," Katram sniffed. "But I suppose it does make more sense for us to be against the tower. Very well." He gestured for the other mages to follow and the group headed toward the stairs leading up to the battlements.

"You never have put much faith in magic, have you, Highness?" Odata said as she watched the mages threading their way through the swirl of moving bodies filling the yard.

"Not true. I've always had the utmost faith in magic," Raidan countered. "I've lived with Alasiri's premier mage for over forty years, so I'm quite familiar with what magic can and can't do. It will give us a much needed advantage, but it can't save us in the end if we fail militarily."

Morio shifted from foot to foot. Raidan glanced at the other man's face and it looked as though the Lord of Ayame had something especially bitter in his mouth he had to chew.

"What's troubling you, Morio?" Raidan asked.

Morio took a deep breath, much like a man does before diving into deep water. "I don't like having to say this, especially now," he replied. He looked through the gates at the frenzy of activity beyond.

Raidan felt a flash of annoyance. "Please say what you need to, my lord!" he growled.

"Very well." Morio's black eyes narrowed as he spoke. "It's about Prince Raidu. I've had a chance to observe him closely these past weeks, and it pains me greatly to say this, but I must. If you should fall, then I don't have much faith in his ability to lead. He is simply not ready!"

"If not my son, then who?" Raidan asked. A swell of anger rose within him, threatening to sweep away all his self control. "You've already made it clear you won't support my niece Jelena. If not my son, or my brother's daughter, *then who?*"

Morio remained silent for a few heartbeats. "I don't know," he admitted. "It seems disaster hems us in on all sides."

"Do the other lords lack faith in my son?"

Raidan saw his answer in Odata's eyes. "Your great lords will obey your orders, my lord Prince," she murmured.

"I need to attend to something," Raidan said. "Stay here. I'll return shortly." He turned on his heel and stalked away. As he passed through the gates, he heard Odata calling after him, but he ignored her. He had no real errand. He just needed to walk.

Morio thinks disaster hems us in and my son is not fit to lead. The worst of it is he's right!

Raidan's bleak thoughts beat against the inside of his head like bats as he moved along the base of the wall toward the west tower. The area lay deserted; the companies camped here had already vacated it. The fading stars overhead presaged the approach of the new day.

Sakehera's forces should already be in place and ready to engage the Soldarans.
The storm is almost upon us.

"Prince Raidan!"

The hail came from somewhere up ahead. Raidan halted in his tracks and peered into the darkness. He could just make out a figure trotting toward him.

A scout, perhaps?

He waited while the figure approached.

"My lord! I'm so glad I found you!" The voice sounded familiar; Raidan felt certain he had spoken to this man before.

"Have you something to report to me, scout?" he called out.

"Yes, my lord...something very important." The man stopped a stone's toss from the prince and bowed.

Raidan moved closer so he could see the man's face. "Goddess!" he exclaimed. "You're alive!"

"Yes, my lord. Very much so," Ashinji Sakehera said.

Chapter 20

SHOWDOWN AT THE PASS

"Captain Sakehera! Where have you been all this time?" the prince demanded.

"That is too long a story for right now, your Highness." Ashinji raked his hands through his tousled hair. "I've ridden from Sendai to find you." From the look of the camp, Ashinji guessed the army stood ready to march.

I've gotten here with barely a moment to spare.

The prince's armor clinked as he moved closer. "You came from Sendai? Then my niece must know…"

"Please, my lord, you must listen. I don't have much time!"

Prince Raidan frowned. "I'm listening," he said.

Ashinji took a moment to gather his wits and clear the fog of weariness from his mind. It struck him that Raidan might not know of his brother's death. "Your Highness, the king is dead," he said.

The prince nodded. "Yes, I know. Lady Sonoe has come to Tono to take charge of the mages, per my wife's orders. She informed me of my brother's passing."

So that's how she plans to complete the spell that will open the Void. She's going to use the other mages to boost her power.

"Where is Sonoe now, your Highness?" Ashinji had already scanned the camp and had detected nothing unusual, but then, the entity controlling Sonoe's body would shield itself well.

"She rode out with your father a short while ago. Lord Sakehera is to hold off the Soldarans for a time at the valley entrance, and Lady Sonoe offered to help with some diversionary magic. What's all this about, Captain?" Ashinji could sense the prince's growing impatience.

"My lord, your wife must have told you something about Jelena's…about the magic she carried within her, and what the Kirians needed to do about it." Ashinji spoke quickly now.

"Yes, she did." Raidan paused, then asked, "What happened? Did the Kirians succeed?"

Ashinji tried to keep his voice from breaking, but he couldn't. "No my lord. They failed…Jelena is dead."

Raidan gasped and uttered a soft curse.

"One of their own betrayed them," Ashinji continued. "Sonoe must have been in league with the enemy all along. At the crucial moment, when Jelena's death released the magic within her, Sonoe opened a way for the enemy to escape its prison. She had a double betrayal planned. She tried to enslave the spirit by speaking its true name, but it was ready for her."

Ashinji shuddered at the memory of Sonoe's hideous demise. "She paid for her betrayal with her life. The thing that came here two days ago is not Sonoe! It only wears Sonoe's flesh. The Kirians call it the Nameless One, but it's the undead spirit of your ancestor, the sorcerer king Shiura Onjara. Somehow, Sonoe found out his true name. He…*it* is now in possession of the very thing the Kirians fought so hard to keep from it."

The prince's eyes focused inward, as if he were trying to fit pieces of a puzzle together and make sense of it in his mind. "My wife kept a great deal from me, I see," he murmured. His gaze sharpened with his next words. "I sensed something had changed about Sonoe, but I couldn't figure out what. At times, when we're together, a very strange sensation comes over me and once, I accused her of trying to scan my mind without my permission."

"The spirit's goal is simple, Highness. It wants to conquer the material world and enslave every living thing," Ashinji explained. "To accomplish this, it needs an army that can't be defeated by ordinary means. It also requires the deaths of all living Onjaras. The spirit may have been attempting to weaken you, drain you magically, which is why you felt the way you did."

"Yes, that could be," Raidan replied thoughtfully. "But how does the ghost of my dead ancestor plan on raising an army?"

"The magic Jelena carried within her is a key of sorts. The Nameless One has it now, and with it, he can open a gate into another dimension, a place the Kirians call the Void. According to their ancient writings, it's not a void at all, but rather a terrible place full of creatures so unlike anything in this world, there are no words to describe some of them. These creatures will be bent to his will by the power of the magic contained within the White Griffin."

"The White Griffin never leaves the hand of the king, and my brother is still in Sendai," Raidan interrupted. "Unless…"

"Yes, my lord. Sonoe has it, or rather, the Nameless One does," Ashinji confirmed. "He stole it, and at the same time, he nearly killed my mother and the other Kirians. My lord, he has everything he needs to complete the spell and open the Void."

High on the ramparts, horns blared—three short blasts followed by one sustained note. Their clarion chorus rolled across the valley and the gathered troops below. The army stood ready to move into position behind the castle.

Raidan ran a hand over his sable hair. "I hope you're here with a plan to stop this," he said quietly.

"I'll need to get close to Sonoe," Ashinji answered. "When I do…"

"Say no more," the prince said, raising his hand. "Take a horse and ride to the pass. You'll find her there, and Sakehera…" the prince called as Ashinji turned to go, "I'm saddened more than you know about Jelena. Her death must count for something. Stop this Nameless One. *Stop him!*"

Ashinji nodded. "I will, Highness…I mean your Majesty."

Open the spirit box and speak his name. That's all I have to do. Somehow, I don't think it will be quite that simple.

Determination warred with despair within him as Ashinji bent low over the neck of the galloping horse, hurtling through the predawn darkness toward a showdown he knew he dare not lose, but yet felt uncertain he could win.

Prince Raidan's admonition still rang in his mind.

Stop this Nameless One. Stop him!

But what if I can't?

The Kirians believed he could, else they never would have sent him.

What if they're wrong?

He could feel the horse beginning to tire, but relentlessly, Ashinji drove it forward. He knew he drew close, for he could hear the sounds of battle ahead—steel ringing against steel, shouts of anger, cries of pain. A brilliant flash of blue illuminated the dark mouth of the pass, now squirming with movement that, from this distance, looked like termites swarming from a crack in the earth.

Before he left camp, Ashinji had armed himself with a bow, a quiver of arrows, and a sword, but he doubted if he would get close enough to the fray to need any conventional weapons. He had no armor to protect his body, and no plans to do any non-magical fighting, at least not now.

He felt certain Sonoe and any other mages she had with her would be well back of the line. He planned to dismount at a distance, then move forward on foot, sticking to what cover he found, and trust he could conceal himself magically from the Nameless One. He had been practicing; when first he had approached Tono Castle, he imagined himself enshrouded by the surrounding darkness. He had walked virtually undetected through the bustling camp, and dropped his concealment only when he had located Prince Raidan.

Avoiding detection by a trained mage would be far more difficult than hiding himself from soldiers and camp servants. He had the advantage of distraction on his side, though. Sonoe was preoccupied with harrying the Soldarans. He counted on her remaining so focused on the battle that she would not detect him until it was too late.

With each passing moment, the sky grew lighter. Soon, Ashinji realized, he would lose the cover of darkness. He reined in the flagging horse, and when the animal stumbled to a halt, he vaulted to the ground and darted in among a stand of alders. A small stream gurgled past the roots of the trees. The ground ahead opened out into fallow fields covered in broad-leafed weeds and wild grasses. A dirt path ran along a drainage ditch, leading arrow-straight toward the battle.

The horse meandered out into the field and bent its head to crop the grass. Ashinji, rather than imagining himself part of the darkness, sought to merge with the landscape, to become no more than a ripple kicked up in the grass by the breeze. With that image lodged in his mind, he left the shelter of the trees and set off.

Another flash of blue light alerted him to the mages' position, back and to the right of the epicenter of the battle. He changed course and left the path, angling across the uneven earth. Crickets chirped in the coarse clumps of grass. A ground-nesting bird, flushed from its hiding place by some unseen predator, skittered off on a low trajectory, its wings making a whirring noise as it flew. The smell of soil, still moist from the spring rains, filled his nostrils with the rich, dark scent of fecundity.

Ashinji glided along like a wisp of morning mist, silent and invisible. From over his left shoulder, the first rays of the new sun stabbed heavenward, bathing the heights with gold. The light raced down and across the valley floor toward him, putting the night's shadows to flight. Up ahead, he could see the battle.

He spotted the black boar on gold of his father's banner, marking the place where Lord Sen stood, directing the action. He wondered if Sadaiyo was there as well, but then decided his brother most likely stood in the thick of things, claiming his share of kills. Sadaiyo might be vicious, sadistic, and manipulative, but cowardice had never been one of his faults.

The elves held their own, at least for now. They had the advantage here at the bottleneck of the pass, where Sen could use his smaller force to maximum effectiveness. The Soldarans found themselves blocked in and pinned down just inside the cut, while withering arrow fire from the elven archers raked their position.

Ashinji didn't know the exact battle plan, but he could guess.

Father is fighting a holding action here, in order to delay the Soldarans for a time. This must be part of some sort of ambush. There're troops on the ridges, waiting for Father to lure the Soldarans into the trap.

So far, things seemed to be going according to plan. Ashinji had no idea when Lord Sen would give the order to retreat, but he knew he had to get to Sonoe before that happened.

He reached down to touch the bag at his belt that held the spirit box. He found it hard to believe something so small could hold an entity as powerful as the Nameless One.

But it's not truly nameless, is it? In truth, its…no, his name will be his undoing. All I have to do is speak it.

Ashinji slowed to a halt, then hunkered down to the ground, searching with both eyesight and magical sense for the creature that wore Sonoe's flesh. He had no trouble finding her—she glowed like fire in the fresh daylight—and he was relieved to see that she stood well apart from his father's entourage. He began to whisper; he didn't know why, but it just felt like the right thing to do.

"Grass, wind, earth, grass, air, earth, air,..." Cautiously, he crept forward.

He paused a stone's throw behind the former Kirian. She stood unmoving, arms relaxed by her sides. Ashinji could not see her face, but he heard her voice, murmuring in a singsong cadence. With his own chant still on his lips, he freed the spirit box from the pouch at his waist.

Abruptly, Sonoe's arms jerked up and twin blue fireballs exploded from her fingertips, arching high overhead to fall, spinning and sparking, amid the seething mass of humans bunched at the mouth of the pass. As the fireballs detonated among the screaming Soldarans, the concussive force of the blast hit Ashinji like a fist, not so hard that it knocked him over, but strong enough to push the breath from his lungs.

Strong enough, also, to stop his incantation.

Sonoe turned and saw him.

Her eyes, once green but now blood red, narrowed.

"You!" she hissed.

Ashinji opened the spirit box and shouted, "Shiura Onjara, I command you to leave that body and come into this vessel!"

Nothing happened.

Ashinji's heart sank as the creature laughed—a deep, throaty, sound. He looked despairingly at the spirit box in his hands.

What did I do wrong?

"Fool!" Sonoe rasped. "Did the Kirians think I would be caught so easily? Then they are even more stupid than I thought!" Before Ashinji could react, she rushed him with unnatural swiftness, and her fingers locked around his throat like a vise. "That they sent *you* is further proof of their weakness!"

Ashinji grabbed Sonoe's wrists and attempted to break her grip, but he might as well have tried snapping iron bands. Her fingers squeezed; his senses shredded like clouds before a strong wind.

SHOWDOWN AT THE PASS

The spirit box tumbled to the ground.

Without warning, Sonoe released him and he fell back, choking and gasping. His knees buckled and the earth rushed up to slam him in the head. As he lay helpless, the sound of multiple battle horns brayed, signaling the retreat. A great roar—the noise of many voices raised in a shout of triumph—filled the air.

Get up! his mind screamed. *Move! You can't stay here!*

Desperately, Ashinji scrambled to his feet, dizzy and nauseous.

Where is Sonoe?

He looked around, groaning from the pain in his neck as he turned his head.

Sonoe had gone, vanished like dew at sunrise. The elven forces were in full retreat, fleeing back toward the castle.

As he bent down to retrieve the spirit box, the Soldaran army came pouring from the mouth of the pass like flood waters over a broken dam.

Shit! I'm standing right in their path!

He turned and ran.

The ground beneath him shook from the impact of thousands of pounding feet.

This is madness! I can't outrun an army!

He staggered to a halt and swung around to face the oncoming wave. A line of cavalry raced ahead of the infantry and within moments, they would be upon him. He drew his sword and raised it, two-handed, in preparation, then began to chant.

The cavalry line reached him…and parted like water around a boulder. The horses seemed to know he stood there and swerved to avoid him, but their riders appeared oblivious to his presence. Ashinji waited until the line had almost passed, picked his target, then swung.

The human toppled over his mount's rump and hit the ground with a rattling crash. The horse careened off at an angle, away from the advancing line. Ashinji rushed the fallen man, prepared to strike again, but the human lay sprawled in the churned earth, unmoving. A quick scan told Ashinji the man had been knocked senseless. He lowered his sword.

Even in war, even on a human, I'll not commit murder.

He looked around for the horse. Like all good war mounts, the animal had ceased running when it sensed its rider had fallen. It stood a spear's throw away, tail swishing. Off to his left, the first Soldaran infantry units rushed past, ignoring him.

Sheathing his sword, Ashinji approached with caution. The horse, catching his unfamiliar scent, tossed its head and whinnied.

"Easy, now. Easy," Ashinji murmured in Soldaran. He reached out and touched the horse's simple mind, soothing it, reassuring it as to his benign intentions. The animal lowered its head, ears drooping. When he stepped up and took hold of its reins, then swung himself into the saddle, it offered no resistance.

Ashinji sat still for a few heartbeats, extending his magical sense outward in search of any clue as to which direction Sonoe had gone. He felt nothing. Logic told him she would have followed the Alasiri forces; after all, the creature that controlled her still needed to keep up its charade, at least until it deemed the time had come to execute its spell. He had no idea when that would be, so Ashinji knew he needed to find the former Kirian, and soon, before he lost all chance to stop her.

Since the creature now appeared immune to the compulsion exerted by speaking its true name, Ashinji would have to come up with some other way of capturing it.

But how, he thought. With no formal training, he had only his own inborn Talent and instincts to guide him.

I have to think of something...Goddess help me!

He drummed his heels against the horse's flanks and set off at a gallop after the Soldarans.

Chapter 21

CONFLAGRATION AND DELIVERANCE

Ashinji caught up with the lead Soldaran infantry units and galloped alongside, just out of arrow range. He did not know what the humans saw when they looked his way—a riderless cavalry horse, perhaps—but whatever they saw, none of them raised any alarm. They remained totally focused on the pursuit of Lord Sen and his troops. Ashinji tried not to think about the sheer vastness of the Soldaran force now invading the valley; he had to concentrate on finding and stopping the thing that had once been Sonoe.

The vanguard of the invading army would soon reach Tono Castle where Prince Raidan waited to spring his trap. Ashinji guessed Sonoe would make her move then.

As Sen's force drew near, sharp blasts from horns atop the castle walls signaled that those within the fortress stood ready. Ashinji hauled back on the reins and his mount skidded to a stop. Twisting first one way, then the other, he scanned the landscape.

Damn it, where is she?

Sen had wheeled around to face the charging Soldarans.

Any moment now, the trap would be sprung.

The human foot soldiers whooped and brandished their weapons as they closed in. The cavalry couched their spears and bent low for the final charge.

From atop the highest battlement of the castle, a single, sustained horn blast sounded. A heartbeat later, massive fireballs, some blue, others white, rained down from the rocky ridgelines. They fell amongst the Soldarans and detonated with terrible force, flinging the bodies of men and horses high into the air. The humans' cries of triumph morphed into screams of pain and terror.

At the same time, the elven forces hidden among the crags to either side of the castle poured down the slopes in a headlong plunge to the valley floor. The archers reached the flats first and they immediately launched a deadly hail of arrows into the flanks of the invaders. Ashinji narrowly missed getting skewered as he flung himself off the horse to the ground. Instinctively, he threw up a protective magical shield around him, just in time to deflect another rain of arrows. He could do nothing for the horse. It went down in a tangle of thrashing limbs, pierced by at least a half-dozen shafts.

I've no training for this! Ashinji thought as he realized he had no idea how to maintain the protective shield for longer than a heartbeat or two. Fear began to scratch at the back of his mind, but he pushed it aside.

No! I can't let anything distract me!

The elven forces were almost upon him, and the Soldarans had re-organized and braced themselves to meet the new threat.

Lord Sen charged just as the massive gates of the castle swung open to allow the troops within to rush out. Simultaneously, the portion of the elven army hidden at the rear of the fortress streamed to the front on either side.

The Soldarans were surrounded.

Ashinji's heart sank.

Goddess, we're so badly outnumbered! How are we ever going to drive the Soldarans out?

Despite the fact that the elves' plan had worked to perfection, Ashinji feared only a miracle could save them now.

"Out of the way, mage!" a voice screamed. Ashinji just had time to jump aside as a rider swept past him, and then the charging elven foot soldiers overtook him. He stood rooted in place as they surged by. Some of them cursed him for being in the way, others yelled at him to take cover. A second officer rode by and ordered him to blast the enemy with a fireball.

Goddess! They really do think I'm one of the mages!

Conflagration and Deliverance

The lines met and clashed with a great roar.

Ashinji fell back, uncertain what to do. His soldier's instincts ordered him to join the fight, but just then, his magical sense caught a faint tingle, a whiff of what he had been searching for.

He looked toward the castle and *knew* she stood there, on the wall below the western tower. A heartbeat later, he felt a powerful stirring, like a vortex, drawing energy toward it from the surrounding aether.

Sonoe...Shiura...is opening the Void! I'm too late!

"Noooo!" he screamed.

A great tearing sound echoed against the walls of the castle, like the very fabric of the universe had ripped asunder. A crack like a lightning bolt appeared in the air above the struggling armies, except it was the *absence* of light, rather than the presence, that defined it. An unnatural wind swept down the valley, picking up strength with each passing moment. It lifted streamers of debris and sent them whirling into the slowly expanding gash of darkness.

At first, the men and women locked in battle below seemed not to notice, but as the violence of the wind increased, more and more of them stopped to cry out and point overhead. Weapons dropped and human and elven voices swelled together in a chorus of confusion and fear.

I've got to get up there now! Ashinji thought.

He stared at the castle wall in desperation and *willed* himself to the top.

A heartbeat later, he landed face-down with bruising force on paving stones. After a terrifying moment of confusion, he realized he had somehow reached the battlements. He tried to rise, but his limbs refused to obey.

Move, move, move! his mind screamed, and after what seemed like an eternity, he managed to shift his head to the side.

What he saw filled him with horror.

He lay against the wall opposite where Sonoe now stood, arms raised, before a howling maw of darkness. Her flaming tresses whipped about her face like a tattered banner as a river of dust swirled past her straining body into the vortex. A pile of bodies lay heaped at her feet—the corpses of Sonoe's fellow mages.

Ashinji could see shapes moving just beyond the tear, milling about as if uncertain whether to hang back or charge through. The former Kirian spoke a Word of Power and the tear expanded. Soon, it would grow big enough for the creatures waiting on the other side to easily pass through.

Ashinji struggled to throw off the strange paralysis that gripped his body. He concentrated on moving a finger, then his hand, then both hands, until he managed to push himself into a sitting position with his back against the parapet.

A black fog of exhaustion threatened to extinguish his consciousness. He fumbled at his belt, searching for the spirit box, then remembered he had lost it. It had proven useless, anyway; he would have to think of something else.

Sonoe seemed unaware of his presence. Ashinji could see the White Griffin glowing pure as starlight on her left hand. Despite how the Nameless One planned to use it, the ring's magic remained uncorrupted by the evil of its creator.

The magic is still pure, Ashinji thought.

The solution came to him in a sublime flash of understanding.

The fundamental natures of the two energies—the positive polarity of the White Griffin, the negative of the Void—would not allow them to exist in concert. If brought together, they would cancel each other out!

Ashinji staggered to his feet, gripping the cruel edge of the parapet with tingling fingers. The rush of air into the vortex had grown to near gale force. One by one, the wind was lifting the corpses of the slain mages and pinwheeling them into the violet-shot darkness. In a few more heartbeats, it would suck him in as well.

Sonoe spoke a second Word of Power and Ashinji cried out in pain as its force ripped through his body. Through the shimmering aftereffects, he rallied his last reserve of strength.

Jelena, I loved you even before I knew you were real, and I'll love you forever, even beyond death. We'll be together again soon, I promise!

With a whispered entreaty to the One, he released his grip and lunged.

He slammed into Sonoe and the force of his charge carried them both over the parapet into the mouth of the Void. A shriek like tearing metal assaulted his ears and then he was falling, falling, into the limitless dark.

Light exploded around him, blinding and glorious.

He felt his body disintegrating in the mighty conflagration.

His last thoughts, before oblivion claimed him, were of the most beautiful girl in the world, and of how lucky he was to have known her love.

Conflagration and Deliverance

&

"Ai, Goddess!" Taya hissed, clutching her head. Amara reeled as the first shockwave hit her mind.

"It seems as if your son has succeeded," the princess said through gritted teeth.

The second shockwave hit and both mages moaned with pain.

"Ashi," Amara whispered.

&

The sky lit up like the very sun itself had exploded. A geyser of light erupted from the dark tear overhead, cutting a swath of destruction through the milling mass of people below. Those in its direct path were reduced to ash in the blink of an eye. The lucky ones on the periphery escaped instant death, but many fell, the exposed parts of their bodies badly burned.

Before the gates of Tono Castle, the defenders watched, awestruck, as the cohesion of the Soldaran army fell apart. With its principal commanders dead and its ranks shattered, morale collapsed and those who could still run turned and fled. As the human forces streamed back down the valley toward the pass, the terrible wound in the sky dwindled to a thin, ragged black cut against the blue, then closed with an audible *snap*.

Raidan shook so hard, he could barely stay seated on his plunging stallion.

"What in the Goddess' Name just happened!" Sen shouted, struggling with his own mount.

A miracle, Raidan thought.

The prince clung to his horse until the animal finally ceased rearing and stood still, its neck and flanks in a lather. He looked around for an aide, spotted Mai Nohe, and waved him over. "Start spreading the word to the captains. I want our forces to follow the humans, nip at their heels, see to it that they really do leave."

"We should station at least five companies at the pass for the next few days," Sen added, pulling his blowing horse up next to Raidan's. "We wouldn't want 'em sneaking back in while we weren't looking."

"Yes, my lords!" Nohe saluted and galloped off.

The prince and the Lord of Kerala sat their horses in silence for a time. Finally, Sen spoke.

"The One works in ways too mysterious for us mere mortals to understand. She has delivered us from a terrible fate, yet the price she exacts is so very steep."

Just how steep you have yet to find out, my friend, Raidan thought. He had no idea how to break the news to Sen about his beloved younger son.

Should I even tell him at all?

Sen believed Ashinji had died over a year ago. His grief, while still a part of him, had become manageable.

Why tear open those wounds again?

Because, as a father, he has the right to know of his son's sacrifice. I can't keep that from him.

Raidan noticed the castle guards, along with some of the bolder serving staff, had ventured forth onto the field and now wandered among the dead.

Damn it! I gave strict orders that no civilian be allowed outside the castle walls! We still have the plague to deal with! His chest tightened with fury.

"Prince Raidan!" Raidan turned in the saddle to see a soldier running toward him. The man skidded to a halt, breathing hard, and pointed to the east. "My lord, you must come at once." he cried, hopping from foot to foot.

"What is it, soldier?" Raidan called out, his anger forgotten.

"It's Prince Raidu, my lord. He has fallen! You must come now."

Raidan's body turned to ice. "Where does my son lie?" he shouted.

"They've taken him to the base of the eastern tower, my lord."

Raidan didn't wait for the soldier to lead the way. Raked by his master's spurs, the stallion sprang forward into a gallop. The prince bent low over the horse's neck, his mind consumed with only one thought.

I must get to my son!

He found Raidu lying in the deep shade cast by the high castle wall, surrounded by a group of Meiji troopers. Someone had folded a cloak and had placed it beneath the younger prince's head. Even before Raidan had dismounted, the soldiers had melted back and bowed their heads in deference.

"My lord Prince." A woman stepped forward—a grizzled veteran and a sergeant by her insignia.

Conflagration and Deliverance

The prince recognized her. "How is my son, Sergeant Mata?" Raidan forced the words out through lips that had lost all feeling.

"We did everything we could, my lord, but none of us here are healers. I'm sorry, my lord." The woman lowered her eyes.

Raidan removed his helmet and tossed it aside, then knelt beside his son's body. For a time, he just looked.

My child…it's as if I'm seeing you for the first time! Your eyes, so like your mother's… your mouth, so like my own. I'll never see you smile again. Those hands, so strong and clever…they'll never clasp mine again…

Raidan made himself examine the wound that had taken his son's life. Great skill, or incredible luck, had guided the point of a sword in below Raidu's jaw, just above where the plates protecting his throat ended, lacerating the main vessel. His death had been swift.

"Bring my son to the castle yard," Raidan ordered.

Four of the troopers sprang to obey. They gently gathered up the slack-limbed body in a makeshift sling and hoisted it between them. Raidan walked alongside, holding Raidu's cool hand in his. Word of the younger prince's death had already spread like wildfire, and by the time they reached the gates, a crowd had formed. Raidan indicated the troopers should lay Raidu's body on the gravel.

"Let me through. I want to see my brother!"

The crowd parted to let Kaisik, who had stayed behind with the castle guard, through to his brother's side. When the boy saw his brother lying on the ground, he broke down. Kneeling beside Raidu's body, he covered his face and wept.

"Kaisik, my son," Raidan murmured gently, laying his hand on the boy's heaving shoulder. "Your brother gave his life to protect the elven people. He would not want his death to be your undoing."

Kaisik looked up at his father with anguished, streaming eyes. "Yes, Father, I know," the boy whispered. "I loved him. He always looked after me…I'll miss him."

Raidan wanted to fall to his knees, gather both his sons in his arms and give vent to his own grief, but he couldn't.

Not in front of my army.

"Your Highness." Sen appeared at Raidan's elbow, then said in a low voice, "I'm so very sorry, Raidan. You know I understand."

"Yes, my friend, you do."

"Let us take Raidu to the chapel," Sen urged. "Odata's priest can see to his body."

Raidan felt numb. He heard and saw everything around him, but it seemed as if he no longer inhabited his own skin; instead, he watched from a distance as his body moved and spoke. "Yes, yes. That would...yes," he murmured, then without thinking, he added, "Sen, your own son..."

"Is safe, my lord. He took our Kerala contingent out to guard the pass."

Raidan shook his head, realizing Sen had misunderstood, but before he could say anything further, a commotion at the gates drew his attention.

A scout had just arrived. She pushed through the crowd to reach him and bowed.

"Your Highness, the enemy has reached the pass and they show no signs of slowing down. The humans have fled the valley!"

A great cheer rose up, but died quickly as those assembled remembered the terrible tragedy that had befallen their prince.

"We've survived, against all odds." Raidan raised his voice so all in the yard could hear. "Do not restrain your joy because of my loss. The Empire is beaten!"

For now.

Chapter 22

THE FINAL CONFRONTATION

So dark...cold...
      Can't move...

He tried to take a breath, but could draw no air into his lungs.

Where am I?

Surrounded, imprisoned, crushed by a great weight...

His eyes, nostrils, mouth, filled with...

Dirt!

I'm buried...alive!

I'm alive!

Struggling against the earth that held him captive, Ashinji clawed his way through soil and gravel, up toward where instinct told him he would find air, light, and life. When his scrabbling hands broke the surface, he heaved himself free, staggered to his feet, then clutched his belly and doubled over.

He spent an eternity choking up gobbets of dirty spit, and when at last he could breathe without coughing, he stood upright and looked around, eyes and nose streaming.

He had emerged from beneath the roots of a lightning-blasted tree that stood like a lonely sentinel atop a small hill. The moon sailed high overhead, a silver crescent amid a field of stars.

Where am I?

His head felt thick and fuzzy.

Off to his right, he saw a constellation of rosy, earthbound stars arrayed before a wall of deeper darkness.

Campfires…that's an army out there, but which one?

Crickets sang among the shrubs bearding the hill. A nightjar swooped by overhead. Ashinji brushed dirt clods from his hair and dug a small pebble from his right ear. In his slightly befuddled state, he couldn't decide what to do. He sank to the ground and rested his head on his knees.

I've got to think…

He had no explanation for how he had come to be entombed beneath a dead tree far from the walls of Tono Castle. The last clear memory he had before regaining consciousness was of going over the parapet, the creature that had been Sonoe struggling and shrieking like a mad harpy in his arms.

The world is still here…That means I did the right thing, but how did I survive?

He sat for a while longer until the fog in his head cleared.

I must be near the mouth of the pass. That camp is too small to be the Soldaran army. Besides, if they'd beaten us, why leave behind any troops out here? There'd be no reason for them to guard the pass. No, that camp must be ours.

Ashinji climbed to his feet, then took a mental inventory of his body. Aside from a few scratches on his face and neck, he seemed to be intact. No serious pain, all parts present and accounted for. He could not say the same for his clothes, however, which hung in tatters from his limbs.

He tried to conjure a magelight, but could only manage a spark, which flared on his palm for a heartbeat, then sputtered out. He reached into the well of energy that fueled his Talent, and to his dismay, found it flickering near total depletion. Pulling the shreds of his clothes around him as best he could, he started walking toward the camp. The moist ground felt good beneath his bare feet. A bark of laughter escaped his cracked lips.

What a fearsome sight I must be, all ragged and caked with dirt! No one will recognize me!

With brutal suddenness, the memory of the knife biting into Jelena's breast flashed before his mind's eye. He stumbled to a halt.

I've killed my wife and taken my child's mother away from her! How can I live with that?

He groaned aloud and lifted his face to the coolly glittering stars. The pain simmering in his gut exploded into anger.

THE FINAL CONFRONTATION

If I hadn't been denied my birthright…if I'd been trained as a mage, maybe I could have found a way to defeat the Nameless One without having to kill Jelena, my one true love!

No. This is useless, raging about what might have been. What's done is done. If we hadn't gone through with it, then everything would have been lost, gone, devoured by the Void.

A streak of light flashed across the heavens.

A falling star…maybe it's a sign.

Ashinji took a deep breath and let the anger drain from him.

Perhaps the Kirians will succeed in bringing Jelena back. Dare I hope for a miracle?

He started walking again.

He had gone about two dozen paces when he heard a whistle off to his right, followed closely by another to his left, then another straight ahead.

Elven sentries. Ashinji sighed with relief.

First thing…food. I need to eat. It's been at least two days, I think. Then, some fresh clothes. Can't very well go about naked, can I? Then…then I have to find Father…and Sadaiyo.

I wonder how Sadaiyo will react when he learns his despised little brother has returned from the dead?

How will I react when I see him?

How many times had he cursed Sadaiyo's name the past year?

Too many to count.

Every time he had stood on the sands of the Great Arena in Darguinia, sword in hand, facing death yet again for the sport of humans.

Every time I got cut…every time I had to kill to survive…

Every time a human spat on me and called me 'tink'.

Yet, to his surprise, despite how hard he tried to dredge up the bitter anger that had kept him going those long months, Ashinji found the fires he had just survived had burned his soul clean of hate. He would never feel anything close to affection for Sadaiyo—too much had happened between them—but he knew now he could, if not forgive, then at least choose not to seek revenge.

"Stand right there, you!" a voice commanded in Soldaran.

Ashinji froze in his tracks. In his emotionally and physically exhausted state, he had not sensed the other, out there in the dark.

"You should have run faster, human. Now, I will have your ugly round ear for trophy, yes?" The sarcastic tone cut like a lash, an old, familiar sting. Ashinji sighed. He had not wanted it to happen like this.

"Don't shoot," he replied in Siri-dar. His voice emerged from his throat as little more than a rusty whisper.

"Who are you and what are you doing out here so far from camp? I almost shot you, you fool!"

Ashinji remained silent, and waited. A figure emerged from the darkness and halted a stone's throw away, leaning forward to scrutinize him.

"I said, who are you? Answer me, man!"

"Someone you never expected to see alive again, Sadaiyo."

Ashinji's brother recoiled in shock. "No! It can't be you! You're dead!"

Ashinji stepped closer so his brother's eyes could verify the truth.

"What, no 'welcome home, Little Brother, I missed you, I'm so glad you're alive?'"

"I saw you die! How can you be here now?" Confusion, anger, and fear rolled off Sadaiyo in waves.

Warily, Ashinji eyed the bow in his brother's hands. "I'm a lot tougher than you thought, Brother, and not so easy to kill. I've got the scars to prove it."

Sadaiyo's eyes narrowed. "Where've you been all this time, then? Why didn't you come home sooner?"

"I couldn't, and that's all I feel like telling you right now. I've just been through something too complicated to explain and I'm worn out. All I want to do is see Father, eat a little and then sleep for a very long time." He brushed past Sadaiyo and started toward the camp.

"Stop!" Sadaiyo growled.

Ashinji halted and turned to face his brother. He braced himself for what he knew was coming. "Sadaiyo..."

"I don't know how you survived, nor do I care. What I do know is that I can't allow you to return." Sadaiyo's hand tightened on the grip of his bow.

"I didn't come back to expose you, if that's what you're afraid of," Ashinji responded. "I couldn't do that to our father. He needs you too much right now."

"Liar!" Sadaiyo spat. "I'm sure you can hardly wait to tell Father about how I left you to die at the hands of the humans."

THE FINAL CONFRONTATION

"But that's what you did do, Brother. I cried out to you for help and you chose to let the humans take me. *You knew…"* Ashinji faltered. An entire lifetime of hurt threatened to drown him. The very thought of Sadaiyo witnessing his tears made him sick with anger, but the pain pushed too hard and strong.

With frightening swiftness, Sadaiyo raised his bow, drew, and fired. Ashinji sensed the attack coming and threw himself sideways, but exhaustion slowed his reflexes. The arrowhead grazed his neck, slicing a stinging furrow into his skin just above his collarbone. He turned and ran.

A second arrow whistled past his ear.

Can't fight him now. Too tired. I have to find somewhere to hide!

He stumbled on the uneven ground but somehow managed to stay on his feet. His legs felt like lead weights and his lungs burned with each breath. Even though he did his best to run in silence, he knew Sadaiyo could track him with ease, even in the dark.

A rocky outcropping loomed ahead, like the weathered bones of a giant, mythical beast. He used the last of his failing strength to scramble into the sheltering rocks. Wedging himself into a crevice, he waited.

Becomethedarkbecometherockbecomethedark…

A tiny puff of breeze tickled the back of his neck. A single bead of sweat rolled down his forehead and along the bridge of his nose, then hung suspended for a heartbeat before dripping off his face. A furtive scrabbling sound from above, like tiny claws upon rock, made him look up over his shoulder, every sense strained to the breaking point.

Sadaiyo won't stop until he's killed me…If only I wasn't so tired!

He had come so far, endured so much, that to die now, like this, seemed a very bitter fate, indeed. At least he could take some small comfort in knowing his father would eventually learn the truth. Amara would not rest until she had discovered the fate of her younger son, and when she did, Sadaiyo would finally be exposed. Ashinji wished with all his heart his parents could be spared that terrible pain.

Then fight! a voice in his head demanded, a voice that sounded very much like Jelena's. *Don't let Sadaiyo murder you! Fight back with everything you've got!*

I can't. I have nothing left. I just want to lie down and sleep.

No! Wake up, Ashi! He's coming!

His ears detected the barest whisper of sound—a faint scuff of leather on rock. Ashinji twisted out of his hiding place just as an arrow splintered on the stone where, a heartbeat before, his head had rested. Heart in his mouth, he peered into the darkness, up to where he could now feel Sadaiyo lurking, poised to shoot again. He swallowed hard and made a decision.

Summoning the last of his physical strength, he surged upward while at the same time, he consumed the dregs of his magic to weave a cloak of temporary invisibility. He pulled himself onto the narrow, flattened top of the outcrop just as Sadaiyo raised his bow into firing position. Confused, Sadaiyo hesitated for an instant, as if he could hear but not see his target. Ashinji slammed into him, and they went down hard. The bow flew from Sadaiyo's hands and spun over the edge of the outcrop into the darkness.

Sadaiyo let out an incoherent roar, like a crazed beast. Savagely, he pummeled Ashinji with his fists, growling with each blow. It took everything Ashinji had just to protect his face and head. An especially brutal punch to the midsection nearly did him in.

"I hate you, you sniveling little piece of *shit*!" Sadaiyo spat each word like a stone from a slingshot. He stopped beating Ashinji, but kept him pinned to the rock. "Father loved me before you came slithering out from between our mother's legs and stole him away from me! I'll *never* forgive you for that!"

"Father never stopped loving you, Sadaiyo, but your own poisonous jealousy made him stop liking you!" Ashinji gasped.

"Liar! Shut your... stinking...lying... hole!" Sadaiyo's fingers tightened around Ashinji's throat.

"Don't do this to our family...Sadaiyo, please!...You know you'll never get away with it...Mother is a *mage*, for Goddess' sake. She'll know...the instant she sees you!"

Ashinji had to keep Sadaiyo engaged or his brother's rage would overwhelm him again and he knew he couldn't hold out much longer.

This needs to end now!

"Brother, *please!*" he wheezed. "Think about your wife and son! Their lives will be ruined if you do this!"

Sadaiyo's fierce grip loosened a tiny bit, giving Ashinji the opening he needed. With a heave and a twist, he threw Sadaiyo off him and scrambled to his feet. Blinking sweat and blood from his eyes, he dropped into a fighting crouch, struggling to stay focused through the pain.

Sadaiyo stood very still now, arms dangling at his sides, a darker shape silhouetted against the night sky. A cloud of rage still enveloped him, and the feel of it made Ashinji shiver with dread.

"Brother. Please! Stop this now before you destroy everything you hold dear."

"The dearest thing I had was Father's love, and you destroyed *that* the day you were born," Sadaiyo replied, his voice dripping with bitterness. "Oh, how he mourned your death! His dear, beloved Ashi! It made me sick to my stomach to watch. I did think, though, that in time, he would get over losing you and turn to me, love *me* again. He was just beginning to, Little Brother, and you are *mad* if you think I'll allow you to come back and ruin things now!" With those final words, he charged.

Ashinji had no time for thought, only reaction guided by years of training and the instinct for survival. As Sadaiyo slammed into him, Ashinji grappled his brother's shoulders and went down on his back, thrusting his knees into the other's stomach. The momentum of Sadaiyo's charge carried him up and over Ashinji's prone body. Ashinji heard, rather than saw, his brother skid to the edge of the outcrop.

"*Noooo!*" he screamed, and tried to grab any part of Sadaiyo he could, but he failed.

Sadaiyo fell without a sound.

Ashinji crawled to the edge of the outcrop then peered down. The night concealed the final evidence of his brother's fate, but he did not need the confirmation of his eyes to know. He felt the moment of Sadaiyo's passing as his brother's raging soul fled his broken body.

Ashinji collapsed to the cool stone and let grief take him.

The moon and stars had begun to fade by the time Ashinji finally summoned enough strength to climb down from the outcrop. When he reached the ground, he did not search for Sadaiyo's body. That would be asking too much of himself. Instead, he turned then headed back toward the encampment. He stumbled as he walked, and once, he stopped then sank to his knees, overcome with dizziness. He knew he had suffered serious injury and would need a doctor.

He did not think about the events just past—he couldn't. The terrible pain behind his eyes made clear thought all but impossible. It took every bit of strength he had left just to focus on getting his legs to move.

"Stop right there!"

For the second time that night, a familiar voice challenged him, this time at his back.

"Don't...shoot," he whispered. He heard a hiss of surprise.

"It can't be...*Lord Ashinji?*"

Ashinji turned around to find his old friend Aneko staring at him, her face a pale blot in the darkness.

"Ai, Goddess!" She approached to within touching distance, raised her hand as if to caress his face, then let it fall. "Lord Ashinji...it really is you," she whispered, then gasped in dismay. "My lord, your clothes...you've been hurt! I'll go fetch Lord Sen!"

Before she could go, Ashinji grabbed her forearm. "No, Aneko," he said. A torn lower lip and aching jaw made speech slow and difficult. "I don't want to cause a commotion. Better if you bring me a cloak or something I can cover myself with. I'd rather just slip into camp quietly."

"Of course, my lord, but..." Ashinji sensed her confusion and fear for him, but Aneko had always been one of the steadiest of the Kerala guards. "You wait right here, my lord. I won't be but a moment."

True to her word, Aneko returned quickly, a voluminous length of cloth in her arms. "Couldn't find a cloak, my lord," she explained. "A horse blanket will have to do."

Ashinji chuckled, despite the pain. "A beggar can't be too picky, can he?" he replied. He tossed the blanket over his shoulders, pulled a fold over his head, then indicated with a nod that Aneko should lead on. Anonymous in his makeshift cloak, he followed the guardswoman through the camp.

A few early risers made note of his passing, but most of the camp still lay wrapped in sleep. Aneko's powerful emotions trailed her like smoke on the dawn air—elation, concern, and curiosity in equal measure. He knew she wanted very much to question him, but her discipline and deference kept her curiosity at bay. They walked in silence until Aneko halted before a tent distinguished from the ones surrounding it only by its larger size. The flap had been pinned back to allow in any stray breezes. Muted conversation, mingled with the sound of a man's laughter, soft and relaxed, drifted out, followed by a snippet of song. Ashinji's breath caught in his throat.

Aneko stood aside, waiting for him to enter the tent ahead of her. Ashinji hesitated. "Aneko," he murmured. "Go in to my father and tell him someone is here to see him."

"Yes, my lord," Aneko replied then ducked into the tent.

The voices stopped as soon as the guardswoman entered. She delivered her message and Ashinji listened for the reply.

"Who is it?"

"You need to see for yourself, my lord."

Ashinji stepped through the entrance, letting the blanket slip from his shoulders as he did so, then moved forward into the light.

Sen lounged in a camp chair, a wooden tankard in his hand. Misune sat beside him on a stool, her brother Ibeji sprawled on a cushion at her feet. Sen looked up to greet his visitor and his words froze on his lips.

The tankard slipped from his fingers.

Misune leapt from her stool with a startled shriek. Ibeji bolted up, staring.

Like a man moving through a dream, Ashinji's father drifted to his feet, his face white.

"Father," Ashinji whispered.

Sen lurched forward then swept Ashinji into his arms.

"My son!" he sobbed. "My son is alive!"

A memory from childhood pushed its way to the fore of Ashinji's consciousness just then. He had been very young, a baby really, playing by himself, when he had fallen into a deep hole. He found out much later that it was an old, forgotten well. He had crouched in the dark, bruised and crying, too young to fear death but old enough to fear he would never see his mother and father again.

After what seemed like forever to his child's mind, Sen came to rescue him. Ashinji remembered how his father lifted him into his strong arms then held him close, how he had felt completely safe and how quickly his fear had evaporated in the heat of his father's love.

It feels like that now.

"How is this possible?" Sen whispered. He held Ashinji at arm's length, shaking his head. Tears spilled from his eyes and dripped off his chin. *"Ashi...* Ashi, my child! Where have you *been?"* Ashinji tried to speak but his own tears trapped the words in his throat.

"Never mind, Son." Sen pulled him close again. "I can see you've been through a terrible ordeal. There'll be time to hear all about it after you've gotten some rest."

Ashinji nodded against his father's shoulder. He could feel his body letting go and his mind slipping away. "I just need to sleep a little, that's all," he murmured.

"Here...come over here, Son. Lie down on my cot."

Ashinji allowed his father to steer him to a folding bed behind a curtain. He sank down with a grateful sigh and closed his eyes. He heard his father ask Ibeji to go fetch the doctor.

Father, your Heir is dead. I killed him, but I had no choice. I'm so sorry.

"I can't understand you, Son, you're mumbling. Don't try to talk. Just sleep, now."

Please forgive me, Father!

"I love you, Son."

Chapter 23

THE UNBREAKABLE BONDS OF LOVE

When Ashinji awoke, he turned his head to see his father slumped in a camp chair at his bedside, dozing. He pushed himself onto his elbows, then collapsed back, grinding his teeth against the pounding agony behind his eyes. That pain, along with an assortment of other aches, served as a potent reminder of the ordeal he had survived.

Sen stirred, then jerked awake with a snort. He rubbed his eyes then focused on Ashinji's face. "Son, you're awake. How're you feeling?" Sen's voice was soft and gentle.

"Like a wagon rolled over my head," Ashinji groaned. He ran his tongue around the inside of his mouth. "Ugh! My mouth tastes awful!"

"That's probably the medicine the doctor's been forcing down your throat these last two days." Sen paused for such a long time, Ashinji looked up with concern. He could see his father struggling with himself about something.

"Father, what's wrong?"

"Ashi, I...no...it's too soon. You need to rest. We can talk about things later."

"You know about Sadaiyo," Ashinji murmured. The memory of his last, terrible encounter with his brother atop the rocky outcrop flooded his mind. For a few heartbeats, he could not move or speak.

"I know my eldest son is dead, but I don't know how he died," Sen replied. "I also know my youngest son whom I'd given up for dead, my favorite child whose loss I thought I'd never get over, is, by some miracle, alive. Ashi, I don't understand any of this. I need to know what happened, but I can wait until you're stronger."

"Father, I..."

"No, Son. Not now. I'll send for the doctor. He'll bring you something to ease the pain in your head. Then, you can sleep awhile longer. After that...if you're ready, we'll talk."

Ashinji did not argue. His head hurt too much. Instead, he closed his eyes and let his mind drift. He managed to rouse himself enough to swallow the draught the doctor brought, but then he let go again, and slept.

&

Maaamaaa!

Who calls to me with my baby's voice? Are there spirits here on the other side that can do that?

Maaamaaa!

Who are you? Why do you torment me so, calling to me that way! I can't be with my baby, not here, not in this place. Stop, please!

Jelena...listen now and follow my voice...Come to me.

I know you, too! But you can't be here, either. Please, please stop torturing me! Leave me alone to rest in peace...Isn't that what the dead are supposed to do?

You are not dead, Jelena. Not any more. It is time to return to the living world. Follow my voice and I will guide you back.

Why should I listen to you? It's peaceful here...quiet...no pain...I like it here.

Your daughter is calling you. Can't you hear her? She needs her mother.

My baby...is that truly her?

Maaamaa!

Yes, Jelena. She is waiting for you. Now, come.

All right...yes, I'll come. For my baby...Hattie! Mama's coming!

Jelena opened her eyes.

The Unbreakable Bonds of Love

Ashinji opened his eyes. He still lay on his father's cot, sweating beneath a pile of blankets. He freed himself from the stifling weight then sighed with relief. While he had been asleep, the remnants of his clothes had been removed, and the worst of the dirt sponged off him. The pain in his head had subsided. Cautiously, he sat up then swung his legs to the floor.

The golden light of late afternoon filtered in through the canvas walls of the tent. How long he had been asleep this time, Ashinji could only guess, but by his urgent need to relieve himself, he figured at least an entire day. He reached under the cot, groping for a chamber pot. A few heartbeats later the curtain separating the sleeping area from the rest of Lord Sen's tent rustled and a manservant peeked around the edge.

Sen's valet Kamiro smiled. "Lord Ashinji, I thought I heard you moving around. Are you hungry? I've got a little cold soup, if you're up to it."

Ashinji pressed a hand to his rumbling midsection. "Soup sounds good," he said with a small grin, though it hurt his injured lip to do so. "It's good to see you, Kamiro. Is my father around?"

"It's good to see you, as well, my lord. Lord Sen has just left to, er, answer nature's call, which is what it looks like you need to do. I'll go fetch the soup."

The valet left Ashinji to his privacy and when he returned, Sen followed hard on his heels.

"By the One, it's good to see you looking better, Son," Sen exclaimed. "I do believe there's some color back in your cheeks." He took the soup bowl out of the valet's hands. "Thank you, Kamiro. I'll take over now."

"Very good, my lord." Kamiro bowed then exited. Sen handed the bowl to Ashinji, then pulled up a stool beside the cot and sat.

"Have you left my side at all these past days, Father?" Ashinji asked.

Sen shrugged. "Only to take a piss now and then." He laid a hand on Ashinji's shoulder then squeezed. "Our people are overjoyed, Son, that you've been returned to us. I think most of the Kerala levies are camped outside this tent, waiting for you to come out."

Ashinji raised the bowl to his mouth then drank, wincing a little as the salty broth stung his injured lip. Sen remained silent while his son ate.

After he had sipped the last drops from the bowl and set it aside, Ashinji dared to look into his father's eyes. He saw the unconditional love and acceptance for him that had always been there, but he also saw his father's sadness and bewilderment.

"Do our people know about Sadaiyo?"

"Yes, Son, they do." The pain Ashinji heard in his father's voice stung his heart. He knew telling his father the whole story would be one of the hardest things he would ever have to do.

The words came haltingly at first, but once started, they flowed more easily. He left nothing out, and after he had finished, he lowered his head and wept. Sen embraced and rocked him, just as he had done when Ashinji had been a boy, soothing his childish hurts as only a father could.

Except that these hurts will never fade completely.

After a while, Sen spoke. "That you survived to return to me is truly a miracle for which I can never offer up enough thanks," he murmured. "I don't deserve the Goddess' blessings, not after what I've done."

Ashinji pulled away from his father in surprise. "What do you mean, Father? You've done nothing wrong."

"Yes, Ashi, I have," Sen insisted. "I refused to admit my behavior toward your brother was unfair, that it caused him great pain, and in turn, I refused to see how he punished you for my transgressions. I tried to love Sadaiyo as I loved you, Ashi, but...Goddess help me, I just couldn't! I knew from the moment I first held you in my arms that we would share a special bond, you and I. I could never explain it—still can't—but it's there, and it's stronger than ever."

"I said this to Mother and I'll say it again to you, Father. You and she mustn't blame yourselves for what Sadaiyo did to me," Ashinji replied.

Sen sighed, blinking back tears. "I just hope your brother has found some peace at last."

"Father, what happened during the battle in front of Tono Castle? How did we manage to defeat the Soldarans? We were so badly outnumbered."

Sen shook his head. "It's hard to believe it, even now...'twas like nothing any of us had ever seen, Son. A miracle, many are saying."

"A miracle? What do you mean?"

"Well, what would you call a pillar of fire pouring down from the sky? It blasted away half their army in the blink of an eye! Turned 'em to ash, just like that! Hurt a lot of our own people as well, so every miracle has its price, I s'pose. The Goddess has to dole out a little hurt for so much good fortune."

So that's what it looked like, Ashinji thought. He gripped the edge of the cot and stared into Sen's face. "Father, there's a lot more I have to tell you."

Sen's eyes widened. "About what, Son?"

"About that miracle. About what really happened. A lot of it has to do with Jelena."

"Jelena?"

"Father, Jelena is dead, and I killed her."

❧

Ashinji felt no surprise to learn that his father already knew most of the major details of the Kirians' plan. Sen and Amara had always told each other everything.

"Your mother swore me to secrecy. I had to lie to Keizo, my friend and my king. Goddess' tits, but that was hard. She promised me the Kirians had everything in hand, that the plan would succeed…She left out the part about having to kill Jelena, though." Sen scowled, and seeing his father's anger, Ashinji laid a hand on his forearm.

"Please don't be angry with Mother. She hoped with all her heart the Kirians could find a way to accomplish their task without…without killing Jelena, but in the end, they could not."

"I wish they'd left you out of it, Son. You shouldn't have had to do what they asked of you. It wasn't fair."

"They had no one else. If I hadn't agreed, then none of us would have survived."

Father and son gazed at each other without speaking for a few heartbeats. Ashinji broke the silence first.

"Father, you knew about my Talent, didn't you?"

Sen looked away. "I'm sorry, Ashi," he murmured. "Your mother knew, even before you were born, how strong your Talent was. She and I both agreed…we felt it would be easier on you if she blocked your magic. That way, it wouldn't be so hard for you to accept what our tradition decreed for you, that as a second-born child of my House, your life was pledged to the king's service."

Ashinji remembered how much anger he had felt toward his mother when she had admitted what she had done.

There's no anger left in me for any of this now. I've lost too much to waste time being angry.

"I always knew a soldier's life wasn't what you wanted, Son," Sen continued, "but you never complained. You did what was expected of you, and now…" Sen cradled Ashinji's bruised face between his hands. "You are my Heir now, Ashi," he whispered.

Ashinji lowered his head, unable to look his father in the eyes. "No matter how I felt about my brother, I never wanted him dead."

"I know," Sen replied. He let his hands slip down to Ashinji's shoulders, gave them a squeeze, then dabbed his leaking eyes on his sleeve. His melancholy expression brightened a little.

"Now that you've recovered enough to travel, I'm ordering this division back to Tono Castle today. We should be on the road to Sendai within the week. I'll send in Kamiro with some clothes for you." Sen rose to his feet, pushed aside the curtain and left.

Ashinji lay back on the bed and closed his eyes. A hodgepodge of aches plagued his body, but nothing so severe that it would prevent him from walking, or even riding when he had to.

After assuring himself his body could function, albeit in a diminished capacity, he turned his mind to the task of assessing the state of his Talent. The energy fueling his magic had begun to replenish itself, but it had yet to reach full strength; even so, he decided to reach out with his mind to try to search for the familiar thread of energy that had bound him and Jelena together.

He sensed nothing.

Maybe I'm still too weak, he thought. He couldn't bring himself to admit the other possibility.

Kamiro bustled in, bringing a fresh set of clothes. "May I assist you, my lord?" the valet offered.

Ashinji opened his eyes. "No thank you, Kamiro. I think I can manage," he replied. The valet bowed, placed the clothing on the cot, bowed again, then departed.

THE UNBREAKABLE BONDS OF LOVE

Dressing himself proved to be a little more difficult and painful than Ashinji had anticipated. A mass of bruises covered his torso where Sadaiyo had pummeled him, and it hurt to raise his arms. After pulling on a pair of sandals then raking his fingers through his disheveled hair, he stepped out of the tent into the late afternoon sunshine.

A ragged chorus of cheers greeted him, causing him to start in surprise. A large group of Kerala soldiers stood before the tent, just as Sen had said.

Aneko stood at the forefront. "On behalf of all of the Kerala troops, I want to welcome you back, my lord," she said, grinning.

Ashinji scanned the faces before him, seeing a new, deeper level of devotion in each one. Until this moment, he had given no thought to the full measure of profound change Sadaiyo's death had wrought upon his life and future. He had no choice but to face it now.

It's true. I really am the future Lord of Kerala.

Aneko stepped forward. "I'm very sorry for your loss, my lord. We all are," she said, then added in a low voice, "For the first time, though, I feel confident about Kerala's future. I apologize if my words offend you, my lord, but it's true and I know all my comrades feel the same." She glanced over her shoulder at the assembled troops.

"In the face of such love and loyalty, I can feel nothing but pride and love in return," Ashinji replied. "I only pray I'll remain worthy of your devotion." He raised his voice so the entire group could hear. "Thank you all."

"Let's hear it for our young lord!" Aneko shouted.

The soldiers' cheers flew into the cloudless sky like bright arrows.

"My lord Prince, General Sakehera has returned."

Raidan raised his head from his clasped hands. "Thank you," he murmured to the messenger. "I will go down and meet him."

In truth, it'll be good to get a little fresh air, he thought. *Priests and their incense! Why'd he have to burn so much, anyway? My throat is raw!*

The new king had spent the last few nights in the castle's chapel, keeping vigil beside his son's body. The chapel attendants had washed the dead prince then redressed him in his armor, and now the body lay on a bier before the altar. Stiffly, Raidan rose from his knees, massaging the ache in his lower back.

He looked around and spotted Kaisik, asleep on a bench by the east wall. Wincing with pain, he made his way over to the bench then stood a moment, looking down at the boy.

Kaisik has always been the most fragile of my children, the one who feels everything most keenly. This burden he must now take on was never meant for one such as him.

"Kaisik," Raidan murmured, reaching down with a gentle hand to shake the boy's shoulder.

"Mmmm."

"Wake up, Son. It's morning."

Kaisik's eyes fluttered open, blank at first, then clouding with grief as memory returned. He levered himself up into a sitting position, his gaze settling on Raidu's body. "I keep praying for it all to be a bad dream," he whispered.

"If only that were so. Come." Raidan gestured for Kaisik to follow him. The messenger waited, fidgeting, by the chapel door. Raidan raised his eyebrow.

"My lord Prince, you won't believe this news!" the man said in a rush. "General Sakehera's son, the one everyone thought was dead? Well, seems he's very much alive! He's with the general now, my lord!"

So. Young Sakehera has not only succeeded in his seemingly impossible task, but he's somehow managed to survive as well. A miracle upon a miracle.

Raidan nodded his head in silent respect. He looked up at the sky and saw that much of the morning had already passed. He had lost all sense of the flow of time while kneeling by Raidu's body in the smoky dimness of the chapel, aware only of the bitter truth of his eldest son's death.

With the messenger leading the way, Raidan left the chapel then walked down the gravel path to the main gate of the castle, Kaisik trailing after him like a mournful ghost. He spotted Sen standing amidst a group of his Kerala troops. Of Sen's eldest son, he saw no sign, but Ashinji stood beside him, his face cut and bruised as if he had been in a vicious fight. A shrouded body on a stretcher lay on the gravel between them.

"The elven people owe you a debt of gratitude too great to repay, Captain Sakehera," Raidan said as he approached.

Ashinji's gaze dropped to the body, then back up to meet Raidan's. "I only did what I had to do, Highness," the younger man replied.

The Unbreakable Bonds of Love

Raidan shook his head. "You are far too modest, young man. You forget that I know a little about what you faced." He turned to Sen. "I'm sorry I didn't tell you that I'd seen your son alive, my friend. I tried, but then the sorrow over my own son's fate overcame me and I couldn't speak."

"It seems we must both endure the same agony this day," Sen replied. He bent over the shrouded body then pulled back a fold of the cloth to reveal the face of his eldest son.

"Ai, Sen!" Raidan exclaimed in dismay. "But how…I saw your Heir alive and well after the battle!"

"An accident, old friend. A terrible, senseless accident took the life of my son." Sen had never feared to show his emotions, and he made no effort to hide his tears now.

"Your son shall lie beside mine in the chapel until we are ready to depart. When we return to Sendai, the death rites shall be performed for both of them in the Royal Chapel."

"I am honored, Majesty." Sen bowed his head into one hand and rested the other on Ashinji's shoulder.

"I am sorry for your loss, Majesty," Ashinji said. Raidan inclined his head in thanks, and, looking into the younger man's eyes, he saw the terrible truth, and felt no surprise.

Perhaps, in a general sense, Sadaiyo Sakehera's death was an accident. I saw this coming a year ago, back when Sen first returned to Sendai with his sons to begin work on the planning of Alasiri's defense.

Such poisonous jealousy between two brothers could only have ended in tragedy.

Raidan looked at his own son, standing bleak and hollow-eyed beside him, and realized that even though he had misunderstood the bond between Kaisik and his brother, the two of them had understood it perfectly well, and had cherished it.

For that I will always be grateful.

Raidan reached out to lay a hand on Sen's shoulder. "Come to the great hall, my friend, and together, we will drink to the memories of our sons."

Chapter 24

REFLECTIONS AND FAREWELLS

J elena opened her eyes, then squeezed them shut again.

"Where am I?" she whispered.

Why does everything seem so bright? "Am I dead?"

No, Jelena. You are most definitely not dead. You are home, child, and you are safe.

"Oh." She tried to move, then realized her mistake. "Uhhhhh!"

Keep still, Jelena. You are badly injured. You must lie still.

"What happened...Hatora! Where is she?"

Shhhhh, child. Don't fret.

"Where...where...is Ashi?"

Sleep now, Jelena.

❦

"Jelena, can you hear me?"

"Mmmmm."

"Jelena, it's me. Time to wake up, love."

"Ashi?"

"Yes, love. Wake up, now."

Jelena opened her eyes. Ashinji looked down at her, smiling, as beautiful as an angel. "How long have I been asleep?"

"Eleven days."

REFLECTIONS AND FAREWELLS

"Eleven...is it over? Did we..."

"It is and we did."

"Oh." Jelena pondered for a moment what that meant, then turned her mind inward, searching.

The blue fire was gone.

&

On the twelfth day of Monzen, three days after the army returned to Sendai, the Rites for the Dead were sung in the Royal Chapel of Sendai Castle for Raidu Onjara and Sadaiyo Sakehera.

After the High Priest and Priestess had consecrated the bodies, an honor guard carried each man to his own funeral pyre. The pyres stood side by side in the courtyard of the chapel, the prince's a spear's length higher than Sadaiyo's.

Each man's father lit his own son's pyre and as the flames consumed the kindling and roared to life, a chorus of clerics raised their voices in a hymn to speed the departed souls to the bosom of The One.

Though still weak from her ordeal, Jelena insisted on accompanying the rest of the family to the funeral. As Sen and Amara's daughter-in-law, she wanted to show her support for them in their time of mourning; as Raidu's cousin, she also wished to stand with her uncle and aunt, the new rulers of Alasiri.

Throughout the service, Ashinji betrayed no outward sign of his emotional turmoil. Jelena felt his terrible sorrow through the mental link they shared, and the tears she shed fell for him and no one else.

That night, both families came together to share a quiet repast and memories of happier times.

The following morning, the morticians collected the charred remains, pulverized them then sealed them into ornate urns. Raidan carried Raidu's urn down to the tomb complex beneath the chapel where generations of Onjaras slept in dusty silence, then laid his son to rest.

Sen and Amara had Sadaiyo's urn packed in a sturdy hardwood box for the journey home to Kerala. Sen wanted to depart before the end of the month, in order to get home in time to try to salvage the last of the spring planting.

GRIFFIN'S DESTINY

※

Two days after Raidu and Sadaiyo's funeral rites, the royal morticians brought King Keizo's body up from the crypt where he had been placed in a temporary coffin until the return of his brother, then laid the king out on the main altar of the chapel. Multiple preservation spells had kept the body from immediate decay, but over two weeks had passed since the king's death and even the most potent preservation spell had its limits; for this reason Raidan ordered that the corpse remain shrouded.

The sun rose and set three times and still, the line of folk waiting to pay their final respects to their deceased king did not abate. City folk and farmers from the countryside, minor nobility and merchants, laborers and off-duty soldiers, okui and hikui alike; all stood united in their collective grief. All believed the king had died of the plague—Raidan decided it served no purpose to allow the people to know the truth of Keizo's death.

As for the fate of Sonoe, the King's Companion, the official version of events stated she had perished while taking part in the magical defense of Alasiri, and that her body had not been recovered.

When Jelena learned of Sonoe's betrayal and the circumstances of her death, she cried, not for the betrayal itself, but for the lost soul of the woman she called her friend. Even though she knew everyone else involved disagreed, Jelena chose to believe the friendship she had shared with her father's consort had been genuine, at least on some level. Sonoe had fallen under the control of an entity whose corrupting power had proven impossible to resist. Jelena remained convinced her friend had been a victim of the Nameless One, just as she, herself had almost been.

Jelena chose to forgive Sonoe, and in doing so, she let go of the terrible hurt Sonoe's betrayal had caused.

※

On the morning of the nineteenth day of Monzen, Raidan lit the sacred fire and Keizo's body burned atop a magnificent funeral pyre in the center of the vast parade ground fronting Sendai Castle.

To Jelena, it seemed as if the entire population of the city had crammed itself into the castle grounds, shoulder to shoulder, to witness the final rites for their king. As the flames shot higher and dense black smoke roiled into the sky, the wailing of the crowd grew louder. The castle guards struggled to keep the people back from the searing heat of the pyre, but finally, one man broke through.

Jelena gasped as the man raced up to the fire, clutching something in his hands. He halted then flung the object high into the air. The sunlight glinted off the blade of a dagger. It disappeared into the roaring inferno and after bowing to the pyre, the man turned and staggered back into the crowd.

Another man followed the first, then a woman, then another man, each one flinging some object onto the pyre. Finally, the guards melted aside and the people surged forward.

"Each person throws a possession of value on the pyre of the king, as a way to show his or her devotion," Ashinji explained. "Now, the king's soul can travel to heaven with tokens of love from his people."

"Should we do the same, Ashi?"

"No. It's a rite for the common people. It belongs to them."

Jelena watched the hail of objects hit the pyre and the tear-stained faces of the people, and for the first time since she had come to Alasiri, she felt like a part of the larger nation, an outsider no longer.

The next day, the King's Guard accompanied the royal family as they bore the urn of the king down to his grave. Jelena walked behind her uncle and aunt, leaning on Ashinji for support. She felt as if the weight of her grief would crush her.

Why was my father taken from me so soon? she raged. *Who do I blame? The gods of my childhood, or the One Goddess of the elves? Can I really blame any god?*

Just before Raidan placed the simple ceramic urn into the magnificent carved marble casket prepared for it, Jelena touched her fingers to her lips, brushed them against the cool clay, then turned and laid her head on Ashinji's chest. As the heavy casket lid settled into place with grinding finality, Jelena wept.

GRIFFIN'S DESTINY

ଛ

Raidan and Taya ascended their thrones three days after Keizo's official funeral. The new king, as one of his first official acts, granted Ashinji a promotion, then released him from his service to the regular army. As Sen's Heir, Ashinji's principle duty now lay with Kerala.

Sen and Amara were anxious to return home, not just to lay their eldest son to rest, but because they had been away for so long. Jelena, too, found herself longing to escape the bustle of Sendai for the peace of Kerala. She missed its verdant landscape of rolling hills and dense forest. Returning to the place where her life had changed for the better felt like the closest thing to a real homecoming. Before she could leave, though, she had one final thing she needed to do.

ଛ

In the little garden known as the Dolphin Bower, so named for the fountain at its center, Jelena waited on a stone bench for a man whose heart she knew she had broken. As she sat clasping and unclasping her hands, she tried to summon up words that might take some of the hurt away, but in her own heart, she knew it was futile. Only time would ease the pain she had inflicted on so undeserving a man.

"Jelena."

Jelena looked into the dark eyes of Mai Nohe and her breath caught in her throat. She had not seen Mai since the day they had said goodbye, just before the army marched south to Tono. On that day, Jelena had hoped and prayed her future would include a life with Mai.

How could either of us have known then that the life we'd planned would never happen?

Mai sat beside her and for several heartbeats, neither spoke. Overhead, amid the spreading branches of a fruitless cherry tree, a mourning dove cooed. The scent of lilacs hung heavy in the air. The stone dolphin poised in the fountain spat a stream of water from its mouth that glittered like a string of diamonds in the sun.

Jelena took a deep breath. "I'm so sorry, Mai," she whispered.

REFLECTIONS AND FAREWELLS

"You have nothing to feel sorry for, Jelena," he replied, looking at his hands. "You believed, as did we all, that your husband had died and you were free to give your heart to another. I knew full well you still loved him just as much as ever, but I counted myself lucky I had even a small piece of your heart."

Jelena reached up to wipe away the tears on her cheeks. "Mai, I..." she began, but fell silent as Mai turned on the bench to face her. Pain and sadness filled his brown eyes, but she saw no reproach.

"I know now what true love is, Jelena, and I know only a fool would stand in its way. I am no fool." He kissed her forehead. "I'm truly happy for you." He stood up. "May you have all the joy and peace you deserve, Jelena."

"And you as well, Mai."

As she watched Mai walk away, Jelena fought the urge to get up and run after him, to beg again for his forgiveness. She knew with certainty the pain of this parting would haunt her until the end of her days.

※

"Goodbye, Uncle."

Raidan took Jelena's left hand and raised it to eye level. The thing that had kept strong her resolve, her father's ring, sized now to fit her finger, flashed in the sun.

"You wear the White Griffin," Raidan stated, tapping the ring with a forefinger. "The symbol of our House. Never forget that you are a true Onjara."

"I won't, Uncle," Jelena replied.

Raidan let go of her hand, then gripped her shoulders. He stared into her eyes. "I can't promise you things will change overnight, Niece. Okui prejudice is a fiendishly stubborn thing, but I can promise you this. I will work hard to win over the council in order to get their approval for full rights for all persons born in Alasiri, be they okui or hikui."

"I know you will, Uncle. Thank you." Raidan bent to kiss her cheek.

The king and queen, Prince Kaisik, and a small group of retainers had gathered before the main entrance of the castle to bid Lord Sen and his entourage farewell. Raidan had provided a large, comfortable carriage for

Amara, Lani, and the children to travel in, along with Eikko, who had begged to be allowed to accompany Jelena and Hatora back to Kerala. Sen had agreed, and so Raidan had released the hikui girl from service at Sendai Castle.

"Goodbye, Cousin. Promise you won't forget me," Jelena said as she embraced Kaisik.

"I'll never forget you, Jelena, not ever!" the young prince whispered.

"Kaisik, I know you think you're not strong enough for the new role you must play," Jelena murmured into the boy's ear, "but you are, Cousin! You are exactly the kind of man Alasiri needs." She paused, then added, "You are always welcome to come out to Kerala for a visit." He bobbed his head against her shoulder and pulled away, scrubbing at his eyes with his sleeve.

"Come, Daughter. It's time we were on our way," Sen said.

"Not so fast, my lord," Taya spoke up. "I've one last piece of business with my niece." The queen reached into her sash, withdrew a small parchment scroll, then held it out to Jelena.

"This is an official writ, inducting you into the Kirian Society. Your bravery and sacrifice have proven many times over that you are a worthy addition to our number."

"But...but, I'm not a mage!" Jelena protested. "I'm not even very Talented!"

Taya smiled. "Your Talent is a lot stronger than you think, child. With training, you could become a competent practitioner, but even if you decide never to study magic at all, you will still be one of us."

"I don't know what to say, Aunt," Jelena replied, shaking her head.

"There is nothing you need to say." Taya leaned in and kissed Jelena's forehead. Jelena sputtered in surprise, for she never would have expected such a gesture from her imperious aunt. The queen smiled again and said, "Yes, child, I know. Now, go. Your husband is waiting."

Jelena looked over her shoulder at Ashinji, who stood a stone's toss away between their two horses, a hand on each bridle. Seeing the pride and love in his eyes made her want to drag him off to a private corner somewhere so she could show him how beautiful and worthy he made her feel.

The whitewashed walls of Sendai Castle shimmered with the growing heat of the day. The royal retainers fidgeted beneath the sun's glare; they lacked the discipline that kept Lord Sen's troops motionless atop their mounts. Jelena gazed at the imposing walls, soaring towers, and swooping blue-tiled roofs of the castle and thought of her father. Even though Keizo had nothing to do with its making, the heartland fortress of the elves seemed very much like him—strong, solid and rooted in the bedrock of Alasiri.

If only we'd had more time together, Father! Jelena thought. She still found it hard to believe only a little more than a year and a half had passed since she had ridden through the gates of this place, a hikui girl whose only social standing came from her marriage to the second son of an important man.

Now she departed Sendai as a full member of the royal family, a princess, and yet, as long as her fellow hikui were denied justice, she would consider her rank a sham and an affront to them. Had she not promised her friend Sateyuka that she would see to it things changed?

With one last, lingering look at the castle, Jelena turned on her heel and strode to where Ashinji waited, holding her dear Willow. He dropped his horse's reins to give her a leg up into the saddle then helped to adjust her stirrups. Only when she was settled did he then mount his own horse.

"What are you thinking, love?" he asked, his head dropped to the side as he gazed at her face. "You look a bit sad."

"I said goodbye to Sateyuka this morning. I never properly thanked her for taking care of Hatora while we were...away." She glanced over to where the carriage stood, hitched behind two placid, shaggy-footed draft horses. "I promised her my uncle will see to it that the hikui receive justice. I hope my promise won't prove to be an empty one."

Ashinji looked away, his face troubled. After a few moments, he said, "Your uncle is an honorable man, just as your father was, but...it's going to take a lot of convincing to get most okui to accept hikui as their equals. Old bigotry dies very, very hard, my love."

"My uncle said something very much like that," Jelena replied.

"I'm giving the estate your father deeded me to Misune's son," Ashinji stated.

Jelena glanced at Sadaiyo's widow, who, though she sat her horse as straight and proud as ever, still could not hide the desolation that cast a pall over her spirit. She had spoken very little since their return to the city, and had spent most of her waking hours standing vigil over her husband's corpse.

"It's the least I can do for the boy," Ashinji continued. "He's been disinherited now that my brother's dead and my father's made me his Heir. At least he'll have land and an income of his own."

"Have you told Misune?" Jelena asked.

"Not yet. With everything that's happened, I just haven't found the right moment."

"I hope she appreciates your generosity. It surprises me, but I feel very sorry for her."

"It doesn't surprise me. You have a generous and loving heart," Ashinji replied. "Hmm, I think Father is ready to go."

After checking on Amara and the children, Sen swung aboard his sturdy chestnut stallion and raised a gloved hand, signaling his troops. Amid the clatter of a large mounted force preparing to move, his voice rose above the noise. "I'll be back for the spring council, Your Majesty!" he shouted.

Raidan inclined his head. "Safe journey, my friend!"

As the Kerala entourage wound its way down the castle hill and through the busy streets of the town, Jelena felt all of her senses engaged as never before. Every sight, smell, and sound she captured and collected like a precious gem, then stored them away in her vault of memory for safekeeping, for she had no idea when she would return.

She reflected on how different her life and circumstances had become. The uncertain, untried girl who'd entered the capital city of Alasiri with only a ring to guide her and hope to sustain her now departed as a strong woman, confident and sure of her place in the world.

She and Ashinji rode beside Lord Sen at the head of the party. As they passed beneath the massive outer gates of the city, a voice called out.

"May the One bless and keep you, Princess Jelena!"

Jelena stared at the swirl of people, expecting to see a hikui face, but to her amazement, a young okui woman waved back at her. Jelena smiled.

Perhaps hearts can be changed sooner than we think!

The road out of Sendai ran southward toward Meizi. The main east-west crossroads lay a day's ride away. The sky glowed bright blue and cloudless overhead, but off to the northeast, thunderclouds rose in dark gray piles over the foothills of the Kesen Numai Mountains. From behind the wagons, a soldier raised his voice in song—a rough, cheerful sound—and soon, most of the troop had joined their voices with his.

Reflections and Farewells

"It'll be good to get back home, children," Sen said.

"Yes, Father," Jelena agreed. "It will."

EPILOGUE

"Misune writes that she'll bring our grandson for a visit at the end of the month," Amara said. The letter from their daughter-in-law had come by post rider that morning.

"Hmmm, good news," Sen replied. "We don't get to see Sentashi nearly enough since Misune decided to move back to her father's house. Perhaps you can persuade her to stay. She and our grandson belong here, with us."

"You know I've tried, Husband. Misune is proud. She's made up her mind."

"Well, she can un-make it," Sen grumbled.

"A runner has just come up from the main gates," Ashinji announced as he entered the day room. "There're two people in a cart waiting at the bridge."

"Visitors!" exclaimed Sen. "This'll give me a chance to break out that new cask of fancy Jagai red your uncle sent me, Jelena."

Jelena smiled. She knew how much her father-in-law loved playing host to their neighbors. It had been a long cold winter, and company would be a welcome diversion.

The family had gathered, as they did every afternoon, in the large sitting room at the top of Kerala Castle to drink tea and chat. Jena and Mariso sprawled on the mats amidst their doll collection, engrossed in a private adventure. Eikko perched in a window seat, amusing Hatora with a game of peek-a-boo. Jelena shared the room's only couch with Amara. Sen and Lani sat on stools beside a small table, a game of mikat in progress between them.

"Oh dear, it looks like we'll have to quit our game, Lani my sweet," Sen said.

Lani pushed out her lower lip in a mock frown. "Father, you only wish to quit because I'm winning, as usual."

Sen's eyebrows shot up. "What? *You*...beat *me*...at mikat?" he sputtered.

"Yes, Father. You know you haven't won against me in ages."

"You'd think an old soldier like me could beat an untried girl at a military strategy game," he growled, but Jelena saw the twinkle of humor in his eyes. "I think you're aiming to take my place some day as Commanding General!"

Lani cocked her head to the side and said, "Perhaps."

Amara lowered Misune's letter to her lap. "I think you and Ashi should go down to greet our guests, Husband," she said.

"Perhaps I'll come as well. That is, if I can lift my enormous body off this couch!" Jelena had just entered her tenth and final month of pregnancy. The large, active child—a boy—had allowed his mother precious little rest these last few weeks.

"Are you sure, love?" Ashinji asked.

"Oh, yes, I'm sure. It'll do me good to get out and walk. I'm tired of sitting." Jelena grimaced as she got her feet beneath her and pushed off. Ashinji stepped forward to assist and, arm in arm, the two of them followed Sen downstairs to the yard. Together, they all made their way down to the main gate of the castle.

The day had turned overcast and blustery, where only yesterday it had been fine and warm—the typical, unstable weather of early spring in Kerala. Jelena shivered, despite her wool tunic and trousers.

Ashinji wrapped his arm around her and pulled her close. "You should have put on a coat," he scolded in a gentle tone.

"I'm fine, Ashi. Don't fuss," Jelena shot back, then kissed his wind-chilled cheek.

"Not a good day for traveling, no, no!" Sen muttered, peering at the darkening sky. "Our visitors beat the storm, but only just." Jelena breathed in the cold air, heavy with the smell of rain, and nodded in agreement.

A brace of castle guards had detained the visitors at the landward end of the bridge. One of the guards spotted Sen and trotted back across the bridge to the gate.

"My lord, it's two humans, a man and an old woman," the guard reported. "Says he's been here before…claims to know the family." The guard's voice rang with sarcastic disbelief. He was new to the Kerala guards, having been in service for less than six months.

Humans! Jelena's heart fluttered with excitement. *Could it be?*

She pushed past the guardsman to get a better look. "Ai, Goddess, Ashi!" she cried, recognizing the tall, dark-haired figure seated on the driver's bench of the cart. "It's Magnes!"

"Let them cross," Sen ordered. The guard touched his forehead then turned to wave to his fellow on the other side. Magnes snapped the reins and the horse leaned into the harness. As the cart drew closer, Jelena spotted a small figure huddled in the back. Even at a distance and swathed in a heavy cloak, Jelena recognized the woman who had raised her.

"Heartmother," she whispered. She spun around to look at Ashinji, eyes overflowing with tears. "Ashi! Magnes has brought my mother here from Amsara!"

Ashinji moved to stand beside her. "This is truly a wonderful gift," he said.

"Magnes Preseren, my young human friend!" Sen called out in Soldaran. "You have returned for long overdue visit!"

Magnes checked the horse and the cart rolled to a stop. "Lord Sen, it is very good to see you," he replied. He set the hand brake then swung down from the driver's bench into Jelena's ecstatic embrace.

"Magnes," she sobbed.

"Hello, Cousin." He stroked her curls then kissed her forehead. "Hello Ashi. You're looking well."

"As are you, my friend." Jelena relinquished her hold on her cousin so he and Ashinji could embrace.

"I've brought someone to see you, Cousin," Magnes said.

Jelena could only nod, unable to speak through her tears.

Magnes moved to the cart bed, gently lifted Claudia out then set her on her feet.

EPILOGUE

"My baby…Is she here?"

"Yes, Heartmother, it's your baby!" Jelena stepped forward and pushed back the hood to reveal the dear face she had not expected to ever see again. "It's me, your lamb."

The muted gray light dulled Claudia's skin to the color of old parchment. The lack of focus in her rheumy eyes revealed her near blindness. Nevertheless, she looked directly into Jelena's face and lifted her gnarled hands to caress her foster daughter's tear-streaked cheeks.

"How are you, child? You look so happy. An' with a new little'un on the way!" One of her hands dropped to rest on Jelena's swollen belly. "A boy, 'tis no doubt. An old midwife always knows."

"I am happy, Heartmother. Happier than I ever imagined possible," Jelena replied.

"Hello, Claudia. Do you remember me?"

A rapturous smile lit up the old woman's face, softening the deep lines etched into her skin by a lifetime's experience. "O' course I remember you, Ashi," she exclaimed. "How could I ever ferget? My prayers 'ave been answered a thousan' times over! My Jelena an' her man are together again, an' I've been given the chance t' see them an' their babies before I die."

Jelena threw her arms around her foster mother and held her close. Even through the heavy layers of wool, she felt the inevitable toll age and illness had taken on Claudia's body. Once, her foster mother had been robust and strong. Now, she felt fragile as a bird. Jelena marveled that Claudia had been able to make the journey from Amsara at all.

A spattering of fat raindrops speckled the gravel. The wind gusted harder, lifting the hems of cloaks and whipping stray locks of hair across faces.

"We'd all best get inside before the rain really starts," Sen urged, starting back through the gate. He added in Soldaran, "Magnes, guards will fetch wagon and horses to stables, you come inside. Ashi will carry mother."

"Oh, no, sir," Claudia demurred. "I can walk, m'lord."

"Come, Heartmother," Ashinji said in a gentle voice. "Let me carry you. It will be much faster if I do." As Ashinji swept Claudia into his arms, she giggled, and for a moment, Jelena caught a glimpse of the young woman her foster mother had once been.

They made it to the steps of the castle just as the rain began to pelt down in earnest. Sen escorted them up to the sitting room, where Amara greeted her human guests as graciously as she would visiting elven nobility.

"Grandmother, you shall sit in our best chair," Amara said, guiding Claudia to Sen's comfortable seat by the hearth. Eikko circled the room, gathering cloaks and handing them off to a manservant waiting at the door.

When everyone had settled in with fresh cups of tea, Sen began the conversation. "So nice to practice my Soldaran. Is, how you say? Rusty."

Magnes chuckled. "Your Soldaran is very good, Lord Sen. Don't worry."

"So. Tell me, young Magnes, how goes situation in Empire? Is Constantia still wanting invasion of Alasiri?" Sen's light tone stood at odds with the wariness in his eyes.

Magnes took a few sips of his tea before answering. "I'm just a farmer now, my lord. My wife and I work our land, run our pottery business and tend to our children."

"Surely, being brother to duchess, you hear things, know things, yes?" Sen pressed.

"Husband," Amara interrupted. "Our guests just arrived. Let us leave serious matters for later."

"No, it's all right, my lady," Magnes assured. "Lord Sen has a right to be concerned. After all, Kerala is Amsara's closest elven neighbor. I can tell you this much. The empress has not given up on her ambitions. She's publicly declared she won't accept the defeat at Tono, and has begun an active program to find ways to counteract elven magic."

"But, how can that happen? Humans have no magical abilities," Ashinji said.

"That is not entirely true," Amara stated in Siri-dar. "Magical ability is extremely rare in humans, but it does exist. The Empire is vast and contains many subjugated peoples within its borders. Given time, enough Talented humans could be found to make up a formidable force…if they are trained properly. That is where the empress will run into difficulty. She may not find anyone with the ability to train other humans to be mages."

Jelena translated Amara's words for Magnes, who then nodded in agreement. "Lady Amara makes a good point," he said.

"So. We've merely won a reprieve," Sen muttered in Siri-dar. He looked hard at Magnes. "You are friend, Magnes Preseren. Sister is another matter," he continued in Soldaran. "She is loyal to Empire, this I understand. I understand, also, you have loyalty to sister. I will not ask you to betray sister, so no questions will I ask about military matters."

Magnes' relief was palpable. "Thank you, Lord Sen. I assure you, if I knew anything at all that I thought might help you keep your people safe, I would tell you."

Throughout the tense exchange, Jelena sat in silence, holding Claudia's hand in hers. Now, she spoke up. "Magnes, so much has happened since I last saw you, I don't know where to begin."

"I've already learned a lot of it from Ashi," Magnes replied. "But, of course, nothing about how all of you survived the war."

Just as Jelena started to reply, a sudden, sharp pain lanced through her lower belly. A warm gush of liquid soaked the couch beneath her.

"It'll have to wait, I think." She turned to Ashinji with a pained smile. "Ashi, your son has decided to come a bit early."

&

Ten days after Jelena gave birth, Claudia died. She passed peacefully, in her sleep, after spending the day with Jelena, Hatora, and the new baby. Lord Sen had ordered she be treated as an honored guest, not as a servant, and so, for the last few days of her long life, Claudia knew what genuine comfort felt like. As a final kindness, Sen gave his permission for her to be buried on the castle grounds, so she would always be near her family.

Magnes stayed on another week. He and Jelena spent many quiet hours together just talking, like they used to do as children. Jelena learned of his reconnection with Livie, and of the daughter they shared. Livie's husband had been killed during the battle at Tono, and out of respect for their bond, Magnes had stayed away for several months. Later, after a decent interval, he had gone to her to declare his intentions and she accepted. Their love for each other had never died. It had remained banked like a pile of glowing embers, waiting for a spark to rekindle it. They had married at the start of the year, and come year's end, they would welcome a new addition to their family.

Jelena, in turn, told Magnes about the strange journey she had undertaken and survived, against all odds. So much had happened to them both that Jelena found it difficult to put it all into words, harder still to believe the two of them had fled Amsara Castle barely three years ago.

When Magnes finally departed Kerala, headed for home and laden down with gifts for his family, Jelena made him promise to return with Livie and their children at summer's end. As she and Ashinji stood at the gate, waving goodbye, Jelena reflected on how much happier she felt now, watching her cousin ride away, than when last she had said goodbye to him. Back then, she didn't know if she would ever see him again.

They watched until Magnes disappeared from view, then turned and walked, hand in hand, back up toward the castle. Ashinji remained quiet, and Jelena could sense something troubled him.

"What's bothering you, Husband? Tell me."

He sighed and shook his head. "I'm just thinking about how much I'll miss you when I go away to school," he said.

Ashinji would be leaving Kerala come the fall to enter the Kan Onji School. Amara had kept her promise to Chiana Hiraino; her son would become the first male of her line to be trained as a mage.

Both Ashinji and Jelena had agreed it would be better for their children if Jelena stayed at home with them. It meant months of separation, a prospect neither one relished, but both accepted the necessity.

"Are you sure that's all that's bothering you?" Jelena prodded. She knew her husband too well to let him get away with such a simple answer.

He stopped walking and gripped her shoulders, turning her to face him. "I don't want to alarm you, but…" His voice trailed off and the look in his eyes made Jelena shiver.

"What, Ashi? Tell me!" she demanded.

"I had a dream last night. I stood in the upper yard, looking at the front door of the keep. The door swung open, then shut, back and forth, as if the wind pushed it. I thought I was alone, but then a young woman appeared. I recognized her immediately. It was Hatora."

Jelena gasped. "You saw our daughter all grown up?"

Ashinji nodded. "She looked, not frightened exactly, but…agitated and… determined. She called to me. She said, 'Father, we have to help them!'"

"Help who?"

EPILOGUE

Ashinji shook his head. "I have no idea. She beckoned to me, then turned and ran into the castle. I tried to follow, but couldn't. My feet had sunk into the ground. I called out to her to come back, but she had disappeared. Then I woke up."

"What do you think this means? Should we be afraid?" Jelena tried to stop her voice from shaking, but couldn't. She knew the power of Ashinji's prophetic dreams. "We have to tell your mother about this."

"It may have been an ordinary dream."

"You don't really believe that, do you?"

Ashinji sighed. "No, I don't. But it may not necessarily mean that whatever it is, is dangerous for us. Still...you're right, love. We must tell my mother."

Jelena slipped her arm around Ashinji's waist and the two of them started walking again. After a few heartbeats, Jelena spoke.

"You saw our daughter...all grown up! What did she look like?"

Ashinji kissed the top of her head. "A lot like her beautiful mother, thank the One. Curly brown hair, not quite as twisty as yours, though, green eyes like mine, golden skin..."

"Your mother says Hatora's Talent is nearly as strong as yours. Perhaps she'll be a great mage someday. If what Magnes says is true about the empress looking for Talented humans to use as weapons against us, we'll need strong mages as a defense, and we'll need a strong Kirian Society to lead them."

Ashinji nodded. "Whatever the future has in store for us and our children, right now, we are all safe and happy," he said.

Yes, we are, Jelena thought. She skipped out of Ashinji's embrace. "I'll race you to the gate!" she cried then sped away.

Laughing, Ashinji ran after her.

BOOKS IN THE
GRIFFIN'S DAUGHTER TRILOGY

*Griffin's Daughter**

Griffin's Shadow

Griffin's Destiny

*Winner 2008 IBPA Ben Franklin Award for Best First Fiction

ABOUT THE AUTHOR

Leslie Ann Moore has been a storyteller since childhood. A native of Los Angeles, she received a doctorate in Veterinary Medicine from the University of California. She lives and works in Los Angeles, and in her spare time she practices the art of belly dancing. Moore's first novel, *Griffin's Daughter* won the 2008 IBPA Ben Franklin Award for Best First Fiction.

Breinigsville, PA USA
26 January 2010
231384BV00004B/25/P

9 780982 514504